MW01139330

The Wrath of Cain

By

Kathy Coopmans

© 2015

The Wrath of Cain © 2015 Kathy Coopmans
Cover Design © 2015 Sommer Stein
Photography © 2015 Eric David
    Battershell

This is a work of fiction. Names, characters, places, and incidents are products of the author's imagination or are used fictitiously and are not to be construed as real. Any resemblance to actual events, locales, organizations, or persons, living or dead, is entirely coincidental. All rights reserved. The unauthorized reproduction or distribution of this copyrighted work is illegal. No part of this book may be used or reproduced electronically or in print without written permission by the author.

All rights are reserved.

To Shane. My Hero.

Prologue

"I can't believe we just got married! Married, Cain! Can you believe it?" I exclaim in delight at my boyfriend of two years, Cain Bexley.

No, I take that back; he was my boyfriend. Now he's my husband.

"Calla Bexley!" Cain yells at the top of his lungs as we walk out of the courthouse in downtown Detroit where we've just gotten married.

It all happened so fast that I still can't believe we pulled it off without either of our families finding out. Maybe that's why Cain said we should come to Detroit to get married instead of holding the ceremony in my hometown of Bloomfield Hills, a small community on the outskirts of the city.

Our fathers hate each other, and that is putting it mildly. I guess you could call the two of us forbidden lovers. My parents are even less lenient than Cain's dad, and that is putting it mildly, too.

This bullshit between our fathers goes all the way back to their time in high school, where my dad was the big jock and Cain's dad was the big party animal, and part of the notorious Sinners of Revolution MC.

Who gives a shit, right? That's what we kept telling them all. Let it go, I would tell my dad, but nope, he wouldn't listen. He would always carry on about the fact that Jed Bexley had been chasing after my mom. Wouldn't leave her alone, always trying to get her to go out with him and all that high school drama crap.

I remember the first day I came home and told my parents I had a date, a date with the boy I'd secretly had a crush on since elementary school. A boy who was a badass. No one, and I mean no one, messed with Cain for the simple fact of who his dad was. Me, on the other hand... I saw Cain for who he really was, just a teenager like myself trying to get through school and make it to the next chapter in our lives.

My dad was furious when I told him who it was, and forbade me to go out with him. I was crushed. I cried and begged him to please let me go. He refused, told me straight to my face that he was no good for me, and if I ever went out with that boy, he would send me away or lock me in my room.

I snuck out and did it anyway, with help from my mom, of course. She's the only one who has been on my side. I know for the most part it's because she loves me, but she has a soft spot for Cain, too.

She knew he didn't grow up with a mother. He lost her when he was three years old in a tragic accident. An elderly couple slid on some ice and lost control of their vehicle, slamming right into Cain's mom and crushing her body against a parked car. Cain doesn't talk about her at all; says he has very little memory of her. It's sad. No child should ever have to grow up without a parent.

For two years Cain and I have snuck around seeing each other whenever we could, both of us lying to our fathers. It's been hard, but we've managed to do it. I could go on and on about this feud between our fathers, but not today, and hopefully not ever again. Now that we're both eighteen and married, there isn't jack shit they can do to us.

"Come here, wife," Cain growls in my ear.

He pulls me into his arms, kissing me deeply as we come to a stop in front of his bike, the Harley I love so much, painted in the blackest of blacks and all decked out with shiny chrome. The only other color on the bike is a white Calla lily painted on the side, which he had done just two weeks ago for my birthday.

His tongue swirls with mine as he sits sideways on his bike, his long legs stretching outwards. He pulls my body flush with his. I inhale the deep smell of his leather vest and all that is Cain.

"So, I think we should just get this over with and go tell both of our parents, because I am not hiding anymore from any of them. I want them all to know you're mine."

"Okay," I manage to squeak out.

He knows when he nibbles on my ear and neck it turns me on. If we weren't here in the middle of this busy street, I would straddle him on this damn bike and fuck him hard, ride him like I have done so many times. One of the reasons I love his bike is that when the weather is warm, we love to have sex on it. Trust me when I say it sucks in the winter when we have to sneak around in his truck, trying to find a place to park in the middle of all that snow.

"Your parents first, or mine?" he now asks.

"Mine," I say.

He hands me my helmet and I tuck my ponytail inside, climbing on the back of his bike as best I can with a knee-length skirt on. I tuck it underneath me as Cain swings his long leg over and starts the bike up. My hands wrap around his middle and I clasp them together over his tight abs, but on second thought, I reach down and give his cock a quick squeeze through his jeans. He cranes his neck back to stare at me with the same desire in his eyes that I have in my own.

"You want that cock, don't you, Calla?"

His eyes roam over my face.

"Always," I grin.

With a knowing smirk, he flips down his visor and races toward I-75.

He only slows down when we pull onto my street, removing one of his hands to give my knee a light squeeze of reassurance. Those nervous butterflies start flapping their wings in my belly when I see both of my parents' cars parked in the drive.

"We can do this, Calla. You're not alone now. I'm your husband, and there ain't jack shit they can say anymore."

He shuts off his bike. The loud rumble dies off, but before either one of us climb off, my father is jumping down off of the porch and getting right up in Cain's face.

"Where the hell have the two of you been?" he screams loud enough that our neighbors on both sides of our house come running outside.

"John!" my mother hollers from right behind him.

"Don't fucking John me, Cecily. I want to know where this motherfucking punk took my daughter."

Cain stands face to face with my dad, never wavering or backing down, and glares right back at him.

"Calla, what have you done?" Mom asks in her sweet voice, a look of disappointment set in her expression.

Swallowing hard, I grab my husband's hand as he helps me off of his bike.

"Dad, stop it," I say sternly.

"I'm the parent here, Calla, not you."

Dad's gaze stays locked on Cain when he speaks.

"Don't talk to my wife like that."

Cain's harsh and protective attitude has me moving quickly to stand in between the two men. I stare up at my dad, his eyes shooting not daggers, but bullets into Cain's head as they dance rapidly across his face.

"Calla," Dad says as he looks down at me.

"Tell me what he just said isn't true. That you didn't marry this piece of shit!"

I feel Cain stiffen behind me.

"Dad, that's enough. And yes, I did marry him. I love him."

My dad scoffs and his next words slice right down the center of my body, severing my heart.

"If that's true and you are now a Bexley, then you are no longer a part of this family."

Then he just turns and walks away, no explanation, no nothing, slamming the front door so hard that I jump. But when the one person who has been by my side this entire time looks at me with displeasure, I start to shake and my world crumbles as tears begin to fall freely from my eyes.

"What have the two of you done?"

My mother is crying now. Cain has his arms wrapped around my waist.

"Look, Mrs. Greer, we love each other. This feud between our fathers has nothing to do with us," Cain says.

"No, it doesn't, but the two of you just running off and getting married like this is going to make this situation so much worse than it already is."

"What situation?" I ask. "Dad and Jed haven't even spoken to each other in years."

"No, they haven't, but you both know better than to do something like this. What about college? What are the two of you going to do about that? You've already been accepted into the University of Michigan. You leave in a month."

My heart starts to pound and then I become furious with my mother, which I have never done before.

"Mom, it's only an hour away. We have it all worked out."

"Look, I believe in young love; that's why I supported you two. But this is unacceptable, Calla. You can't just run off and get married without telling anyone. Why would you keep something as big as this from me?"

"I'm sorry," I say sincerely.

"Sorry isn't good enough. This is a mistake, one the two of you should have thought through before you ran off and did something as rash as this."

"You knew, didn't you? That's why the two of you came barreling out of the house like you did. You knew we went and got married and you told Dad, didn't you?" I seethe.

"I did. I found all of this material on marriage housing in your room and I put two and two together when you didn't come home last night from Lexi's house." She grabs my arms.

"I don't think you realize the severity of what the two of you have done. And you!"

She points her finger at Cain.

"How could you do this? You of all people know how important her education is. You'll be a distraction to her and she will never become a lawyer like she has always wanted to be," she accuses, scowling at the both of us.

"Mrs. Greer, that's not true. I already have a job, and we've been accepted into marriage housing. I have always supported her and I will continue to do so. We came here hoping for your blessing. You know I would never do anything to stand in the way of what she wants. Unlike our fathers."

He hesitates for a moment, which gives my mom the perfect opportunity to start right back in.

"I won't give the two of you my blessing, not now, anyway. I'm more than disappointed in the both of you."

Mom pinches the end of her nose and closes her eyes. When she opens them again, they are still wet from her tears and concern is etched across her face.

"You are my daughter, Calla, and I love you more than anything, so I will support you. As far as your dad goes, he'll come around eventually. I know he didn't mean what he said. Now, what do you two have planned for the next month before you leave for school?"

She looks at the two of us.

"Please tell me you have something planned."

"We're staying at the compound," Cain finally says.

"Really? And your father is okay with this?" she questions, her hands going to her hips.

"He doesn't know, either. We thought we would tell you first," I say.

She shakes her head.

"Good Lord, you two. Cain, how about if you go tell your dad, and I help Calla pack some of her stuff? I can bring her over there later tonight, and for right now she can go inside with me and we can try to reason with her father."

Cain squeezes me tightly.

"Fine, as long as you promise to bring her to me."

"Of course, I will," she promises as my husband turns to me.

"I'll see you later tonight then, babe. Okay?"

He spins me around in his arms, kissing my forehead.

"Are you sure?"

"Positive. If anything changes, I promise I'll text you."

He chuckles, but it doesn't reach his eyes. I know he's just as scared to tell his dad as I have been to tell mine. More, even. Cain's father has been grooming him to take over the club once he retires. When he finds out about me, there is no telling what he will do or say. I place my arms around his neck and lean up on my tiptoes to whisper in his ear.

"I love you. Just remember that and everything will be fine."

This time his smile does reach his eyes. I stand there and watch my husband drive off then turn back to my mother, who still looks disappointed. I feel terrible for being the one to put that look on her face when all she has ever done is support me, love me, and remind me every day that my happiness is all that matters to her.

She grabs my hand and waves to our nosy neighbor as we walk up the sidewalk to our house, but when we climb up onto the porch, she pauses at the doorway.

"Let me talk to him while you go up and pack a bag. It will all work out, I promise."

Her smile is tight, making me nervous and frightened, her smile is telling me something she can't. I can feel it, and all I want to do is run back down the stairs, jump into my car, and go after Cain.

I rush up to my room, pull my already packed suitcase out from under my bed and toss it on top. I gather up a few more pairs of shorts, t-shirts and panties, then stuff them inside and close it up. Clasping the handle and lugging the case onto the floor, I turn back around and exhale deeply as I say goodbye to my childhood room full of so many happy memories.

I drag the suitcase downstairs and sit on the couch. It's been almost an hour since Cain has been gone. Those earlier feelings slowly dissipate with each passing minute. No news is good news, I keep telling myself.

My parents emerge from the backyard, my dad walking right past me and into his office, slamming the door shut. My mom sits beside me.

"It didn't go so good, huh?" I ask, scooting forward and placing my elbows on my knees. I curl my hands into fists and rest my chin on them.

"Not really. Just give him some time, sweetheart. Give us all some time. You ready?" she asks coolly.

"Yes. But I can just take my car, if that's okay with you?"

She nods. No talk of what to expect on your wedding night. No talk about anything at all. Just a simple nod and a kiss on my cheek as I grab my suitcase and practically run out of the house and to my car.

The Sinners of Revolution Clubhouse is in Sterling Heights, about a half an hour from my parents' home. My palms are sweaty, my mouth is dry, and I am shaking as I pull up to the gated drive leading in. Two security guards with rifles stand outside, forcing me to come to a stop. I push on the button to roll my window down. An older, dark-haired man with the longest beard I have ever seen sticks his head inside my window, inches away from my face.

"Well. When the news traveled that young Cain up and got himself married, they didn't say she was a pretty little thing. Welcome, young lady. I was told by the Prez himself to send you right up."

He taps the side of my car, then backs away. My nerves settle in an instant. If everyone around here is as nice as he is, then we should all get along just fine for the next month. I drive slowly up the paved road. The winding trees sway back and forth with the warm, light breeze that sweeps into the car.

After a moment, the compound comes into view. Every type of Harley in every color you can think of is sitting out front. The garage is open, and I can see men inside working. The 'club whores,' as Cain calls them, stand outside smoking and giving me the evil eye as I drive by. I hold my breath as I come to a stop in front of the office, where Cain told me to meet him when I texted him to let him know I was on my way.

I shut my car off before exhaling and climbing out. If I'm going to be one tough ass bitch of a lawyer, I may as well face my fears now. I need to suck it up and deal with Cain's dad.

My flip-flops smack against the wooden steps as I climb. I tug on my jean shorts as I knock on the door. They're too short, and I hate them, but for some reason Cain loves them and asked me to wear them when I showed up.

The door swings open and a beautiful, dark auburn-haired woman smiles at me. This I know to be Cain's step mom, Darcy. He has told me all about her; how she has settled his father down from all his whoring around.

"Hi," I say with a wave.

"Hi, Calla. Come on in. Jed's in his office and wanted to talk to you for a minute. I'm not sure where Cain is. He should be here any minute, I would think."

She gestures me inside. I follow her to the office where she opens it and we both step inside. Shit, his dad is huge! All I can see is broad shoulders and muscles bulging everywhere. Holy shit!

"Don't let him intimidate you," Darcy whispers.

My gaze works its way up to his face, which is twisted with a shit eating grin.

"Well, Calla Lily Bexley."

Damn, this man could swallow me up whole. I'm not moving from this spot. I don't think I could move if I tried.

"Hi, sir," I manage to squeak out, much to his amusement.

"There ain't no sir around here, girl," he laughs.

"And I'm not too pleased about you marrying my boy, either. But what the fuck am I gonna do about it? You'll soon find out for yourself that a prissy ass little bitch like you isn't cut out to be an old lady to a Sinner."

He eyes me up and down.

"You are a pretty little thing, though. Look a lot like your mother, and thank Christ for that."

I know what he means, but I'm too damn scared to say anything. He's talking about my dad... screw his ass! He may be Cain's father, but he's a fucking prick.

"Jed, be nice to the poor girl," Darcy warns him, smacking his arm.

He merely gives her a 'don't fuck with me' look.

"Just get her the hell out of here."

He waves us off, then slaps Darcy on her ass. She lets out a little yelp, but bends and kisses him on his mouth. He pulls her in closer, one hand grabbing her boobs and the other a handful of ass. When he lifts his face from hers, his patronizing stare cuts through my brave façade, sizing me up to see if I can handle the kind of shit that goes on around here.

I can tell by the way he looks at me that he can smell my fear. I know all about the women; people fucking and sucking each other off in the corners. At parties. In their rooms here at the compound. I also know something this snarly bastard doesn't know. His son wants nothing to do with this. He wants to go to college and be a cop. And he wants to be with me.

I have failed this part though, only because I have been caught off guard. Bound and determined not to let him get to me, I follow Darcy as she walks around his desk and toward the door.

"Come on, let's go find your husband and have some girl time. Leave this grumpy ass to deal with the shit that his boy is all grown up and in love," she says cheerily.

"I like you," I say as she takes me outside and points me in the direction of their house, which is directly behind the compound.

"I like you, too. Sorry about that back there," she adds, jerking her thumb towards the office.

"He's pissed at Cain. The two of them go at each other's throats all the time. But a piece of advice."

She stops and places her hands on my shoulders.

"Stand by your man. Don't ask any questions, and do your own thing. We're a club; we all work outside of here. Have our own families. We're not like some of the other clubs who deal drugs, guns, and all that stuff. We're just a group of people who like to ride, party, and have fun. The men who are married don't cheat on their old ladies. The ones that don't have an old lady can do whatever the hell they want, with whomever they want. Oh, and one more thing… stay away from Emerald Jefferson."

"Who?"

The name vaguely rings a bell. I know I've heard that name somewhere before. More than likely from Cain.

"She's Jed's VP Monty's daughter, and she is a little bitch. She's been after Cain for years."

"Oh," I say, a little shocked.

I know if Cain had mentioned her to me, I would definitely remember. I've really never been the jealous type. Cain has never given me a reason.

"Good to know, and thanks again."

I wave and watch her walk back the way she came.

I practically sprint across the yard to the house. Excited to finally be alone with Cain, I jog up the porch steps. Do I knock or just go in? I choose to just go in and let him know I am here. I head straight up the stairs, where he's told me his bedroom is, and tap lightly on his closed door. No answer. I twist the knob slowly, with visions of him lying in bed waiting for me.

Gently I push it open, my excitement bursting from within me. Then, my eyes go wide and my heart drops to the fucking floor because my husband is in his bed. But not with me, his wife.

"Cain!" I scream.

She turns around, her long, blonde hair swinging right along with her. Her fake boobs getting groped by his hands. A crud smile flashes across her face as she sees me watching her glide up and down on my HUSBAND'S DICK!

"Calla!"

I just look at him, confused, hurt, and angry, and run. Not once do I look back.

Chapter One

Six Years Later

Six years. Seventy-two months. Two thousand and ninety one days and way too many damn minutes it's been since my feet have stepped on American soil.

And here I am sitting in my Mercedes coupe shaking like a bitch while I wait in line to cross over the Canadian border into Michigan.

What was supposed to be the best day of my life all those years ago drove me here when on my wedding night I found my husband fucking another woman in his bed. Not just any woman either, she was the one I was warned about by Cain's stepmom moments before I went into his house and caught him. Stupid whoring club slut.

Nice, wouldn't you say? I was young and naïve like my mom said when I told her we eloped to get married. I wasn't smart enough back then to realize I had been set up to walk in and find him with some skank riding him.

My mind went blank and I drove across the border to Canada and never once came back. I threw my phone in the river and ended up in a bed and breakfast just outside of Windsor, Canada.

Those first few days I stayed locked in my room until the owner, Mrs. Henry, knocked on my door. When I didn't answer, she let herself in and found me in the same clothes as when I had arrived. A fucking mess is what I was. She convinced me to call my parents, which I did, and both of them came to me trying to convince me to go back home.

My dad was on a rampage, wanting to kill Cain for hurting me, but my mother made him calm the hell down. I stood my ground and told her that I never wanted to see either one of those dickheads again.

Even with Windsor being right across the river from Detroit, it took a little convincing and two weeks of my mom staying with me to get her to let me stay. Meanwhile, she ignored all of Cain's phone calls. He left voice mail after voice mail until she finally turned her phone off, leaving him no way to get in touch with me at all.

Didn't stop the asshole, though. He resorted to going by their house continuously, pounding on the door, pleading and begging my father to tell him where I was. Dad hated him before he cheated and even more so after. He told him nothing. Cain continued going to my parents' house every day for about a month, sitting outside in his car when my dad stopped answering the door. One day he just stopped. Fell off the face of the earth, just like I did.

My name is still Calla, but my last name is no longer Bexley or Greer, which was my maiden name. It's now Calla Bexley-Henry, which wasn't easy to do. It's complicated but it's legal.

Legal because I am still fucking married to that piece of shit. Which brings me back to the here and now. I don't want to be married to him anymore. Going through all the bullshit of living in a foreign country, filing for taxes and most of all, lying to the last man I dated.

It took me four years to even want to look at a man, let alone go out with one. Even then, I just dated here and there; nothing serious. My body would constantly tighten up the minute they would try and touch me. Until I met Mikel Voskov.

Mikel is a hockey player. We met at an ice skating rink, naturally. His team was there with a group of fourth grade students whose class won a fundraising event, the prize being a night skating with the Canadian Ducks with Mikel as their goalie.

My eyes watched him, the way he bent down to the level of every child he spoke to and smiled, his attention focused on them.

I accidentally plowed him down turning a corner on my skates too sharply, and fell right on top of him. I laughed right along with him, for the first time in years. I had forgotten how good it felt to laugh. I missed it. I missed the longing looks from a man. The feeling of being cherished. A simple touch, a kiss, all of it. Mikel gave me all of those, and so much more.

After going out for several months, he told me he loved me. He wanted me to move in with him, get married. But how can anyone get married when they are still married to someone else?

He was heartbroken when I told him. Who could blame him? I never want to see the look on another man's face that I did on Mikel's. I hurt him by lying and betraying him the way I did. Never again. Cain is not worth it.

You keep saying he's not worth it. Why haven't you done anything about it before now? Why did you wait until a perfectly good man walked into your life to get a divorce? whispers the charming little devil on my shoulder.

I'm almost twenty four years old and tired of living a lie. I want to live, have a real life; an honest life. I also want to finish law school, move on, and forget about Cain once and for all.

I've stalked him online since he returned a year after I left; Google is quite friendly in telling you everything you need to know about a person. He never did fulfill his dream of becoming a cop. He is now the President of his dad's club, The Sinners of Revolution. A club that was once just that, a club, but now it's all kinds of screwed up. The Sinners are involved in illegal activities in every sense of the word.

Cain has changed so much; he's not at all the man I expected him to be, and I want no part of the fucked up life he has created for himself. Pictures of him and his notorious club are everywhere across the internet. He lives and breathes for them. He's untouchable, they say.

The one thing that hasn't changed much about him is his looks. He still looks like the young man I fell in love with all those years ago. Dark hair, rock-solid body. That delectable, dipping V. I've stared into those eyes for hours on my computer, praying that he is living in a cesspool of regret in the darkest reaches of hell for ruining my life. Fuck. I hate him.

Pulling my car to a stop, I hand the border control officer my documents and tell him I am crossing the border to visit family. He winks flirtatiously at me as he hands me my Visa and passport back.

Pulling back into traffic, my heart rate accelerates as I cross over into Michigan and get on the interstate to head to the one place I dread more than anything. A part of me wishes he wouldn't even be there, the other part of me hoping he is just so I can shove these papers in his face.

"Keep telling yourself you hate him, Calla. Remember what you saw," says the angel on my other shoulder.

I love her so much more. I flick that devil off my other shoulder and put a smile on my face, even though I suspect it's not real.

I come to a stop at the gas station a mile down the road from the compound. I sit for a few minutes, my breathing all kinds of erratic. My hands are shaking. I can do this. I have to, for no one other than myself.

What if he's with someone else and I walk in on him fucking her like before? What if he's doing drugs? All kinds of shit starts going through my head. Maybe I should go get my dad. He would be more than happy to shove these papers at Cain.

"No, Calla. You can do this. Just walk in there and be nice. He has to want this over just as much as you do."

The sound of my own voice and words calms me. I glance at myself one more time in the mirror. My long, dark hair is flat-ironed straight. My greenish-blue eyes are made up with a sultry look, and my tight, red pencil skirt and low-buttoned white sleeveless shirt make me feel like a badass. Top it all off with my black Jimmy Choo stilettos and I am one hell of knock out, if I do say so myself.

Just like last time, I pull up to the gate, which is heavily guarded. My eyes bulge when the biggest man I have ever seen taps a gun on my window. There are tattoos up and down his arms, and a colorful snake tattoo that looks real drapes around his neck, its mouth covering his right cheek, hanging open as if ready to strike.

I'm so freaked out I'm unable to move. I'm studying to be a lawyer, for God's sake. I shouldn't be intimidated by this man, but I don't like the deeply entrenched feeling I'm getting in the pit of my stomach that something terribly wrong is happening around here. What the hell has Cain done with this place?

I jump clear out of my seat when his gravelly voice crashes through my window as if he were sitting right next to me.

"This isn't a carpool parking spot, little mama. Get the fuck out of here."

He taps my window one more time then turns his bulky frame away from me. My hands continue to shake when I lower the window just a crack.

"I'm here to see Cain," I squeak.

He stops but never turns back around.

"Is that so? Boss man went and got himself a high class hooker instead of dipping his dick into that Emerald whore, huh? Well, he never told me about you... so like I said, get the fuck out of here."

Two steps is all this big bear of a man gets before my fear turns into full-fledged anger. My heart goes from cold to glacial knowing Cain's still with her.

"Look, you son of a bitch. I am not a hooker. Now do whatever the fuck you do when someone is here to see your so called 'boss man,' and tell him his wife is here."

"The fuck?" He jerks his head back.

"You heard me, you damn moron. Now call him."

I cross my arms over my breasts, drawing his stare directly there.

"You're Calla?" he asks curiously.

That's odd, and instantly has me on edge again. How does he know my name and who I am?

"Yes," I spit out.

"And how did you know my name?"

"Well, Jesus Christ. He's a damn fucking fool. And to answer your question, all of us around here know who you are."

"Come again?"

"Look, woman. I don't have time to stand here and talk to you. My shift is over. I want a cold beer and my wife. So I'll let you in. Cain should be in his office. Or in the bar. Anything else you want to know you can talk to him, but..."

He steps into my space.

"Cain may look like a sweet man on the outside with his clean-cut self, but he's definitely not the same man you once knew. He's one cold-hearted son of a bitch. Whatever went down between the two of you years ago did a number on him. Take my advice, sweet cheeks. A lot of things have changed around here, and this isn't the place for someone like you. Now that's all I'm gonna say."

He turns his back to me again and I swallow the lump in my throat as his callous words about Cain settle in my head. Hearing the gate creak open, I bite back the big 'Fuck you, too' I'm dying to deliver to him and climb back into my car, praying for God to help me get the hell in and out of here as fast as I can.

Chapter Two

Calla

I've only been here one time. Either I missed the looks of this place in the excitement of getting to Cain all those years ago, or things have really changed. There are people milling around everywhere. Scary-as-all-hell looking people. There is one big building with neon lights flashing. Loud music barrels through the door as people stroll in and out. What is this place?

This is the life Cain has built for himself. My eyes observe it all. I keep my focus on trying to find a place to park and not on the men whose beady eyes I can feel on me as I come to a stop in front of the building, the same one where Cain's dad's office used to be.

I don't know if this is where Cain will be or not, or if there's another building somewhere. My instincts tell me to stay in my car, turn around, and get the hell out of here, but there's a magnetic force tugging at me to stay. So I do. I snatch up my purse along with the divorce papers and get out of the car, hitting the key fob to lock it.

As I make my way to the door, I ignore the various cat-calls and name calling coming from these assholes.

"I'll tap that ass!"

"How much to suck my cock, bitch?"

Feeling more pissed off than scared, I push open the door, my mouth gaping when I step inside the dimly lit room. Oh, my God. This place has turned into a bar? The internet never mentioned that little fact. The guard did say Cain could be at the bar, but it never clicked for me that this is what he meant.

This is nothing like what I remember at all. Pool tables sit side by side in the back. The dance floor lies deserted in front of an empty stage. The loud music is coming from the old-fashioned jukebox up against the wall opposite of me. The bar itself is long, trailing the whole width of the room.

All the men are wearing black leather vests, which are adorned with a motorcycle on the back and the saying 'Live Fast- Ride Hard' along with the club name 'Sinners of Revolution.' Some of them have arms draped around women who are dressed normally, like me, but a few of the women hardly have clothes on at all. Here and there I see females also wearing the club vest.

My feet stay deeply rooted to this spot. No one is even giving me the time of day; they're all in a circle in the middle of the room in what seems to be some sort of meeting. I'm observing them all, and whatever the topic is, they clearly don't like it. The veins in the men's necks are bulging, and many hands are clenching into fists.

And then I see him, my darling husband, in the center of it all. His arm is dangling around the neck of the slut whose face I will never forget. She's fucking beautiful. Her long, blonde hair flows in waves around the flawlessly made up porcelain skin of her face. She's the only one not paying any attention to what Cain is saying. Instead, her head tilts to the side, recognition of who I am written across her face. I watch her intently as she snakes her arm around his waist, showing me she is staking her claim. I lift a brow, grinning back. You don't have a damn thing to worry about, sweetheart. The cheater is all yours.

I glance back at Cain. The pictures on the internet do him no justice at all; he's still fucking sexy. If he were a stranger, I believe I would drop my eyes right down to his package and forget my own damn name.

He makes eye contact with each member of the circle as he continues to talk, his voice too low for me to comprehend exactly what he is saying. I take a tiny step forward and the movement attracts his attention.

Suddenly, his gaze snaps to me, his arm dropping from around his slut as his eyes search my face almost as if he is trying to figure out if it is really me. And then his deep blue eyes travel to that magical spot on my neck where he knows I used to love being kissed by him.

A groan threatens to escape me when deeply buried memories resurface of the way his warm mouth would linger there. My nipples harden and my core aches from just this one look, but I refuse to let my own eyes roam his cut physique, afraid they will betray me like my body is doing now.

I stand there like a wallflower, watching him closely as he continues his personal tour, lingering on my breasts before heading south. His eyes darken when they land on my legs, made even longer by my stilettos.

The room suddenly falls quiet, heads turning on a dime to see what the man in charge is staring at. Hushed whispers start to echo from the onlookers.

"It's her, isn't it?" several women ask.

No one answers. Cain moves toward me and the group splits apart as if he was a damned god, leaving the two of us the openly scrutinizing each other as he stalks my way, anger and disapproval pouring off of him.

Under normal circumstances, the vibes radiating off of him might make a person uncomfortable, but I'm not moved in any way, shape, or form by the displeasure seeping out of him. He's used to making people feel that way. I can sense it. He's no longer a boy, but when I look at him, really look, I can see traces of his younger self behind those cold eyes.

He approaches me, coming to a stop within my reach. My instincts kick in. I'm here for one reason only, and I won't kowtow to him. What I want to do is reach out and slap his pretty-boy face.

No words are spoken for several long, drawn-out minutes until the high-pitched voice of his Goldilocks bitch sounds out from behind him.

"What are you doing here?" she hisses snidely.

"Shut the fuck up, Emerald."

The sound of Cain's voice startles me, so deep and masculine, very different from the young man I knew before.

"Everyone clear the hell out of here!" he orders.

Like devoted cult members, they do exactly what they are told by their leader. Each man passing him slaps him on his shoulder, while each woman looks at me with malevolence as if I have come here to stake a claim on what they all believe is theirs. I roll my eyes at a few of them, telling them silently to go fuck themselves.

"That means you, too," he barks at Emerald.

"Hell, no! I'm not leaving you alone with her."

Her honeyed words have me spitting out a low laugh.

"Don't worry, sweetheart," I say condescendingly. "He's all yours. I just need a few minutes of his time and you can carry on with whatever it is your slutty little self normally does."

I gesture with my hands for her to leave. She scrunches up her nose, aiming her pointer finger at my chest.

"You bitch! How dare you come in with your here with your fancy clothes and expensive shoes and call me names? You know nothing about me or what it is I do!"

I'm a little too quick for her. Taking hold of her by the wrist, I twist her around, pulling her arm up behind her.

"Listen here, babe... I know all I want to know about you. I could smell your nasty, used up snatch from over there. Now I need a few minutes with your fuck buddy here and then the two of you can go back to doing whatever the fuck you want, but until then, you will give me the time."

I release her arm and give her a little extra shove.

"Just go, Emerald. I'm curious as to what my wife has to say."

"Fine!"

She storms past us, slamming the door behind herself. All of a sudden I am freaking the hell out on the inside now that Cain and I are entirely alone. One of us has to break the silence in this eerily quiet room. Cain's cold, narrowed eyes have me sucking in a sharp breath. He's looking at me as if he can't decide whether he wants to kiss me or hurt me.

Fuck him and his death glare. I'm not about to back down. He's the one who turned me into the cold-hearted bitch I am today. The one who will never fully trust another man for the rest of my life.

"I want a divorce. I have the papers right here for you to sign, and then I will be gone."

Reaching inside my purse, I retrieve the papers, shoving them in his direction. He doesn't move a muscle to try and take them. He doesn't even blink.

"Goddamnit, Cain. Just take them and sign."

I shove them at him again. This time he rips them out of my hand and flips them over his shoulder, scattering them all over the floor.

"Jesus! What are you doing?"

I move to step around him to collect the papers. His arms slashes out, gripping my upper arm, pulling me directly into him so our fronts are pressed firmly against each other's. I can smell the alcohol on his breath.

That little devil on my shoulder has a mind of her own. She's urging me to dip forward and sneak one little taste of that sweet, spicy scent. Fucking traitor!

Cain continues to stare, his grip tightening. The way his rock-hard body is pressed against mine, I can feel the firmness of his chest and the length of his erection boring into my stomach. I don't like being manhandled and I sure as hell don't like the man standing so close to me. He's pissing me the fuck off.

"What am I doing?" he growls. "Shouldn't I be asking you that question?"

"Let go of me now, Cain. I'm not messing around, and to answer you damn question, I'm here because I want a divorce. This was never a marriage to begin with and now it's in my way. Can you just sign the papers? Please?"

All of a sudden I become all too aware of what kind of man he has turned into when he switches our position, backing us up until my spine is firmly resting against the wall behind me.

"It's in your way?"

"Yes. I'm engaged," I lie, hoping he can't tell. It's the first thing that came to mind.

"You're lying."

He dips his face closer to mine. He still smells the same. All man. Intoxicating. Addicting. I need him to get away from me. I'm on edge and even quicker to defend myself while being trapped beneath his brute force. Anger rears its ugly head.

"I'm not. It's been six goddamned years, Cain. Besides, even if I'm not engaged, what the hell business is it of yours, you son of a bitch?"

"I'm not signing, Calla. Never!"

On impulse my free hand comes up to push him back, but he's firmly rooted in place, not budging at all. He brings one of his legs in between mine, nudging them apart. The slit on my skirt threatens to give way.

How dare he try to turn me on? How fucking dare my pussy clench with a familiar ache? How dare my eyes want to divert down to his dick? I'm just as mad at myself for being a disloyal little tramp as I am at him.

"You don't know me anymore. I don't know you. I never knew you. You're a cheat. A drug dealer. A gun smuggler. And a fucking coward. I want nothing to do with you. I hate you. Goddammit, get away from me!" I scream.

"Shut up."

He gathers both of my hands in his and lifts them over my head. I shake my head back and forth, my long hair flinging all over the place. I'm about to go stark raving mad. It's been so long since he's touched me. His rough hands feel the same. I'm on the verge of asking him to touch me here or kiss me there. He threads our fingers together and I clamp down on my tongue. Why after all this time is he doing this? Doesn't he want his freedom, too?

"Calla."

The sound of my name coming out of his mouth, as gentle and smooth as it used to, is my undoing. My mind tries in vain to block out how much I've missed having him this close, his lips only a hairsbreadth away from mine. A tear slips from the corner of my eye. I don't want him to think I'm weak or for him to see he is getting to me. When he speaks again, my head is down. I keep it this way and close my eyes.

"You will never marry another man, not as long as I'm alive. You're mine, Calla. I've waited way too fucking long for you to come back to me, and I will be damned if you are leaving here without hearing me out."

The man before me has changed from the one I knew all those years ago. I can tell he is used to getting what he wants, and he may be the boss around here, but there is no damn way I will let him stake a claim on me after what he did. He threw away his rights the day he decided to fuck that whore. I feel like spitting in his face and then tearing his damn head off.

"I don't want to be married to you anymore. I just want to be free. I'm not yours; I never was. You proved it, you bastard, on our wedding night, of all days. So, no, you egotistical son of a bitch. I belong to myself. Now step the hell back away from me and sign those papers. Or don't. Either way, I will get my divorce from you."

The corners of his mouth turn up in a smug grin.

"Did Bowie let you in the gate the minute you told him who you were?" he asks, completely ignoring my previous statement. The question throws me off guard.

"What the hell kind of question is that? Of course he did. He said he knew who I was. And by the looks of it when I walked in here, everyone does."

I pull my brows together, trying get some clarity as to why he's asking.

"There is so much shit you have no motherfucking idea about. It's a damn good thing you've been in Canada all these years. Better yet, you were smart enough to change your name, although when I finally found out where you were it killed me not to come after you and bring you back were you belong."

He almost sounds hurt, even regretful. I'm not buying his bullshit. An unsettling feeling begins to well up inside of me. He found me, and he never came for me?

"Y-you knew where I was?"

"Fuck, yes, I knew where you were. I know every fucking thing about you. I know how many men you have fucked. I know where you went to school. I even know where you buy all those lacy, sexy as hell bras you have a fetish for. And one more thing, I sure as fuck know you aren't engaged. You're my goddamn wife, so yes, I know every motherfucking thing there is to know. And to answer your other question, they all know I'm married. A few of them even know what you look like."

His body pushes into mine, his mouth lingering at the base of my ear. Oh, dear lord. He is hard. I'm talking steel hard, and way the hell bigger than I remember him being. The distraction nearly causes me to miss his next words.

"They were all told if you ever came here to let you in. And to never let you out."

Chapter Three

"What?"

I am transfixed by horror. Cain is out of his damned mind if he thinks I am staying here in his den of illegal activity. I writhe free of his firm hold and slap him across the face, the sound echoing loudly in the room. He flinches slightly, backing away and giving me enough room to breathe. My chest heaves up and down with uneven breaths.

"You can't keep me here against my will, Cain. What the hell is wrong with you? Good God, have you been doing the drugs you sell? Because you are fucked in the head if you think I'm staying here with you while all this shit happens right in front of me. Besides, my dad will come looking for me soon. I'm done talking to you. I'm leaving."

He grabs my arm, bends, and hoists me into the air, his other hand planted firmly on my ass as he throws me over his shoulder.

"Put me down!" I shriek, kicking and doing my best to inflict damage with my stilettos while dangling upside down.

"Shut your mouth, Calla."

He's too strong for me. I still try and put up a fight as he retreats across the floor. His strides are quick as he takes us outside, the gravel crunching underneath his black boots.

"Cain, don't do this. You have no right!"

I see the legs of several men and hear them calling out to him about getting some. He is getting nothing from me but a kick in his damn nuts when he puts me down. I'm getting tossed around like a rag doll.

"Help me, you fucking assholes!" I scream.

Cain chuckles.

"No one is going to help you. Now shut the hell up, or I will tape your mouth shut and tie you to my fucking bed until you do as you're goddamn told."

Before I can retort, he abruptly stops at the sound of a shrill voice behind us.

"Cain, what the hell are you doing?"

Emerald. Even though I am hanging upside down, I know it's her by the desperation in her voice. I feel Cain swivel around.

"Can someone get this cunt the fuck away from here?"

"No!" she wails. "Damn it, Cain, what's going on?"

"Don't tell me what the fuck to do. It's none of your goddamned business. Now fucking leave before I have you thrown out."

Oh my God, if I didn't hate her so much, I just might feel sorry for the bitch. Without another word to her, Cain turns his back and strides away, leaving her standing there shouting and cursing the both of us.

I have no idea where we are going until I feel and then see him climb a few steps. Panic sets in. Memories flood my mind from the one and only time I was in this house. I start to pound on his back with everything I have to get him to release me.

He continues across the front porch, ignoring the beating I am inflicting on him. Once we're inside, he stomps up the stairs. My heart is beating frantically. Finally, I cave and give in to my raw emotions, and I start to cry.

"Please, Cain, don't do this. I'll beg if I have to."

Still nothing from him. I screech through my tears when he tosses me onto his bed. He pulls my shoes off, tossing them behind his back. My expensive Jimmy's hit the wall with a little thwack. I'm sobbing now, and scared.

"Stop crying. I'm not going to hurt you."

He's gentle when he squats down in front of me. I refuse to look at him. My anger at myself for being so weak consumes me.

"Let me go, Cain. You don't want me here any more than I want to be."

The bed shifts when he sits down next to me. I stay still, for the first time admitting I'm scared of this Cain Bexley I do not know. All kinds of fucked up scenarios are invading my head. I should have brought my dad with me. No one knows where the hell I am.

"You're shaking."

A warm, rough, calloused hand settles on my knee. I flinch from the contact.

"Listen to me for just one minute. There are a few things you need to know."

I keep my head bowed down, my hair shielding him from seeing my face as I watch my tears land on my skirt one by one.

"Fuck me. The last thing in this world I ever wanted to do was to hurt you again, baby. Before I tell you anything, I need you to know that."

I close my eyes. Every bit of hurt from that horrible night comes rushing back. Him calling me baby is breaking me all over again.

"I had to do it, Calla. My dad left me no choice."

My head snaps up at the mention of his father.

"What do you mean, you had no choice?"

He sighs, pulling his hand away from my knee. I avert my gaze from his down to the spot where I can still feel the warmth of his skin on mine.

"The day we got married, I came back here, and told my dad about us like I promised you I would. But it didn't go as we'd hoped. He was pissed off, started saying shit I had no idea about. All this time I thought we were just a club... a group of people who liked to ride. I never knew the bullshit that really went down around here. The drugs. Any of it."

He lets out a frustrated breath.

"He told me everything. Believe me, I was shocked as fuck. He had been lying to me for fucking years, leading me to believe he was legit. At the time I was blinded to it all. My mind was obsessed with you and me, with trying to find a way for us to be together in spite of the hatred our fathers had for one another. It wasn't until after you were gone and my dad brought me in that I realized our parents were right all along. They were only trying to protect you from a life neither of us knew anything about."

I sit here like a mummy wrapped so tightly that I'm unable to move any part of my body except my eyes. Cain starts straight ahead, breathing heavily. I almost feel sorry for him.

"Before I continue, I need you to tell me you believe me. When we were together I had no idea the kind of shit my dad was involved in. The entire club was a farce. He lied to me, too. Do you believe me?"

Tense silence fills the room until slowly my ire subsides. Cain never wanted this life for himself, he was born into it, and had obviously been trained to lead this club before his dad was killed.

Something you learn in law school is that when you study a person to distinguish whether they are lying or telling the truth, their voice is as telling as their face. Analyzing Cain right now, my gut instinct says he is speaking the truth.

My heart, on the other hand, wants to curl up and die. To stop beating. Losing him was by far the most traumatizing experience of my life. I felt meaningless without him. I wouldn't wish that kind of pain on my worst enemy. To top it all off, my parents knew? They knew this entire time and never once told me?

"I'm not sure if I believe you or not," I say slowly. "That's the best I've got for you right now. My mind is trying to absorb a lot here."

I really don't know if I believe him or not. What I do know is that my words must mollify him until I figure it out. I indicate with my hand for him to continue with his story.

"My dad told me I had to do whatever it would take to get you to stay away from me. He was being threatened Calla, by dangerous men. A rival MC called the Savages. We're not talking your everyday 'I'm going to kick your ass' threats. We're talking blood and murder. He tried to keep it from me, but they started threatening to get me, too."

Cain hangs his head for a moment before looking back up at me.

"I can't take back what I did, but at the time, I believed my father and understood that as my wife, your life was in danger, too. By the time I walked out of his office, I had less than fifteen minutes before you were supposed to be here. That's when I saw Emerald. I knew the only way I could get you to walk away from me was by letting you see me with her."

Whatever pain I went through, he went through it, too. His language, his posture, and the way he won't look at me when he's telling me this shows me enough to believe him. Our pain was shared, yet he chose to distance himself from me instead of fighting for our love, our four-hour marriage. Words to honor and protect spoken right before he screwed another woman.

"I believe you," I tell him softly, which gets his attention. He turns to me with a wary smile on his lips, which fades at my next words.

"But... I don't think I will ever forgive you. I just can't wrap my head around any of it. You didn't love me enough to fight for me. To tell your father to go to hell. To jump on your motorcycle and come and get me. You threw me away like the two years we spent together meant nothing to you. There isn't a person in this entire world who deserved to see what I saw, to have that kind of pain to deal with. I never saw it coming. I'm beyond all that pain now. I'm coping. I have a life of my own now."

He remains stoic for several long beats before speaking again.

"I can't let you leave here, Calla. There's too much danger out there for me to let you go."

His words trigger more frustration. Standing, I lash out with the little bit of self-worth I have left.

"You can't make me stay here. What part of that don't you understand? My God, I said I believed you. We can both move on and chalk this up as the one big mistake we will make in our lives. You can settle down with Emerald or God knows who and have little motorcycle riding, gun shooting fucking babies for all I care."

I don't have the will to be strong any longer. Everything is too much all at once. Seeing him again after all this time, noting all the changes in his body that make him even hotter now than he was even then, has made me feel the loss of every one of those six years that have gone by. My limp body sags to the floor and I cry. I cry because it's killing me to be in this room. I cry because the man I once loved is so damn close to me, and he's not mine anymore.

I don't know how much time passes, but somehow I pull myself together, lift my wet face off of the carpet, and meet the eyes of the man who betrayed me.

"You're a heartless bastard!" I scream.

"That I am. But not when it comes to you. When it comes to you, my heart beats. It fucking beats so damn fast you have no idea. Now look, I know you're confused. Your world is suddenly fucked up. But I swear to you, if I let you leave here, you won't make it a mile down that road before someone either takes you or puts a goddamned bullet between your gorgeous eyes. This isn't a fucking joke. It's not up for discussion. Until I fix this war with the Savages my father got this club into, you will stay here."

I arch an eyebrow at him.

"The Savages, huh? You're the one who chose this life, not me. So why would someone want to put a bullet through my head?"

Instead of answering, he scowls.

"Jesus Christ. The less you know, the fucking safer you are."

I lift my hands up and shove my hair out of my face, letting out a bitter laugh as I do. This is crazy. I came here for a simple divorce, one I was sure would come easily, and now I find myself being held prisoner for reasons unknown to me. I mean, come on. How much crazier can this shit get?

"Not sure what you find funny about this whole thing, babe. Care to share?"

I look at him in mock astonishment.

"You don't find this funny? After six years I finally decide I want my freedom from a marriage that was wrecked before it even got started. I came here expecting to get just that and now I've been told that my husband fucked some slut on my wedding day to protect me. Then he disappears for God knows how long, comes back here and runs some gun smuggling, illegal biker club, knowing where I've been the entire time. And now he's going to kidnap me to save my life? I'm sorry, but I find this to be quite comical."

Scooching my back up against the wall, I reach for my shoes and slip them on my feet.

"I'm leaving."

I turn on my heel preparing to walk right out of there when his hands grasp me around my waist from behind. I let out a scream as I'm hauled backwards with my damn feet dragging on the floor.

"Son of a motherfucker! Do you want me to tie your gutsy ass up?" he barks, tossing me face-first onto the bed.

I begin to kick. He growls when one of my pointy-toed shoes connects with some part of his body. His strong hands grasp me by both of my ankles as he manhandles me to the edge of the bed.

"Cain, this is kidnapping. I'm done playing games. Let me go!" I demand.

"Fuck it. I tried being nice. To treat you kindly. You leave me no other choice."

In a flash, he flips me over and his full weight crashes down on top of me, pinning me down with both his hands and his stare. I suck in a very much needed breath. My traitorous body heats up when I feel his erection press into me and the arrogant prick knows it. He smirks, insistent on making sure the hardest part of his body is pressed against the now wettest part of mine.

"Do you remember the first time we fucked? How you screamed my name so damn loud when I tasted your virgin pussy for the first time. When I popped your tight fucking cherry?"

He is like a supernatural shape shifter changing from good to evil. Suddenly, the weak woman I became a few moments ago returns and I simply lie there, appalled by his words.

"Let's clear this shit up right now," he says harshly. "You are not leaving here. You will shut your fucking mouth. This isn't high school or college or even fucking Disney World. This is my club, my house and my goddamned rules. You will stay in my house, you will do what I say, and you will sleep in my fucking bed. When I decide to fill you in on more, I will, but until I do, you will stay right the fuck here! Now, do I make myself clear? Because I've got shit to do, and even though this was a pleasant surprise, I was in the middle of a meeting I need to finish."

He shoves himself off of me, his look lethal and downright chilling.

"Stay," he commands, pointing his finger at me like a dog. "And let's get the record straight. We are not a gang. This is a club and a damn bar. We don't do drugs. Never have, never will."

With that, he turns and strides out of the room, slamming the door behind him. Just like that, he's gone. And me?

I'm trapped.

Chapter Four

Cain

"Motherfucking cock sucking son of a motherfucking bitch!"

I'm an asshole. She's here. The one person in my life that I love is here, and I just treated her like a piece of shit under my shoe.

As much as I might regret the way I dealt with her, for her own protection, she will have to do what I say and talk only when necessary for as long as she's here, which for her will be like pulling her own damn teeth. The Calla I know would never keep her mouth shut. I'm fucked either way I look at it, but she's safe here and for now that's what matters to me the most.

She's even more strikingly gorgeous than I remember. I've seen over a thousand pictures of her over the years, and not a damn one of them compares to seeing her in person.

Her hair, though. My God, that hair. The thick mass used to be curly, the long locks hanging down the middle of her back. But now? Fuck. It's sleek and straight, sitting just a few inches above the curve of her ass.

Her ass, which was right in my face when I slung her over my shoulder. My cock is still hard thinking about the way her skirt hugged that plump, firm, and shapely backside that connects to the longest pair of legs I have ever seen.

And her tits. Fuck me with those, too. They've grown. My woman always had a nice rack, but now I could look at them for days... fondle them for hours and suck on them for the rest of my life.

My fingers twitch thinking about the way they would feel in the palms of my hands.

And her pussy. I have never forgotten how incredible she feels. I know for a fact how pink, wet, and tight it is. I can picture her smooth mound, the way it tastes. The way her muscles clenched my cock. Clutching. Squeezing tightly, as if she never wanted me to come out. I never wanted to. I could live inside her forever.

My beautiful wife doesn't have any clue as to the lengths I've gone to in order to keep tabs on her all these years. I know her every move; her monthly visits to the day spa where she treats herself. Her school schedule. Her friends. I know every damn thing. Hell, I went as far as assigning my friend Manny as her personal bodyguard. Sick fucker that I am, there were several times I had him set up video in her room just so I could watch her sleep, and listen to the soft sounds of her breathing.

It's not just her body that first caught my attention all those years ago. It was her brains. She's brilliant. Queen of her own mind. She was never afraid to speak it, to say how she felt. And here I am crushing her as if she's the one who hurt me, when it's the other way around. I've single-handedly destroyed my marriage and my life, all for this fucking club. I hate it and everything it stands for.

The Sinners is not the same as it was when my father was alive. We no longer do anything illegal. All right, that's not entirely true. They don't do anything illegal. For me, this club is a front for the shit I do. It sure as hell isn't drugs, as Calla obviously thinks. Drugs can fuck you up. You start selling that shit and the next damn thing you know, you're fucking using it. Hooked. No fucking way do I want any of that shit around here; the things I do are bad enough.

For the record, I recognize my own hypocrisy regarding the law. I wanted to be on the good side of the law my entire life. My dad went and screwed it all the hell up for me by lying.

We're just a group of people who like to get together and have a good time for the love of our bikes, son.

Liar. If not for his lies, everything could be different right now. I could be inside that house making love to my wife. Be a cop like I wanted to be. Instead, his death left me with no choice but to try to clean up the brewing pot of shit-stew he created. That's entirely not true, either. I was given a choice of doing right or wrong, and I chose wrong. But to me, I chose wrong for the right reasons.

Here's where the problem lies. I turned this place around, into what I wanted it to be; a clean-cut bar, the way it should have been all along. We're legit. Everyone has well respected jobs. Families. The whole nine yards. One man left when we found out he was dealing, and he's the piece of shit who killed my father and Darcy to get back at me, all because I shut his shit down.

When I found out Kryder Banks was into dealing, we came down hard. He and his entourage of drugged-out coke and heroin addicts broke the fucking law every damn time they left here, selling to little kids, or moms who should have been using that money to feed and shelter those kids.

Kryder was given the choice to either back the hell off, or leave. He chose the latter. Went in with the Savages, or so I thought. He had been a member of that club for years and brought that shit in here. Now that lying son of a bitch is one of the biggest drug dealers in the Midwest. Or he was, until the pussy ass disappeared.

Bringing myself to a halt, I look back at my old house; the house I haven't stepped foot in for several years. I wonder to my asshole self why I even brought Calla there. Why I left her in a room where the last time she saw me I was balls deep inside of Emerald.

Little does she know, I did it to save her life. Save her from this shit that surrounds me. I'm a bastard for doing that to her, and I'm an even worse bastard for telling her half the crap I told her and then storming out like I did. I'm completely fucking this up with her. The best thing I can do is stay as far away from her as I can, finish this meeting, and get lost in a bottle of whiskey.

Fuck me, I wish I could get lost in her right now. I wish I could take us far away from here and start the hell over.

I just need some space and time to think.

I wasn't expecting her to come here today. I knew she would one day, but why the fuck didn't Manny give me the heads up that she was headed here? Fuck, I ought to beat his damn ass!

I won't, though. He's one of a handful of people I trust. The one person who has kept my wife safe all these years while I've pretended to be a man I'm not. I almost gave myself up to her a few minutes ago when she sat on my floor and cried. And then I went and fucked things up even more by tainting the one night in my life I will never forget; the night we lost our virginity to each other.

It kills me to see the pain in her eyes that she's trying so damn hard to hide. She's changed, but no matter how hard she denies her feelings for me, I know she still cares. I know she still loves me in spite of all that bullshit about wanting a divorce so she can move on. Fuck. The truth is, she's not mine anymore. But God, how I want her to be.

My emotions are normally well hidden under my dark exterior. Being a brutal son of a bitch does not permit me to be liked or loved; it gets me feared. They say I'm ruthless, a man who takes what he wants and stops at nothing. A take-no-prisoners kind of man. And if you cross me, my fists become my weapons of choice.

I've got so many sins on my hands. Murder is not one of them, but I would do it for her if I had to. I would do anything to keep her safe.

I don't give a shit about anyone except for the woman who I want nothing more than to give this all up for. She's my weakness; the one person who could cure my soul, the only one who can bring me to my knees and get my head spinning out of control. It's going to take my balls to turn into brass to be a prick to her again. To make her think I don't care when all I want to do is bring her into my arms. Tell her I never once stopped loving her.

Damn it! My chest explodes with rage. I fucking can't do it. She needs to think I've gone bad.

I'm still trying to figure out who is the mole in this club. Everyone around here knows I'm married. They were all sworn to keep their damn mouths shut or suffer the consequences of my wrath, but someone talked. That's why Manny was sent off to Canada to take care of her. This shit is so deep that I wanted to keep my wife as far away from it as possible.

Now that she is here by my side, I need to stick to my master plan of finding the assholes who killed my father, starting with Kryder Banks. He knows I'm after his piece of shit ass. Ever since word got out about Calla, he's been laying low, keeping his whereabouts a secret while he has his parasites do all of his dirty work.

Even though every part of me wants to go back and take my wife in my arms, I have shit to get done. Turning around, I take about five steps before I see Emerald stalking my way with a determined look on her face. I need to end this shit with her here and now.

She's been nothing but a means to an end for me for years. All she has ever been to me was a quick release for my dick, and she knows it. The pitiful bitch has been begging me to let her ride on the back of my bike, to officially make her mine. Little does she know that I know what the cunt does when I'm not around... she's on her back or on her knees for Coon.

I laugh at the nickname we gave him. Coon Dog. All he likes to do is fuck doggy style, and doesn't give two shits if someone watches him do it, either. He's into that kind of exhibitionist shit. This is how I know he's been screwing around with Emerald. Don't care either. He can have her. That bitch screams louder than a banshee when she's being fucked. Good thing I tune her ass out. Every woman I've been with, I tune them out and pretend I'm inside Calla.

These bitches around here have been fucked by so many hen-pecked pussy-whipped sons of bitches it isn't even funny anymore. I have never fucked another woman bareback. Never gone down on another woman, either. None of them have sucked my cock, and I sure as hell won't kiss them.

Emerald gets close enough to reach out and try to touch me.

"Come on, Cain. Talk to me, please."

"Go home. Get out of here, NOW!"

I make it to my office, settling into my chair to discuss business when my VP Beamer walks in, all six foot seven of him lean and tatted up muscle. Those tats look damn good on him; they fit his badass persona to a tee. Me, on the other hand? I have one tattoo, in a spot no one has seen except me and the man who put it there. I never had the desire to mark myself with one unless it meant something to me. This one means every damn thing to me.

Call me crazy for marking my dick with a tattoo. I don't give a shit. It's never been a problem to keep it from any of the women I've screwed. None of them touches my dick, sucks it, or looks at it. I get straight down to fucking and then kick their asses out the minute I get my balls off.

"You got news for me, brother?" I ask Beam, while pulling out a bottle of Johnny Walker Blue Label and two shot glasses. I set them down on my desk and glare at my friend.

"Nothing, man. No one's talking. It's like he disappeared." He shrugs. "You know me, I'll keep digging. Someone's bound to talk."

His eyebrows shoot up when he notices the two shot glasses.

"You know I'm not drinking that shit, right?" he smirks, then reaches into his back pocket and pulls out a small pint of his cheap Jim Beam.

And there you have why we call him Beamer. I shove a glass across my desk at him.

"Best shit in the world right here," I say as I crack open my bottle, take a deep sniff, and pour my shot. Beam does the same with his.

"Cheers, man."

Both of us suck down our favorite drink like it's water. This type of stuff should be sipped and savored. Not with me. I love the ever-so-gratifying feeling of the burn as it makes its way down my throat, settling into my stomach. I need to get shit-faced, forget about today, and worry about tomorrow when I wake my ass up.

"I heard about Calla coming here," Beam says with concern.

"Yeah, man. She's here," I reply brusquely.

"And?"

"And what?"

"How'd it go?"

"She wants a divorce. I'm not giving her one. I've waited way too long, wasted six years that I could have spent with her. She'll never get me to sign. She's in my old house. Until we kill that rat bastard who gutted my dad and threatened her life, she stays here."

He doesn't need to know any more than that, so I quickly change the subject. I grab my bottle of Jack and head towards the door with Beam, intent on getting drunk. The minute I walk out the door and head towards the event in the back, I roll my eyes.

Emerald strides towards me the minute I'm out the door, circling around beside me. She loops her arm through mine as if she owns me. I want to rip my skin off when her fingertips graze down my arm. I grind my teeth like crazy at her audacity. She knows not to touch me unless she is told.

"Jesus, woman. Get your hands off of me," I growl, jerking myself free. "I thought I told you to leave. You're not wanted here, Emerald."

The minute I plop down in my chair she sits on my lap, which pisses me off.

"Come on. What the hell?"

My best friend Manny shakes his head from across the yard as I try to dislodge her. Yeah, screw you too, asshole. I flip him the middle finger. Dickhead knows I'm going to go postal on his ass the first chance I get for not giving me the heads up that Calla was on her way.

"Jesus, Emerald. What the hell?"

I grab her arm and pull her back into the compound, heading straight for my office. Her smile widens across her face. I know what she's thinking. She thinks I'm going to fuck her back here and everything is going to be fine. She couldn't be more wrong. I'm about to set this bitch straight.

Chapter Five

I lay here staring up at the ceiling in the one room that brings back the worst day of my life, chastising myself over and over in my mind. How could I have been so stupid? This is not me. I'm not weak. I really thought I had moved on. It's been over five years since I have allowed myself to cry. A man who did what Cain did to me was not worth one more tear.

I'm so confused. I don't know what to make of his sweet-to-mean cycle, either. How can someone ask for an apology, then in the next breath spew out hateful, stinging words?

He has left me here with so many unanswered questions. Like, who in the hell are the Savages, and why would they want to kill me? I've been gone, I know nothing about this new life of his, except the things I have read or heard. I even went as far as telling my parents that no matter how much I begged them to tell me details about Cain that they were to never convey anything, and they didn't, no matter how hard I cried.

The more I think about my mom and dad, the less angry I become with them. Even though I'm not a parent, I do understand the fact they were only trying to protect me from a life that would bring their only child nothing but danger. But why? What could be so bad that someone would want to hurt me?

And then there's the fact that Cain knew where I was this whole time. Did he have someone spying on me? Following me around? He said he knew everything right down to knowing how many men I have slept with. Two. I have slept with two men, which I know damn well is a far smaller number than the women he has been with.

I can't say that I blame any woman for wanting to have him. The way his hard body felt up against mine, I could have evaporated right into it. Cain has always been muscular, but not like he is now. His strong, well-built frame demands attention. I could feel how full and well defined his pecs were when he pinned me to him. How his t-shirt strained across his broad chest, his stomach feeling like a slab of granite.

God, why am I even thinking about him in this way? He nearly destroyed me, and now he's doing it again.

Rolling over on my side and curling up in the fetal position, I suppress a loud groan, my thoughts on major overload. It's then that I see several pictures all in familiar frames sitting on top of a dresser.

He's kept them all; every last photo of the two of us together, and there they are, staring me dead in the face. Sitting up, I swing my legs over the edge and grab the one that calls out to me the most.

I run my fingers over the contours of Cain's face. It saddens me to see how happy he looks in this picture and how unhappy he truly looks today. That day several years ago is a day I will never forget; the day we were finally able to show each other how much we loved one another, and he threw it all back in my face. I hate him for the vulgar way he spoke about that day, as if it meant nothing to him. It meant everything to me, and he made it sound like I was just another random fuck.

"What happened to you?" I whisper.

Instead of placing the photo back in its spot, I heave it across the room. The sound of the broken glass incites me to destroy every damn photo, every fucking memory. I take my anger out on them all, listening to each one shatter as it hits the floor.

When they are all gone, I look around, my chest heaving in anger as I take in my surroundings. How dare he leave me in here, in this room, on this bed where I caught him fucking his slut?

Grabbing my beautiful shoes and shoving my feet into them, I make my way to the door. Realizing I need my purse, I search the room frantically for it. Where the hell is it? All he did was walk in here and toss me on the bed, but it's gone.

"Goddamnit. Where is it?" I scream.

Did I drop it somewhere?

Not bothering to look for it anymore, I yank the door wide open and descend the stairs as quickly as I can. I'm going to find a way out of this place one way or another.

I feel the warmth of summer cover me when I step onto the porch. It's almost dark now. I have been here way too long. I inhale deeply, the scent of pine wafting up my nose along with a whiff of smoke from a nearby bonfire.

The sound of people talking and laughing loudly has me heading in that direction. There has got to be someone who will help me get out of here. It's not until I stumble upon the party that I forget exactly where it is I am. I'm in his territory. These are his people and this is his world. No one is going to help me get out of here, not if he's told them not to.

I search the crowd of people for him and he is nowhere to be found. I'm shocked by what I see. Jesus, don't these women believe in wearing clothes? Skirts so short, their ass is half hanging out. Tops so low cut that if they bend over, you are sure to get a full view of their boobs. No one notices me standing here in this dark corner with my mouth hanging wide open as they all party, beers or liquor bottles in hand. The music is so loud I don't even understand how you could carry on a conversation. I've been to several college parties and they've all been exactly like this. This is a flipping fuckfest.

"Calla?" a powerful masculine voice says in my ear, alarming me.

"Manny?" I place my hand over my heart, surprised to see Cain's best friend from school. "You frightened the hell out of me."

His deep chuckle rumbles around the music.

"Sorry about that."

I freeze when he comes into view.

"Girl. It's been way too damn long since the last time I saw you. And fuck me straight to hell, you're a sight for sore eyes."

Even though it's dark and he can't see me, I roll my eyes.

"How have you been?" he asks.

"Great, until I came here expecting to get Cain to sign for a divorce and find myself being held hostage," I scoff.

"About that..," he begins, scratching the back of his head. "Look, Calla. I know you have no clue what the hell is going on, and I'm one of the very few people here who knows the truth as to why you took off."

I go to interrupt him and he holds up a hand.

"Just listen," he says.

"Shit's been bad for years. I mean, real bad. Cain had it in his mind when he came back after you left him that he was going to set things straight within this club. Do right by you and find a way to get you back. You may not believe me when I tell you this, and frankly I don't blame you, but I'm not bullshitting you when I tell you that what he did fucking destroyed him. He took off when he couldn't find you. He disappeared for over a year, and to this day, whenever anyone asks him where he was, he tells them it's none of their damn business. No one, not even his dad knew where he went."

Manny takes a long drink of his beer. Eyes trained straight ahead as he goes on.

"He hasn't been the same since. He came back bitter and filled with hate for everyone around him. He dug right into learning everything about this place. Told his dad off more times than I can remember. And then a few years ago, those fucking Savages declared war on the club. Shit went to hell and Jeb ended up getting himself killed. Cain fucking lost it when that happened. He turned into a fucking crazy man. No one could reason with him."

A dull ache forms in my chest. I feel for Cain and the fact he was blindsided by all of this, but my heart can't get past the fact that he didn't love me enough to stay true to his vows or the promises he made me. He disappeared for a very long time... we could have left together and tried to work things out. So many things could be different right now if he hadn't given up on us so easily. I turn back to Manny.

"Do you know where Cain disappeared to?"

He chugs back some more of his beer.

"Yup."

"Are you going to tell me?"

"Nope."

I cross my arms over my chest.

"It doesn't really matter. What's done is done. I couldn't care less."

"Keep telling yourself that. Maybe when you're ninety, you'll believe it."

He laughs at his own joke. I don't find any of this funny at all. I want answers, and Manny most likely has them.

"Who are these Savages, and what does this all have to do with me?" I ask abruptly.

"They're the fucking enemy," he says without hesitation. "Why they're the enemy is a story for Cain to tell you, not me. I will say this, though. The Savages have the worst reputation of all of the MCs. They think they can rule every other club out there. Those assholes will kill men, women, even members of their own club. Hell, they've gone as far as killing police officers."

Manny takes another swig of beer as I let that information sink in.

"Jeb didn't take their shit. He was out on a ride with his wife, who was one of the sweetest women I've ever met, constantly going to bat for Cain when he and his dad would get into it. Those evil bastards shot and killed the both of them. From what we all heard, there wasn't much left of the bodies by the time they were discovered. And before you ask how we know it was them, those fuckers carve a big 'S' into their victims' foreheads afterwards. Somehow they found out about you, Calla. They've been threatening Cain with you for several years now and that's why he's left you alone. Why he didn't come after you before that shit went down, well, that's on him."

His words slice me and I feel sick. I wobble on my feet, anxiety curling around my stomach. Invisible hands scuttle up my throat, clawing dreadfully to asphyxiate me. Manny grabs me by the arm and leads me to a picnic table where he helps me sit down.

"You need a drink?"

I shake my head slowly.

"No. I think I need to be clear-headed for this. I just… I can't breathe. Is this like a war? Gangs fighting gangs?"

My heart races. For God's sake, I have had these ruthless criminals looking for me for all these years and Cain has been protecting me? I don't know what the hell to think anymore.

"No. The Savages have a lot of enemies. For years they have thought they ruled the streets of Detroit, but they've been falling apart for a while, now. There's a few of them left out there. The few that want to taunt Cain with you. The main one seems to have vanished. He's out there somewhere."

So a man who is not above killing to get what he wants is on the loose, and no one can find him. The back of my neck itches as if a target were painted on it. I need to know more.

"Who is this man? What's his name?"

"His name is Kryder, and he's a remorseless son of a bitch." A grim look crosses his face. "I can't imagine how you're feeling right now. Cain will kick my fucking ass if he finds out I've told you any of this. He's lost in his own head right now after seeing you today."

I sneer at his comment.

"He's lost? I doubt it. He's been harsh, rude, and inconsiderate since I've gotten here."

"I know, but trust me. Your safety has been his top priority for years."

I crane my head to look up at him.

"It's been you, hasn't it? You've been watching me this whole time, haven't you?"

He simply nods.

"You dirty liar. Not two minutes ago, you just said long time no see. It may have been a long time since I've seen you last, but you've been stalking me this whole time."

"You didn't even know I was watching you. Don't get your panties all bunched up, woman. I didn't stalk. I protected."

Both of us laugh. Now I know why Cain knows so much about me. I'm grateful for whatever reason he felt he needed to have me protected.

"Exactly how long have you been watching me?" I ask.

"I've been living in Canada for the past few years. Cain didn't trust anyone else with your safety, and neither did I. Although today you threw me for a loop when you hopped in your car and drove here."

"Yeah, well. I had been thinking about it for a while now. Today seemed like the day, so I just took off. If I had known all of this was going on, I would have just given you the papers myself, or let them be delivered by a process server and left it up to him whether to respond or not," I say righteously. "Either way, the Canadian courts would have granted me a divorce."

Manny's no fool. He knows damn well I could have had someone else deliver these papers instead of coming here in person. Why didn't I?

He shrugs.

"It's your life, Calla. Never really put much thought into watching you go into the courthouse. You're in and out of there all the time, with law school and all. Do your parents know? About the divorce, I mean."

I shake my head.

"No, they don't know. And you're right, Manny. It is my life. A life I need to start living."

"I agree," he says a little too quickly.

I don't think he believes I want this divorce, but I'm not in the mood to argue with him over it. I want my life back, that's all.

"You really did keep an eye on me, huh?" I reach up and kiss his cheek, lightening the heavy mood that has shrouded us. "Seriously, though. I can't believe you have given up years of your life just to watch me walk around school, or go to parties and study groups. God, you must have been bored out of your mind. My life has been nothing but one big uninteresting bag of books."

"Nah. I had a job to do, so I did it. Besides, we take care of our own around here. I would never be able to live with myself if something were to happen to you. Simple as that. And you were boring for the first year, but you broke free over the past year and a half. Especially after you started dating Mikel."

I don't miss the crossness in his tone.

"We broke up after he asked me to marry him. I lied to him the entire time we dated. That's when I decided enough was enough and I couldn't continue to put my life on hold for a man who didn't give a shit about me. Mikel didn't deserve to be hurt like that."

I'll never forget the regret I felt when I broke his heart. I know what that feels like, to think you know someone, and then to find out everything about them was a lie.

Manny sits down next to me and polishes off the rest of his beer, tossing the bottle onto the ground.

"It's a damn good thing you did break up, though, because that's the first time Cain really thought he was going to lose you for good. I had to talk the fucker down time and time again from driving over the border. He was ready to kill him."

"That's a little hypocritical, don't you think? I mean, he wanted to kill Mikel when he's the one who lied and slept with someone else in the first place. I mean, come on. I get the fact that he's been protecting me, I really do, but that's bullshit and you know it. He lost me the day he married me. The day he decided our love for one another wasn't strong enough."

"Come on, Calla. Loosen up a little. I didn't mean it literally. I just meant for the first time since you left, he didn't think he had a chance of getting you back."

"I was never his in the first place," I say softly.

"You've always been his woman. You just don't realize it."

I stand up, straightening my skirt as best I can.

"Really? Pin your ears back and crack open those eyes, Manny. I belong to no-one. What I want is to climb back into my car, go home, and forget this day ever happened. So if you could be so kind as to tell me where Cain is, I would appreciate it."

"He's in there. You're wasting your breath and your time if you think anyone in this club will let you leave here. Come on," he says, pointing to the bar. "Let me take you."

I sigh, knowing I'm facing a losing battle trying to get out of here. But for the love of God, there has to be another way. Geez. I'll even let the kingpin here drive me to my parents' house himself.

The first step I take I stumble, my shoes catching in the dirt. These poor shoes are going to be ruined before this day is over. Manny's arms go around my shoulders to catch my fall, the two of us laughing at my clumsiness, but it falters when we look up and under the light of the doorway stands Cain. And he's not alone.

Chapter Six

Calla

"What the mother fuck?" he shouts.

Cain brings his arms up on either side of him, his hands balled into tight fists. If looks really could kill, Manny and I would both be dead right now.

"Don't 'mother fuck' me, asshole. You're the one who left her in your dad's house. I'm the one who found her out here looking for you."

Manny releases me. The two men stare each other down while I break away from looking at Cain to snap a dirty look at Emerald. Her sly smile lets me know all too well that she knows something I don't.

I flash my best bitch grin right back at her. I hate this woman. She has Cain and I don't, and if I didn't want to get out of here so badly, I could very well kill her right now with my bare hands.

Emerald sidles up against him, her claws coming out like a vicious cat.

"Come on, baby. Let's go party with everyone else. Unless you want to go back to your place? We can create our own party."

I would love to say something crude to her, but Cain beats me to it.

"Enough, Emerald. We talked about this. We're done here; now go find someone else's bed to crawl into."

Ouch.

"You can't be serious right now? After what we just did in there, you're going to cast me aside a-fucking-gain? You can't do this, Cain. She doesn't belong here. She will never fit in here. I mean, look at her. She looks like a high class whore! She's a killjoy, a dead lay. You said so yourself," she hisses like the nasty snake she is.

"We didn't do jack shit, you lying bitch," he says, turning on her.

Whatever. He probably did fuck her. I keep telling myself I don't care, but the truth is, it hurts. More than I care to admit. However, this bitch and her words are more than I can stand. She's desperate, and I can't say I really blame her. But a dead lay? I'm far from a dead lay. Maybe I should remind him of all the blow jobs I've given him, how he used to tell me I could suck a nail out of a board! Knowing him, that was a lie, too.

And that's the second time I've been called a whore since I stepped foot in this place. He must prefer whores over someone who would have always been only his. I can't believe he would say something like that about me. What did I ever do to him for him to degrade me so spitefully? Moisture begins to build behind my eyes, but I won't cry. Not in front of these two. Not ever.

She speaks the truth. I don't belong here, which is why I want to leave. I can get my own protection. Hell, I'll move clean across the country.

"What the hell kind of game are you playing at, Emerald? I've been nothing but honest with you from the very beginning. You've been nothing but a convenient fuck. And I sure as fuck have never spoken to you even once about Calla," Cain snaps.

He takes hold of her by her arm, jerking her so hard I flinch, feeling the pain he is inflicting on her. I'm not one for abuse on any woman, no matter if I despise them or not. I go to step forward and I'm halted dead in my tracks by Manny.

"Leave him be, woman," he barks in my ear as Cain's voice escalates.

"I'm fucking warning you, bitch, for the last time. Get the hell out of my club and stay the hell away from me. And if I ever hear you spewing lies and bullshit about Calla again, I swear to Christ I will gut you."

My insides start to crumble into a giant heap of shards. I should not have to stand here and endure this lovers' quarrel. My world feels like it's crashing down again. He's talking about screwing her right in front of me. I couldn't care less if he is defending me or not. Fuck them both.

"No!" screeches the hussy. "She is not going to come in here and take what's mine!"

I don't even see her coming until her fist connects with the side of my head, causing me to stumble backwards, nearly knocking both Manny and me to the ground.

One of the heels of my shoes breaks off and that's it; these shoes are ruined. They're one of my favorite pairs and were a gift from Mr. and Mrs. Henry when I graduated from college. I love these shoes. Now I am pissed.

"What the hell?" Cain and Manny holler out at the same time.

Each of the men tries to grab one of us, but I'm not having it. She wants a fight? Well, she's about to get one.

"Get your hands off of me!" I command, causing Manny to release me. I kick my shoes off now that they are ruined and charge straight for that bitch, grabbing a handful of her hair and slamming my fist into her stomach.

"You cock-sucking whore!"

She goes down under my blow, doubling over and gasping for breath, but it doesn't shut her mouth.

"Cain's cock is a delicious one to suck," she taunts.

"Oh, yeah? Well the next time you do, you'll be sucking it with a broken jaw, you nasty cow!"

And that is when the catfight begins. Out of my peripheral vision I notice more and more people gathering around us. I hear shouts of 'Hell, yeah!' and, 'Beat her ass!' and other explicit phrases. I don't know or care if they are talking about me or her. My goal at this moment is to show this cunt bag I mean business.

"He's mine!" she shouts, her high-pitched tone sounding like a child who just got their favorite toy taken away from them.

She comes at me with full force, her face grimacing with as much animosity toward me as I feel for her. The impact knocks us both to the ground, with her landing on top of me. The crack of her open hand hitting my cheek echoes over the noise of the hooting and hollering.

"Please, is that the best you've got?" I goad her.

In a wrestler-like move I flip us over. My skirt rips, exposing half of my pantyless ass. She is now on her back and I let the bitch have it. My hands strike her in the face and chest; anywhere I can land a blow. No tears, no screams. No sound comes from me at all except my heavy breathing as I pummel the living shit out of her. She howls like a wild animal under attack.

"You rotten bitch!" I finally scream as I dig my nails in the side of her head. It's not until I am hoisted up and off of her that she gets in her best shot. Her foot catches me in the stomach, causing me to gasp for air as the wind is nearly knocked out of me.

Strong arms circle around me. Although these aren't the arms of the man I would have expected to comfort me, they are soothing nonetheless.

I continue to kick at Emerald, her ramblings about the things she and Cain have done together hitting me dead center. She's poking tiny holes in my heart as she continues to throw her darts at me, the tip penetrating right through the surface. I hate them all.

Cain snatches her up viciously. Her face is a bloody mess and her mouth is shouting profanities I have never heard before. Classy.

Her muffled cries dissipate as Cain drags her off into the darkness somewhere. I'm shaking, sweat dripping down my face, and I still want to fight. The pent up fury of years towards that woman has finally been unleashed and all I want to do is cut her snarly tongue out of her mouth for claiming Cain as hers. For throwing spiteful, hurtful information about the two of them at me. She doesn't strike me as a woman who will easily walk away. She'll be back. Please, God. Let me be gone by the time she decides to come back. If not, I'll be calling up a lawyer of my own. Next time I might kill her.

"You can let go of me now, Manny," I say calmly.

"You sure? I mean, you're not going to go running after them and attack her even more? Because woman, I have to tell you, that was some badass shit right there."

"Yeah, well, the dumb slut deserved it. She deserved it six years ago. That was just a tiny fraction of what I could do to her. I've never hated anyone as much as I hate that bitch. I hope she goes home and a thousand red hot fire ants crawl up her crotch."

Manny releases me. I turn around and we both bust out laughing.

"Oh, my God. I can't believe I said something like that. That's nasty," I say while still laughing.

"No, it's not. It's the fucking truth. She's bad news. Never liked the bitch."

She may have not wanted to have her face all bruised and bloodied; I hope she regrets it when she looks at herself in the mirror. But she got the reaction out of me she was looking for. Emerald thinks I want her man. If only I could convince my own damn self that her intuition weren't entirely correct.

"He can clean her up. She's his after all." Jerking my thumb in the direction they took off to. I admit to myself it hurts, worse than I imagined. I turn around taking off running. Escaping from this tiresome day. Cain, Emerald, Manny. All of it.

I wrap my arms around myself, my legs carrying me as fast as they will go in bare feet. Not knowing where I'm going, I slow down to a walk on a small dirt path. I hear Emerald's wails in the background overlaid by Cain's loud rumbling. I want it gone, all of it, out of my aching head which is throbbing from where she hit me.

The bottoms of my feet land on several sharp stones; I feel small trickles of blood where they break through the skin. I don't care. I keep moving forward, not knowing where the hell I am or how I would even try to get back. My guess is I've been walking for ten or fifteen minutes before I hear my name being called from behind me.

"Calla! Wait!"

It's Manny. Of course, it would be. I won't deny the fact that it wounds me Cain isn't the one coming after me. He's more than likely comforting his woman right now. I continue to walk, hearing Manny approach me.

"Come on, Calla. Stop."

I don't know what makes me stop, but I do. I feel myself crumple to the dirt on my knees. I bow my head and I begin to cry. My gaze travels up somewhere into the distant black night. Welled up tears from deep inside travel down my face.

"Why, Manny? What did I ever do to anyone to have to suffer like this? I... I just want to go home. This isn't for me. The longer I stay here, the more he's going to hurt me. And her... Jesus, she's a whack job!"

I let loose a paroxysm of choking and sobbing cries, not even realizing Manny has lifted me up and placed me on his lap until I feel the dampness from my tears on his shirt.

"I should have never come here. If I would have known I'd be coming back to any of this, I would have stayed away forever."

"Like fucking hell, you would have. And God damn it, Manny, get your fucking filthy hands off of her."

The reverberation of Cain's voice draws up my spine. My crying fit turns into laughter at his absurdity.

"You have a lot of nerve, do you know that?"

Observing his beautiful face in the moonlight, I feel contempt towards him, even though he has the most intense blue eyes I have seen and a body that makes me want to oil it down and slip and slide all over it.

"My nerves are gone, sweetheart. Now get up. You're coming home with me."

My anger increases in its intensity. I'm not going anywhere with him. No way am I going back to a house that has haunted me for years. Ignoring him completely, my attention shoots to Manny.

"I would much rather stay with you," I say sweetly.

"Hell, no," Cain sputters out crazily.

"And why not?" I retort, tilting my head to one side. "If I have to be here, I would much rather stay with someone who treats me like a human, not someone who leaves me in a room like a captive."

The minute those words fall out of my mouth I know I shouldn't have said them. I'm not full of malice and humiliation like he is.

"You want me to show you what it's like to be held captive?"

At that, Manny stands up on his feet, bringing me right along with him. He places me gently on the ground, his crazy eyes watching Cain's.

"What the fuck is wrong with you, man? Get your goddamned shit together. She's your fucking wife, you asshole. Now, she isn't going with me, because she belongs with you. I love you like a brother, dude, but treat her like your damn wife and not like you treat every other asshole around you. Christ, Cain! Sometimes I think I don't even fucking know you anymore. And fucking tell her the goddamned truth."

Cain sucks in a deep breath. I feel like shit for putting Manny in the middle like this by suggesting I stay with him. Stepping in between the two men, I place a hand on each of their chests, directing my attention to Manny first.

"I'm sorry. I shouldn't have said what I did. I'm feeling helpless, ripped apart layer by layer. Thank you for being a friend. I'll be fine."

I whirl in Cain's direction.

"And you! I'm not staying in that house. If you want me to stay with you, then fine, but have the damned decency to take me somewhere else. Preferably with a spare room, because I sure as shit will not be sleeping with you. Leave me there. Lock me up while you tend to your little club whore. Do whatever it is you have to do, and do it fast, because I want the hell out of here."

"I'm fucking gone," Manny states before he turns back in the direction we came from, leaving me standing in the dark facing a man who I don't know anymore. And if I were to be honest with myself, I'm afraid of this stranger standing before me.

"I'm going to let your smart mouth slip just this one last time. If you ever speak to me in front of anyone like that again, I will take you over my knee and beat your ass. And it won't be the kind of spanking that will bring you pleasure."

I shake my head, dumbfounded. Beat me? Oh, my God. He's cracked.

"What happened to you? I'm regretting ever loving you at all, Cain, because you are being so childish right now. So arrogant. Tell me how I'm supposed to act? Do you want me to sit by your side like a good little girl? Do you want me to be the good wife and stay home? Wait for you to come to me at night, hoping like hell you haven't been with someone else? Or better yet, worry that someone may knock on the door at any given moment and say, 'I'm sorry to inform you, Mrs. Bexley, but your husband is dead'? I'm your wife on paper only, and you're the one who made sure of that. I'm not your plaything. And you will never put your hands me. I'm nothing to you. NOTHING!"

Cain hisses at me and grabs my arm hard, causing me to stumble forward. He's pulling me God knows where, half-dragging me as I teeter back and forth on my bloodied and bruised up feet trying to hold myself upright. I flinch, then cry out in pain.

"Cain, stop! You're hurting me!"

He isn't listening.

"Ow!" I scream, my body tumbling to the ground.

"Fuck!" Cain roars, releasing his grip.

I try backing up, to get away, but he's too quick. He picks me up and carries me in his arms. I want to scream, but my vocal cords are paralyzed. I kick, claw, and escape from this wild animal.

He effortlessly hauls me up a few steps, a light flicking on when we hit the top. I blink my eyes rapidly, adjusting to the light. In no time, the door is flung open. Cain kicks it closed before I get any chance at all to see my surroundings. For the first time since I've known him, reality sinks into my veins. My Cain is gone. He has been replaced by a psychopath. A stranger.

"Sit, stay, and shut the hell up."

He sets me down gently on what feels like a couch. I don't know; it's still pitch black in here.

Cain fumbles around, turning on several lights. Once my vision adjusts to the lighting, I look down my arm and see his finger marks embedded into my skin. My big toe is also bleeding. The side of my head hurts like hell.

Cain looks from my face, to my arm, to my toe, then walks directly out of the room without another word. I hear him swearing and the thuds of cupboard doors being slammed before he walks back in a few minutes later with a wet towel in his hands.

I wish he would talk, say something. Anything at all. I start choking back my sobs.

"Cain, you're really scaring me right now."

I sit there and cry again, getting no comfort from him at all. He's probably going to tie me up, chain me to a bed, and leave me there.

"Give me your feet," he says finally, patting his leg, indicating for me to place them there.

My shoulders sag in defeat and I do as he asks. I'm tired, hungry, and dirty. The slit in the side of my skirt is torn, exposing more leg than I would normally let anyone see, especially the man whose rough hands are delicately touching my feet. Warm, inviting hands, inspecting both the top and bottoms of each foot and then delicately placing them back on his muscular thighs.

His big hands start to work on cleaning up my stubbed big toe. He's gentle when washing away the grimy dirt and blood, though I wince at the sting of the wet towel and try to move my foot out of his hold. He inspects each foot after he has them wiped clean. Reaching down beside him, he brings up a small tube of some sort of antibacterial medication. Working meticulously, he places dabs of the soothing gel on my scrapes.

"Here, drink this and take these," he orders, handing me a small glass of water and two pills I didn't see him holding when he came in a few minutes ago.

I hesitate before taking them, which Cain notices.

"It's aspirin for the pain," he says gruffly. "You have a nasty bruise forming on the side of your face. I know you must have a headache and your feet are hurt. Now take them."

I place both pills on my tongue and wash them down with the entire glass of water.

"Thank you," I mumble, removing my foot from his leg.

His hands begin to trail gently up my limbs. Smooth, circular strokes send a thrill of pleasure up my spine. Never once does his gaze lift to meet mine. He's focused on his task, almost as if he is transfixed, worshipping. He suddenly stops when he reaches my knees.

"You're going to hate me even more for what I'm about to say to you," he says, shifting his gaze to where my hands rest in my lap.

My eyes wander around the room as I wait for him to continue, finally taking in my surroundings. Whose home is this? It's stunning. Everything about it screams a man lives here. Black leather couch, matching chair. Wide screen television hanging on the wall. Dark wood blinds on the windows. That's it, besides a table next to the chair. The deep greenish-blue color of the walls is what really catches my eye, though. It's enthralling. The deep green fades into blue like a changing kaleidoscope. It... it reminds me of my eyes.

I shake my turmoil-filled head. Black furniture, the shades of the walls...

This is his house.

Everything Manny told me earlier bursts forth in my thoughts. Cain's hurting. Seeing this is proof to me that he is. My insides shatter. All of a sudden, I'm not frightened of him anymore.

It's difficult to describe what I am feeling right now, though. It's almost like a jolt, a forceful sensation deep in my gut telling me to hang on for dear life. I'm torn in two directions. Seeing the tormented expression on his face makes me want to reach out, run the tips of my fingers through his hair, and tell him to just say what he needs to say. Another part of me wants to rip his balls off, shove them up his ass, and tell him to go fuck himself.

But even more so, there's something powerful trying to claw its way out from under the surface of my skin, to tear away the brick exterior safely guarding my beaten down heart. Even after six years, I still love him. I try to swallow my emotions before I speak.

"Why would I hate you more? What is it?"

"I'm going to tell you a whole lot of shit you won't want to hear, baby."

He stays calm. Me? I'm not calm. Who knows what I am anymore?

I see him, though. Clear as a crystal blue day. He's fighting against himself. The hurt and anger mix together, creating a war of guilt, fear, and desperation. I should feel gratified he's struggling within himself; instead, I sit here not knowing what to expect from a man I'm still very much in love with. A man I will always love. A man who has done nothing but degrade, destroy, and insult that love. My husband is about to hurt me all over again.

Chapter Seven

Cain

The last thing I want to do is what I'm doing now. She won't listen. This is the only way I know how to make her. I've decided I'm done hiding this situation that is out of my control, beyond her wildest human comprehension.

I have no damn clue if guilt and shame are the same thing. All I do know as I sit here is that I can't even look at her. She's crying again. The sound destroys the last bit of resolve I have left.

I study her openly. She's emotional and distressed, just as I need her to be, but it's going to be tough to stress how important it is for her to listen to me when all I can hear are those pleading noises coming from her.

I look down at my hands. Running them along her smooth legs a moment ago made me feel so alive, yet peaceful at the same time. How badly I wanted to leave my hands on her, to let her beauty and softness penetrate deep into me. To be able to run my tongue up her body, letting her melt into my mouth. I wanted to continue my exploration. Glide my fingers higher, then slide them under her skirt. Feel her thighs clench and tingle from my touch. She is, hands down, the most beautiful creation I have ever seen.

It's hard as hell not to let my fingers run over her smooth skin. Trace the outline of those lips I have missed so much. What I wouldn't do to be able to lean in and kiss her, suck in her oxygen so I could feel like I'm truly breathing for the first time in six years. I love her so much this is killing me. That's right. I fucking love this woman, and here I sit hurting her, abusing her over and over again.

I look down again in disgust. I've never wanted anything in my life, except her. For her to love me. To think about me all day long, counting down the hours until we can be together. For her face to light up the minute I walk through the door. To just be able to be with her, hear her laugh. See her smile. To touch her. Hold her. Hear her say good morning, good night, and I love you, all the things most couples in society take advantage of. Those are my wants, but I'm afraid after all of this is said and done, those wants will become a distant fantasy.

I have a damned mole around here. They've most likely already told that pussy ass Kryder she's here, which means she needs to stay by my side. We can both pretend all we want that we hate each other. Let everyone believe it. But behind these walls, or whenever we are alone, I will prove to her how much she means to me. How much I love her above anyone or anything else.

I'm not dumb enough to believe they will think it, but Calla needs to believe that if the mole thinks I don't give two shits about her, then Kryder will stay the hell away from her and so will whoever he has working on the inside. It may be the one thing that will save her life.

She needs to stay here and keep acting like she hates me, like this is the last place she wants to be. The trick is, she has to do it my way and listen to me. She should have never come back here, damn it. I should send her away. Call her dad and tell him to come and get her.

Can a person truly loathe themselves, I wonder? Self-hate is a dark hole, known by me best of all. I'm nothing but the man I've created for myself. A man left with my own thoughts for years. I've dug my own grave by not being the husband Calla deserves. All I've done, I've done for her, but right now, it's best that she thinks I'm nothing but a rotten prick.

The way she pummeled Emerald, though, I can see she's one strong woman. I stood there and could not move, my eyes not believing how she just flipped her around and punched her repeatedly in the face without a second thought. Yeah, my dick twitched like a happy camper watching her fist connect with Emerald's jaw. She deserved it, the stupid, trouble-making slut, for spouting off a bunch of lies.

I chuckle to myself. Calla can hold her own, especially after what I saw tonight. She sure doesn't need to toughen up; she's got that handled. She actually needs to calm the hell down and hold her shit in when these bitches talk smack to her. Not everyone will go down as easy as Emerald did. I've fucked every single one of the women who hang out around here, and left all of them wanting more. All of them knowing they will never get more.

All of them, except Emerald. She already thinks I'm hers. I've never been hers; I've always belonged to the woman who's sitting across from me. Who's in my home.

Even though I know the truth of who he is, it still gutted me to the core seeing Manny getting to comfort her. That man, friend, family, or not, is going to have to keep his hands to himself. No one touches what belongs to me. Never. And she definitely belongs to me. If I ever hear the word 'divorce' come out of her mouth again, I'm going to lose my shit. Tell her to eat shit. And to fuck that shit.

Enough of the pep talk. I need to move on and get this done.

"You need to listen to me," I begin harshly. "If you don't do exactly what I tell you to do, I'm going to be calling your parents and telling them to plan your damn funeral, because that smart mouth of yours is going to end up getting you killed."

I lift my face to hers to show her I mean what I say, and nearly come undone at what I see.

I'm tortured watching her eyes well up with tears. Her shirt is ripped, exposing her lacy, nude-toned bra with her plump breasts spilling out over the top. That sexy-as-hell skirt has ripped halfway up her leg. This is goddamned cruel. Even though she's a mess, she's still so damn beautiful. Fucking perfect, even with makeup all over her face. There's even a smudge of dirt on her cheek. I'd give anything to reach up and wipe it clean. To see her smile.

When she simply nods her head, I have never hated myself more than I do right now.

Good. This is how she needs to be; scared and utterly frightened. I'm about to thrust her into a vortex, and I pray like hell that her time in law school has turned her into one hell of a dangerous shark, because she sure as hell needs to be a tough ass bitch to handle this life.

God, I'm a sick fuck for doing this. There is no way in hell she will ever forgive me once this is done. If it wasn't for the fact that someone has a hit out on her, I would drag this shit out as long as I possibly could just to keep her near me. The minute this is over she'll be gone, leaving me no choice but to let her divorce me. Hell, she may even kill me herself.

Her lips stop quivering, her gaze going down to her hands resting in her lap. I extend my arm out to her and she flinches. Christ, she thinks I'm going to hit her. And even though her thinking I'm that big of an asshole falls right in with my plans, it makes me feel like shit.

I need to move away from her before I do something stupid like pulling her into my arms. I get up and move to a chair on the opposite side of the room, gather my thoughts, and prepare to tell her every damn thing, starting with the part that needs to make her fear for her life.

"There's a hit out on you, Calla."

I say it without warning, giving nothing to soften the blow. I sit here and watch her shake, her face contorting into a look of astonishment and confusion, making me feel like I've been kicked in the teeth.

"The man who killed my father found out about you a few years back, and he's been looking for you ever since. He knows you're the one thing he can break me with. The only person left who I truly care about. He wants you dead."

She opens her mouth as if she wants to say something, then she closes it just as quickly.

"I have a rat in my club, someone who told this shady, no good asshole about you, and I haven't been able to find out who. I've had everyone in this place followed, had everyone checked out. You name it, I have done it, and I've come up with nothing. Not a damn thing. I'm no closer to finding out today than I was a few years ago when this all came to light. That's why when you showed up I decided to keep you here, where I can be the one to take care of you and not Manny."

Her look of disgust tells me she already knows he's been watching her for me. I can't be angry with him, though; I owe him more than anyone for taking care of her and keeping her safe. He's reported to me daily about her every move; however, now that Calla is here, I will be telling him to stay out of my business. The little shit is trustworthy, but he needs to keep his big mouth shut more often.

"So you found out about Manny. I know you better than you think, so I'm not going to get into it right now with you, but now you know why I have so much information about you. I did what I had to do to make sure no one located you, and he's the only one I fucking trust."

I harden my voice when I continue, demanding her full attention.

"Now, here's the part where you really need to listen to every word I say, and I am not screwing around about it anymore. You don't have to want to be here, but you're going to be. You may as well get used to seeing a lot of me. It's the way it's going to be, whether you like it or not. I get the fact that you have no clue how shit works around here. Like I said before, I don't do drugs. I loathe them. They're the reason that fucker killed my dad and Darcy. There's also a lot of women who hang out here. They like the bikes, they like the men. They respect us. We respect them. We fuck. No strings attached, unless someone makes it that way. I've been with every one of them."

My organs all just about stop working when more tears fall down her face, but I have to push on.

"We're an organization. A club. A private bar. Anyone can join as long as they don't do drugs, don't start fights, and don't try and screw around with anyone's wife. They pay their dues and drink my booze. It's as simple as that. That's the way I want it. And that's the way I need it."

She's so quiet, which is very unlike her. I wanted her to know the truth; well, the truth about this club. We are who we are now. Most of the people here are innocent, normal, hardworking Americans who love the thrill of the throttle between their legs. Nothing more, just the sweet relief of all-American freedom.

"You need to act like you want to be here. Pretend like you and I are trying to work through our shit. And stand by my side. My world is a hell of a lot different from the world you've been living in. When I say do something, you don't ask any questions, you just do it. If by chance I have to leave, you come with me. You get what I'm saying?"

Wrinkles of angry shock crease her forehead.

"You have got to be shitting me!"

"Damn it, Calla. That right there is exactly what I'm talking about. You to need to learn when to speak and when to shut the hell up. These people are just regular people. They leave their marriage problems at home. The men come here to get away from an argument they may have just had with their wife or girlfriend. What part of what I'm telling you don't you understand?" My hands go up in the air in frustration.

"I don't understand why I can't say what I want. Are we not alone in here? And you say you're a club. A respected one, I assume. So what's the deal? Do women not have the same rights around here? Do they just sit around with their tails tucked between their legs, waiting to be told what to do? I mean, what is it?"

"I don't care if we're alone or not. What the hell do I need to do to make you understand this is some serious shit you've gotten yourself into? You should have never come here. Not until I summoned you."

"Summoned me? What the hell are you, some kind of dominant? I may get into kink, but you will never summon me to do shit. You don't scare me. I want out of here. I want my purse back. I want to call my parents. Mom and I talk every day and she has to be going out of her mind by now."

God, the mouth on her. If I wasn't trying to help her, I would let her run her mouth all damn day and say whatever the hell she wanted. But until I get this figured out, she needs to shut the hell up. Word will get out that she's here, and I can't afford to let anyone think I'm weak. And when it comes to Calla, I'm so fucking weak, it's pathetic. The mole could have heard every damn word that went down between Manny, myself, and Calla on that path. Fuck, I have no clue.

My blood pressure is rising. My ass shoots up out of the chair and I take the few steps needed to get to her. Her face turns to panic. If she doesn't want to listen, then by God, I'm going to make her. I yank her thick hair back, putting my face within an inch of hers. She cries out in pain when I tug even harder. I would love to show her just how kinky I can get.

"One, you let me worry about your parents. I'm doing everything I can to protect everyone, and that includes them. Once Kryder and his men know you're here, if they don't already, they could be targets. The less they know, the safer it is for them. Two, your phone has been destroyed. There's ways to track those damn things. Three, I need you to fucking trust me, goddamnit. Four, when we're alone, you can come at me with everything you've got. I get you feel like you walked into a ring of fire, and you're trapped. The things I just told you are things you needed to hear. You need to know what's happening here, and me being an asshole is the only way I seem to get your attention. And five, I'll be as kinky with you as you want me to be. You can dominate me, or I can dominate you. I'll take it either way, as long as the end result is me burying my cock into you."

"You dick! You manipulative asshole!"

"Been called a lot worse, babe."

"Fuck you!" she spits.

"I would love to fuck you, in many different ways. Maybe I should start with this mouth. When was the last time someone fucked this pretty mouth?"

Her lips part at my crude remark. She better not have let anyone else fuck that lush mouth. It belongs to me. This is my territory, my body, my every fucking thing. I dive in for the kill, my mouth crushing down on her brutally. I plunge my tongue inside, demanding that she kiss me back. She doesn't. Her tongue lays flat, not moving as she fights to try and escape me.

I want to seize what is rightfully mine, damn it. To taste, to devour. I become more intense; rougher, even, doing my best to try and make her kiss me back. This is why I have never kissed a woman since her. Her mouth and her lips belong to me. As mine do to her.

I feel tears against my face, making me pull away from her. The hurt in her eyes guts me. I said I'd stay away from her, but I can't help myself. I can't. I've waited too long for this. I rest my forehead against hers and close my eyes. Anything I can do to stay close to her until she decides to push me away.

"Cain, please don't do this. There's too much bad history between us, and you've divulged too much information about your present life. I'm just not that girl anymore."

"You're right, you're not. I'm not that same young man, either. But one thing that has never changed is the way I feel about you. If after all of this is done, you do walk away from me and I never see you again, walk away with that."

Her gorgeous blue-green eyes are glazed over with more unshed tears caused by me. Love should never hurt, damnit. It's one of the few things in life that are free. I happen to have fallen so deeply in love at the age of sixteen that I will never come out.

I love her. I've been without her because I love her so much, I would do anything for her. If she only knew how many nights I would lie in bed with a restless mind and pretend we were still together, planning our future, telling each other everything. Crawling into bed together. Making love at night, then turning around the next morning and doing it all over again.

A hint of a smile curves upwards on her mouth. I will do whatever it takes for her to realize my deep-seated feelings will never change. Her safety is my top priority.

"You'll see I'm telling you the truth, sweetheart. I promise. Just give me time to find him, to make sure you're safe, and then we can talk about us."

There's so much more I would love to say to her, but I'll leave her with the information she needs to digest for now. Backing off, I settle at the opposite end of the couch in silence. Neither of us speaks for the longest time until the loud rumble of her stomach cuts through the stillness.

"You're hungry, and you probably want to get cleaned up," I observe.

"Yeah, I am. This is your house, I take it?"

Her walls are back up, I can tell by the icy way she says 'your house'.

"It's mine," I confirm. "I'll make us something to eat, while you shower."

I stand and turn to her. She's so lost, her expression blank.

"One more thing and I'll leave you to it. We are a club. Most of us do respect our women around here, but some of these guys are old school. They've been in those bad gangs, the ones who treat their women like shit. I'm not going to tell them what they can and can't do outside of here. If the women hear you smart off to me, they might get to thinking that if I let you do it, then they can, too. I just don't want that shit to be on me or on you. We'll talk more later, but for now, just please do what I ask." I point down the hallway. "There's a bedroom with a private bathroom right down this hall. Everything you need to clean yourself up is in there."

She still doesn't look up from the spot she's fixated on. If time is what she needs to adjust, I'll give her that. She needs it. I get it. She came here expecting to get rid of me and instead, she has to live under my roof and be with me twenty-four seven.

I asked her to trust me, but what she doesn't know yet is that I don't trust her. She's bound to run; therefore, my wife will be sleeping with me while she's here. Something tells me I may have to tie her to the bed when I tell her that. Gag her even. In different circumstances, I would love nothing more than to do just that, while I suck on the sweet spot on her neck, lick every inch of her skin, and screw her into a fucking sex stupor. I'd give her all the kink she wanted.

Calla finally decides to speak.

"You said everyone had respectable jobs around here. What is it you do?"

She looks directly into my eyes. If only I could tell her the truth about what it is I actually do. I can't. No one can. I've told her all she needs to know for now. Before I tell her the whole truth about my life and the things I do, I need to gain her trust back. If she finds out I lied to her about anything, I know I will lose her forever before I have the chance to prove to her how much I want her back.

Kryder may be the biggest drug dealer around these parts, but me? I'm the biggest gun thief motherfucker in this whole damn country. But when I look back at her, I simply say,

"I run this bar, Calla. That's my job."

Chapter Eight

Calla

I have two choices. Either I can sit here and bitch and complain, or I can follow his rules. Plain and simple. Neither of these options will get me the hell out of here any faster the way I see it. Justice sucks. I've seen it, read it, know all about it with my six years of studying law. I could argue with Cain until I'm blue in the face, throw every case precedent at him that has ever been created, and I'd get nowhere with him. He still wouldn't let me leave or call my parents to let them know I'm safe.

The truth is, if I wasn't so hell-bent on trying to make myself believe I hate him, I could admit that he's been keeping me safe from this Kryder dude. I'm thankful that I now know someone has been after me, but I'm not about to tell him that.

There is still so much to talk about, so much I know for a damn fact he isn't telling me. He is greatly underestimating the power of my lawyerly instincts. This bar isn't legit. They may not deal with drugs anymore, this I do believe. But guns are definitely a part of whatever is up around here. You can't bullshit a bullshitter, and as most of my professors have told me, I will make one hell of an attorney because I can smell a liar a mile away. I may not have been around him for the last six years, but I can see the lies as clearly as if they were written across his handsome face.

I look up at him again. Cain doesn't strike me as a vain man, but shit, he's been blessed in the genetics department. The way his body is sculpted to perfection, one would think Michelangelo himself carved him just to make women physically and emotionally spent simply by looking at him. A sane woman would want to wrap her hands around his neck and choke him for the way he's been throwing out demands. But me? Oh no. I'm not sane right now at all.

I shake my head; my body has been pushed hard enough today. My brain has taken in way too much information. A shower sounds nice, but a long, hot bath sounds even better.

"Do you have a bathtub? I'd prefer to have a bath. They relax me, and with the information you have provided me with today, I could use it."

I cringe a little as I hear my voice come out in a sexy, deeply alluring kind of way. Do they still make chastity belts? Because my vagina needs one.

Confusion plays out across his features for a moment before his gaze trails up and down my body in a hungry kind of way, making my pussy feel like it could erupt all on its own. The intensity of his fixation on my neck makes me want to tilt my head more just to see what he would do. My pulse quickens, my breath catches, and if I don't quit staring at his mouth, I'm going to be straddling him pantyless in about two point five seconds. I'm getting off track here.

"I have one," he says finally. "It's never been used."

My eyebrows shoot straight up in surprise.

"What? You mean to tell me this is your house, you have a girlfriend, who I assume lives with you or at least stays here, and she has never used your bathtub?"

Now he looks surprised. His eyes widen then quickly fill with anger. Jesus, his face looks deadly.

"That bitch has never been in this house, Calla."

"I, um... I guess I don't understand."

He's never brought her here? Aren't they in a relationship? I mean, sure, I think he treats the twat like shit, and for whatever reason she puts up with it, but come the hell on!

"Like I said, we've both changed. I've got my reasons why she doesn't come here. Why I very rarely stay here. When I decide to share them with you, I will. In the meantime, it's all yours."

He abruptly turns without another word, obviously expecting me to just follow him. I do, though. I follow him through an open walkway where he switches on a light, giving me the perfect view of his ass.

I should not be looking; it only tortures my soul. But good God almighty. If anything, it is even tighter than before. Those black jeans hugging it are the luckiest pair of pants in the world, they truly are. That ass is the reason I never really paid much attention to other men; it ruined me for them.

I slide my glance down, checking out his long, muscular legs encased in big black motorcycle boots. My eyes roam back up across the vest he's wearing over a dark-colored tee. I check everything out, from his robust traps to his expansive shoulders and back. He definitely works out and keeps himself in great shape. I'm glad he still does that for himself, at least.

He turns left into a room and turns on a light. Now I'm mad at myself for checking him out and mad at him for stopping. Damn.

But then I walk further into the room and it takes my breath away. There's a huge, dark brown king sized bed up against one wall. The headboard is made of four wooden rectangles connected by a thin piece of wood. Two matching night stands sit on each side, with the matching dressers sitting against the opposite wall. A fireplace with shades of brown, turquoise, and a very light cream brick runs all the way up to the high cathedral ceiling. On either side of the fireplace are floor-to-ceiling windows covered with wooden blinds, which are closed now. I can only imagine the view behind those windows.

"Woah, this is your bedroom? It's... wow. I don't even know what to think. This is remarkable." I twirl around in wonder. "It all looks... I don't know. New. Don't you sleep here?"

Cain ignores my question.

"Come on. Let me show you the bath."

He sounds pained, which makes me stop and glance over at him. He's standing there with his jaw flexing, arms crossed over his chest.

"No, I want to see this," I insist.

My feet carry me to the edge of the bed. My dirty hands reach out to feel the softness of the turquoise and brown comforter. I draw them back rapidly, afraid to stain the soft fabric. Now I'm close enough to see that an intricate design is etched into the wood, and I peer down to study it. When I do, my entire body lurches backward.

"Th... those are Calla lilies. Good God. I... I don't understand."

Exhaling loudly, he steps towards me, eyes heated. He stops at the end of the bed, his eyes never leaving mine.

"I've never slept in here. Not once. I sleep on my couch. This is our room. At least I hoped it would be our room one day."

"You must be joking me?" I ask, my aggressive tone masking my nervousness.

"I never joke, not when it comes to you." He points behind him. "The bathroom is in there."

"Wait, damnit. You can't just let me see something so meaningful and personal, and then not tell me what it means. Why would you do something like this?"

Cain just stares at me as if I'm the one holding all the answers. His boots smack firmly against the hardwood floor when he turns and leaves. This man has thrown yet another curve ball at me, and this one's hit me smack in the face.

My life was doing so well before I drove into this place. The daunting, unknown life I am being forced to live lies in front of me, and now I stand in the middle of a bedroom that was apparently designed for me, trying to figure out how the hell I'm supposed to manage all of this. Living with him. Being with him all the time.

We're both hurting. So many things have been left unsaid. So many things need to be said. We're going to have to sit down and talk all of this out in a reasonable manner, or else these deep wounds are going to fester and bleed us both dry.

I pad on dirty feet across the room and gasp when I arrive at a bathroom like I've never seen before.

"My God, Cain. What have you done?"

The same colors as the bedroom adorn this immaculate room. The sunken tub is like a small pool sitting right below a giant window, with a brown tiled walk in shower off to the left of it. A long, brown vanity with teal countertops and marbled sinks takes up another wall. I'm afraid to touch a thing in here. It's all so pristine, so unlike Cain and his manly biker dude, bossy, uncontrollable ways.

"Wow. I may skip eating and stay in this tub all night," I whisper to myself.

I ditch my now-ruined clothing as fast as I can and practically run to the tub, where I stand naked trying to figure out how to turn the thing on. Finally I see buttons on the floor and push them as I squat on the cold, tiled ledge surrounding the tub. The drain automatically closes and just like that it starts to fill. Reaching for a knob, I adjust the temp and wait while water splashes into it with whisper soft splatters, like the tiny tears now streaming freely down my face.

My tears drip into the water, drowning along with my emotions. I'm feeling bereft, sad, and lonely with no idea whatsoever how I'm going to come up with the right answer to this solution.

Swiping my hand across my eyes, I stand up and dip my big toe into the water. The warmth stings the cut there. I wince and ease myself forward. Pain pushed aside, relaxation sets in. I press the button to turn the water off and lean back onto the soft pillow-like padding at the opposite end, sighing loudly.

My eyes drift closed as I let the water envelop me, submerging myself completely. My hair fans out to the sides as I sink toward the bottom. When my lungs start to burn, I emerge from the depths of the water and scream when I see Cain standing there at the edge of the tub.

Water splashes over the sides as I try and gather my wits. My heart starts pounding and my breathing becomes short.

"What in the hell are you doing in here?" I yell, mortified.

I'm completely naked, lying stretched out in a tub full of clear water. He can see everything. My brain tells my hands to move and cover myself up, but I seem to be immobilized, as does he. Nothing moves on his body except those damn dark eyes of his, the same as when we saw each other earlier today for the first time. His gaze scorches down my naked body, which is fully on display. At last, his smoldering, sensual gaze moves up to my eyes.

"Fuck me, I have never seen anything more beautiful in my entire life. You're both a blessing and a curse, Calla."

My brain finally catches up with the fact I'm naked in front of Cain for the first time in six years. I sit up in a rush of water and bring my knees to my chest, resting my chin on top of them.

"You... you shouldn't be in here."

"You wouldn't answer me," he says exasperatedly.

"Well, no shit. My head was underwater. That still doesn't give you the right to just walk in here."

"When you don't answer me when I'm standing right outside of a wide open door, not to mention the fact this is my house... well, then I think I have every fucking right. Don't you?"

"No, I don't. You could have just peeked in and seen I was fine and waited. Was this some kind of ploy for you to get me right where you wanted me? Are you so afraid that the minute you turn your back on me I will up and try to leave? Are you going to watch my every move? Or did you have an ulterior motive in suggesting I shower, just so I could strip down naked and you could make damn sure I didn't go anywhere? So tell me what the hell it is, because this back and forth, hot and cold game you've started is really starting to piss me the hell off!"

I glare up at him, not quite able to read his eyes.

What I do know is that the sexual tension between the two of us is so strong, it's working triple overtime. There's only one tiny little obstacle in our way... and that would be our past. The fact that I can't trust him. He broke every bit of it the same day he broke my heart. One of us needs to give in, take charge so we can just fuck and move on.

As if he can read my mind, he stalks right up to the ledge. Again my freaking disloyal eyes travel down. His cock is straining against his jeans. He's clenching and unclenching his fists, and fuck me, his feet are bare. When I meet his eyes again, they've changed. They're still dark and full of mystery, but they also have a hint of amusement behind them now.

I nearly fly out of the tub when he steps in with his jeans on, his big frame towering over me. He reaches down and yanks me up beneath my arms. My wet body crashes against his. It's hotter than a bitch frying in hell in here and it is most definitely not coming from the water we are both standing in.

"I'm done playing games. I'm about to fuck that sweet cunt of yours. By God, you can stand here and try to deny it all you want, but baby, you want my cock buried deep inside of you just as bad I want it there. Now shut the fuck up and kiss me."

A loud moan rises from deep inside of me, escaping without warning. My pussy is doing all of the talking, pressing up against him giving him the answer he wants.

Cain's hands leave my body to cradle my face, his thumbs skimming down my cheeks and running across my lips. His hands grab me by the ass and lift me, so I wrap my legs around his waist and my arms around his neck. I moan again when he doesn't go for my lips first; instead, he hits that spot on my neck. The sensations are too much. My God, his lips feel so good, sucking and assaulting my neck like he's truly missed me.

"Oh, hell!" I gasp.

My legs squeeze tighter around his waist. Rough friction from his damp jeans abrades me and I grind and writhe like a snake against him.

"Fuck!" he roars.

How he manages to get the two of us lying back down in this water is beyond me, but he does. He's on top of me with my head resting comfortably on the soft cushion.

I'm in a daze of wanton desire. Cain pushes my legs apart, palms my ass, and lifts the bottom half of my body out of the water. A smile pulls his lips which has me looking down to see what he is reacting to.

"What?' I ask breathlessly.

"I fucking knew you would be bare down here. This pink pussy uncovered for me to see. Hold on to something, because I haven't eaten a goddamned thing all day."

I bite my bottom lip when his face lowers to my pussy. He doesn't touch me for the longest time, he just stares at it like it's his lifeline. A tiny voice inside my head tells me this isn't the right thing to do, but when his face dips closer and he inhales my scent, those thoughts fly from my mind.

"I've waited six fucking years to do this. To have you in my arms. To have this pussy staring me right in the face. Six years, Calla. Don't you dare ask me to stop. I'm taking what's mine."

Chapter Nine

Cain

Having craved the taste of her for so damn long, I'm now gaping at this glistening wet pink flesh that's within an inch of my mouth. It's like I'm looking at it for the first time. Flashbacks hit me full force of when I tasted her sweet pussy for the first time. Nothing, and I mean nothing, as sweet-smelling has run across my lips since.

Her luscious lips greet me, her clit hard and ready for me to take into my hot mouth. It's fucking beautiful.

Since I haven't had my mouth on any other woman, you would think I'd want to devour her. And I do, but I also want to savor this moment. She wiggles her ass a little, clearly not on the side of savoring. She wants it now, and by God, I'm going to give it to her so good that when she tries to walk tomorrow she won't know if her pussy is aching from the tongue lashing she is about to get or from my cock.

I've never been one to pray, but I sure am now that this is not a one-time thing for her, that all she wants to do is fuck me out of her system. It will never happen. Calla is engraved into my soul. This house I have built has never been my home, not until she crossed the threshold. It's home now that she is in it. Home is her.

I take one long lick, spreading her lips apart until I reach her clit. Her pussy is dripping wet and spread wide open for me to see. I thank God once again for the high quality lighting in this room.

"Oh, hell!" she wails.

Her bud is so hard. It's all I can do not to bite down on it. She cries out more. My tongue circles her clit, moving down between the layers of her tender flesh. Fucking heaven.

I do this gently a few more times before tongue fucking the living shit out of her. My tongue cherishes every stroke, every plunge into her juicy hole. Her clit begs for more attention, and it gets it. I suck it deep into my mouth, tongue swirling, lips smacking every piece of her pussy I can find. Even the tight hole of her behind gets the tip of my tongue.

She's screaming my name, hollering profanities I have never heard her say before. Jesus Christ, I've missed her so fucking much. The way her body responds to mine. The way her tight ass feels in my hands. The smell of her pussy. The sound of her voice. Everything. And fuck, here she is, in my arms screaming and begging me not to stop. No one is going to make her leave me ever again.

I can sense she is getting close. My mouth remains on her clit. My eyes move from the view of her pussy to her face to gauge her reaction when she comes undone for me.

I suck gently, then harder, and even harder. She's staring right at me but her eyes are glazed over. My gaze never drops from hers.

Her pelvis lifts with her impending orgasm, shoving her pussy farther into my face. The air in the room is thick with tension. I ride it out with her. Give her more. Hang the hell on, and keep my mouth firmly around her throbbing clit.

"Don't you stop! Don't... oh, my fucking God!" Calla screams when she explodes all over my tongue. The sweet taste of pure fucking sugar rushes over my taste buds. Pure fucking Cain sugar is more like it. I have never tasted anything so goddamned good in my entire fucking life.

God help me when I remove my mouth from her and lower her body back into the water. Her face is flushed red, body trembling. I'm far from finished with her.

Pushing myself up off of my knees, I feel the water dripping from my soaked jeans and shirt.

"Don't you fucking move, Calla."

Her chest bobs up and down. I need to keep her in this euphoric state. Her mind is too sensitive; it needs to stay focused on us. Unbuttoning my jeans and ripping off my shirt, I climb out, switch off the overhead lights, and push the button to illuminate the tub surround. I stand mute when I see how radiant she looks with her damp hair clinging to her face.

Not a second longer. I need to be with her. Fuck her like crazy. Give her everything I have.

I shuck my soaked pants, freeing my raging cock. It's dark enough in here that she won't see the tattoo inked on my dick. She'll think I've lost my goddamned mind.

"Cain."

Her voice is whisper soft as I step back into the now tepid water.

"Cain. We have to talk."

"No, we don't. We can talk when we're done. What you and I are going to do right now is fuck."

"You... what we just did..."

I silence her with my hand over her mouth.

"Don't you dare. I said we will talk. Don't you deny this to either one of us. If you didn't want me to fuck you, you wouldn't have just come all over my tongue, baby."

I may sound crude, but I don't care; I know she wants me as much as I want her. I'm done talking. I want her fucking mouth.

I grab her for a passionate kiss, swinging my leg around her naked torso and straddling her waist. Water sloshes between us. I'm careful not to put all of my weight on her, but Jesus, I want to see how far I can push her. See how much of my domination she can take. Explore her boundaries.

I'm primal in kissing her, urgency mixing with sexual desperation. When her tongue glides across mine, I completely lose it. She tastes like passion.

My hands go into her wet hair, tugging enough so she arches her long neck and I can escape into the territory of her body I have missed. Her sweet spot. The one that makes her cry out my name like she is doing now.

"Cain. Oh, my."

She sucks in a breath. My mouth glides down the side of her neck. I need those perfect breasts in my mouth.

Her nipples are already hard and protruding. I begin my exploration by lifting one in my hand, my wet mouth licking around them then moving underneath where I kiss and lick and nip. She is enjoying this just as much as I am. Her sighs and moans as she grinds herself against me are all I need to know.

She squirms when I exhale on her nipple so she feels the warmth of my breath. Her body is totally under my control. I can't get nearly enough. I switch my mouth to her other breast while leaving my hand stretched wide, busily playing with the one I just left. They're too damn beautiful for either one of them to be ignored.

"Do you like that?" I ask gruffly after I suck her nipple in deep.

"God, yes!" she moans.

"Tell me what else you like."

"Anything. You could do anything to me right now, and I would love it."

She places her palms down flat on my shoulders. Her pussy grinds into my stomach and my cock aches. Goddamn, he is going to feel so fucking happy when I finally sink inside her.

"How about this?"

My finger roams down her ribcage, along her backside, and down the crack of her plump. tight ass. Her body goes rigid for a beat. She quivers when I circle her puckered hole.

"Yes," she whispers.

"Every part of this body has always belonged to me, Calla. And I'm staking my claim right here and now."

With one last lick of her breast I am at her mouth again, kissing long, hard, and deep while I push my finger gently inside her ass. She clenches with resistance at first, then slowly begins to relax. I stop when I get to my knuckle.

Our kissing becomes more erratic. She nips at my bottom lip. My finger glides out and back in. She whimpers and clenches down again. I grin against her mouth.

"You like that, huh, baby? I got you. You want more, then tell me."

"Just don't stop. Please don't stop."

Her desperation rings loud and clear. My sweet, innocent wife has turned into a fucking naughty sex goddess. My finger goes in deep.

"Like this?" I tease.

Her hips lift up completely. That's it. I pump my finger in and out of her ass. Calla watches me with glazed over eyes. She wants it rough and dirty, making me wonder exactly what the hell she has done with the two other men she has been with.

I cast those thoughts aside just as quickly as they enter my head, tucking them away for a talk we will definitely be having later. I continue to finger fuck her senseless until I feel her grab hold of my wrist, nails slicing into my skin as she comes once again.

"I'm going to fuck you now, baby, but the first time is not going to be in this tub, so come here."

I extract my finger from her. I sit on the edge of the tub with my feet planted firmly onto the bottom of it. With a lift of her ass, I haul her on top of me.

Her brows quirk up.

"What, beautiful?"

"If I'm on top, I'd say I'm the one doing the fucking, wouldn't you?"

She definitely has me there.

Our roles are reversed. Her knees spread wide, giving me a prime view of her pussy. Her hand grips my cock, stroking him up and down and then lightly grazing the tip with one of her fingers. I go up in flames.

Fuck me, my wife is stroking my dick. If I wasn't such a hard ass son of a bitch I could cry right now, I swear to Christ. That is how good she feels. How desperate I am for her.

When she lines her eager pussy up to my dick, sinking down slowly and taking in every inch, I do cry out in a deep groan.

"You ready to be fucked, Cain?"

She shoves me back and I ease my way onto the tile floor. I've never felt anything so good in my life. All I want to do is watch her glide up and down. No words. Nothing, except to feel. Feel the way her pussy wraps around me like warm silk, slinking down my dick. Feel the way she grips me tight when she lifts back up.

My eyes are glued to our connection. My dick is coated with her creamy juices, the sound of her slick heat becoming louder and juicier with every bouncing thrust.

I wanted to dominate her, and now here I am letting her fuck my goddamned brains all over this bathroom floor.

She begins to grind in quick, controlled motions, her wetness smearing on me. And then she ups the ante. My eyes roll in the back of my head when she takes her legs, stretching them straight out to the sides of my head by my shoulders. Her fingers dig deep into my shins, using them for leverage. Her hips start moving in a circular motion and she rides my cock hard and fast like a damned joystick.

"Fucking Christ! That's it, baby. Ride it. Fuck it. Take every inch I have and get yourself off."

I thrust my hips up to meet her, taking her to the depths of carnal bliss. I want everything from her.

All that matters to me right now is to come inside of her. No way in hell am I coming before her. My balls are so fucking tight right now. I clench my abs, hold it in, and watch my woman ride me. Her breasts bounce in every direction, and my hands itch to reach up and mold my fingers around them.

I'm stuck. Transported back in time when it was just me and her, the way it should have been all along. The way it will be again.

"Cain! I'm going to come!" she bellows.

"Fuck, yeah, sweetheart! Come."

With her eyes on fire, smoky and staring right into mine, and her hair going wild in every which way, my wife's body tenses up, her inner thighs spasming against my ribs. She moans in the sexiest way.

"Holy shit!"

She grinds down one last time, and fuck it, I'm done. I grip her hips tightly and pound up into her two, three, four times and fill her so full she will be leaking and smelling like me for a week.

For the longest time we stare at each other. I'm filled with the burning desire to slam back into her, to start making up for the six years we lost. Calla, on the other hand...

I shoot straight up, getting nose to nose and face to face with her, my eyes pleading for her to tell me what's wrong. Her mouth moves, but nothing comes out.

"What the hell, babe?"

I disconnect us and flip her gently onto her back. Tears are pooling out of her eyes. She's sobbing.

"What have we done? I... I can't believe I just did that."

I'm confused.

"Come again." I ask harshly.

"We just had sex."

Regret fills her tear-stained eyes. I instantly become pissed off. I jackknife myself up off of her.

"You have got to be fucking shitting me! Do you want me to say what you can't? What your face is telling me? You regret what just happened."

Does she mean it? She'd better not.

"No. I don't regret it. I'm just..," she stops.

"You're just what?"

"We... we had unprotected sex. I've never had unprotected sex with anyone but you. And I'm not on any form of birth control. I quit taking the pill, shortly after..," she shrugs. "Well, you know. So I've never needed to go back on them."

I'm relieved. It isn't regret she's feeling. I'm glad she's always been safe. That no one has come inside of her but me. No one else should have been there in the first place. That shit's on me. Never again will she be touched by anyone else.

"I've never gone without one, either, since you. So there's only one solution to this tiny little problem. Tomorrow first thing I'm calling a doctor, because there is no way I'm using one again. Not when I just had my first taste of you again. No damned way."

I look down at her red-rimmed eyes. Her face has that freshly- fucked look. In spite of her being an absolute mess, she's beautiful.

"Well about that, too," she says. Then sniffles.

"About what?"

"Don't you think we got a little carried away? We don't even know each other anymore. And aren't you forgetting someone?"

She sits up, pulling herself into a standing position.

"Forgetting who?"

"Uh, Emerald. Your girlfriend, whore, slut, or whatever she is to you."

"Emerald? She isn't jack shit to me. Never was."

"I beg to differ. She hates me as much as I hate her. And you've been with her for years. There is no way in hell she's just going to walk away from you."

"You beg to differ? Am I on trial now? Because that sounds like a bunch of lawyer bullshit to me. When I tell you she means nothing to me, I mean it. I haven't been with her or anyone else for well over a month, and she's damn stupid if she thinks I would choose her over you. The only woman who has ever meant anything to me is standing right in front of me, and if she doesn't shut her mouth and get the fuck over here and kiss me, I'm going to stick my cock in her mouth and shut her up myself."

She sighs, then rolls those pretty little eyes and waltzes right out without kissing me. Fucking pain in my ass already.

This talk is not over by a long shot.

Chapter Ten

Calla

Cain struts out of the bathroom with a towel wrapped around his waist, his confidence following right behind him.

"You don't walk out of an important conversation. You and me, we're talking this out. And quit thinking so much. I promise you, I'm clean."

He tosses me a t-shirt he pulls out of the dresser.

"Here, put this on. Tomorrow I'll get someone to go buy you some clothes."

Catching it in mid-air, I slip it over my head. It's huge, of course, hanging down to just above my knees and practically falling off my shoulders.

I watch him with his back to me. He takes out a pair of shorts, steps into them, and pulls them up and over his ass. He drops the towel and turns around and faces me.

"Very sexy," he smirks.

"I believe you when you say you're clean, but we can't just go around and have unprotected sex. I could get pregnant, too, you know."

His eyes gleam back at me with amusement.

"You're not pregnant. Quit analyzing shit. We'll deal with it. Right now it's getting late, I want to grab something quick to eat and get some sleep. I don't know about you, but I'm exhausted. I don't have jack shit in here to eat except for peanut butter and jelly and some chips. I'll get someone to hit up the grocery store tomorrow, too."

This man is talking like we live together. Like everything is going to be fine between the two of us. We just had sex.

Does he think that's it? That we can just pick up right where we left off and start a happy life together? It's not happening.

I'm too tired, hungry, and way disappointed in myself for letting my stupid lady parts control my actions to argue right now. And since when did he go to medical school to become an OBGYN? With the way my pussy opened up and said dive right in, my eggs more than likely did a cannonball straight into his sperm.

"Peanut butter and jelly is fine. I do have one more question, though."

"What is it?"

I sit down on the edge of the bed and rest my hands firmly in my lap. He moves to stand directly in front of me.

"Well, more like two questions."

"I don't have time for games. I'm fucking hungry."

"Fine. First, I'm not comfortable with someone else buying my clothes. And second, I'm also not keen on some random doctor coming here and seeing me, either. So if and when we-"

He stops me again.

"If and when we what? Fuck? Screw? Have sex? Make love? Is that what you're trying to say? Because trust me, there will be an 'if!'"

He ticks off one finger.

"An 'and!'"

He ticks off another.

"And there definitely will be a 'when!'"

My heart pounds in my chest. I know Cain doesn't like disrespect. He's made this loud and clear. We're also alone here. Just like anyone else, I'm entitled to my own damn opinion. I'm also in control of my own body.

"You and I are happening, Calla Bexley. Deal with it!"

"We shall see," I say smugly, crossing my arms over my chest.

I haven't been called Calla Bexley since the day we got married. It sounds even better than I remember. Cain shoves me back onto the bed, covering me with his big body.

"Listen up. I have answers to those damn questions. I'm only saying them once. You can't leave here to go shopping for clothes. I've told you the reason why. You make a list of what you need and I'll give it to Priscilla and she will get them. And you will see a doctor. I may not have an education, but I sure as shit know there are more options for birth control then condoms. I don't want anyone looking at your pretty little pussy, either, but there is no way in hell I'm letting anything come between you and me again and that includes a goddamned condom. Deal with it."

His arrogance is flipping maddening. I tip my head back in shock.

"And don't look at me like that!"

"How am I looking at you?" I say flippantly, trying to get a little of my own back.

"Like you're wondering who the hell Priscilla is and whether I screwed her or not."

"I most certainly am not! Who you screwed while we were apart is none of my business. Just like what I did is none of yours."

"Bullshit. Everything about you is and always will be my business. And for your information, no, I did not fuck her. She's married to Bronzer. They have two kids, a dog, and a damn hamster. She keeps my books for me. Are there any other questions brewing in that head of yours?"

"Not right now. I'll ask to reconvene to discuss these facts with my client," I laugh.

"There you go, then. Bring it on, Ms. Lawyer. I have nothing to hide."

And this is where I call bullshit. Not out loud, of course. I know damn well he's hiding plenty.

Tossing him a forced smile, I reluctantly agree. I'm too tired to argue with him anymore. As I follow him out of the bedroom and into the kitchen, all I can do is picture myself wearing Daisy Dukes and black biker tank tops. Going braless and pantyless. God, I need to find a way out of here, and fast.

"This kitchen is amazing. The whole house is, actually. Did you build it yourself?"

I sit at the kitchen table on one of the high bar stools. The rounded table looks handmade. A thin strip of dark wood borders the glass tabletop. The intriguing part of it is what's underneath the glass. Shards of what appear to be broken glass in every color are scattered throughout, giving the appearance of a rainbow effect the way one color bleeds into the next.

"I designed it and hired a company out of Canton to build it," he shrugs and takes the last bite of his sandwich.

"It all looks so new."

"It's been done for about a year. And like I told you already, I haven't stayed here. I built it for us. You're here now, so this is where we stay."

Maybe I've been wrong about Cain this whole time. Then again, the way he turns from ice to a blazing hot sun, maybe not. I'm exhausted. I need to sleep and wake up to a fresh mind.

Cain busies himself in the kitchen, putting things away and wiping down the counters. I observe him. He's hiding way too much from me. Would I be crazy to dig around and see if I can find out exactly what it is? Do I gain his trust and make him think I will stay, then run the first chance I get? Or do I stand by his side like he wants me to?

Give it a day or two and everyone will have the cops out looking for me. They'll all be worried, and when that happens, here is one of the first places my dad will look, depending on how much he actually knows. He's hidden a lot from me. He may know everything.

"You ready for bed?"

Cain's voice startles me and my eyes snap to his. His inspection holds me in place. Warmth flourishes in places where it shouldn't, thinking about sleeping next to him all night for the first time as husband and wife. This night should have happened years ago, but it was ruined.

I muster up a fake smile.

"Sure."

It seems to appease him. He walks over and reaches for my hand, then turns off the light, guiding me through the house in the dark to his room.

"I'm just going to use the bathroom. Do you have a spare toothbrush?" I ask.

"I do. It's in one of the top drawers. Help yourself. I shower here and that's about it. I'll have Priscilla get you everything you need."

I stand for a moment watching the muscles in his back flex while he pulls the covers down and adjusts the pillows. Here comes the heat again between my legs. Heat mixed with pleasant pain from the rough sex we had. I've never fucked or been fucked like that before. Not even when Cain and I first started having sex. Both of us were inexperienced, but always wanting to try something new. And like typical teenagers, failing miserably at it.

It doesn't matter. I will play this game. See the doctor. Do what he wants me to do. Stay until he finds this man who wants to hurt me.

With my mind made up, I enter the bathroom, this time shutting the door behind me. I brush my teeth, wash my face, and clean myself up. I stare at my reflection in the mirror, cringing when I see small bite marks on my neck. No matter how good he is at sex, how big his dick is, and how he truly sets me off like no one else, my heart needs to stay guarded around him. He's a man who can't be trusted. A man who will destroy me again if I give him the chance.

There's a lot of songs out there about being crazy. I think they all were written with women like me in mind. I feel like a racquetball being slammed up against the wall with the way my thoughts go from wanting him one minute then the next biding my time to get away from him.

By the time I exit the bathroom, Cain is already in bed texting on his phone, his long fingers moving swiftly across the screen. He glances up at me briefly, turns, and plugs his phone into the charger. God, I would give anything to get my hands on a phone, just to let my family know I'm all right. I'm smart enough to know I can't do that. Not until I investigate for myself this asshole who is after me. An idea goes off in my head. I can use the skills I've worked hard at cultivating to help bring this piece of shit down.

"Come here," Cain beckons.

"Geez. You're like a tyrant on a bossy power trip. I'm coming."

I crawl up the bed and settle my body next to his.

"You're a little hellcat, you know that? You're going to be a great lawyer."

Sweet baby Jesus. He can be nice when he wants to be. I snuggle into him, resting my head on his shoulder.

"I hope so. Speaking of which, you should let me help you find this Kryder guy. I have resources, you know."

I tread lightly with my words. I'm hoping he will let me. It might move things along faster.

"You can help me from here. Work by my side if you want, and we can see what we can come up with. He's vanished. He has others do all of his dirty work; picking up drugs, distribution of them. You name it. Someone else is doing it. We've caught many of his men, and not a single one of those fuckers will talk. It's like they would rather get the shit beat out of them, lose a limb, or worse, die before they betray that animal."

My face crumples.

"Wow. Death, you say? Have you killed before?"

Silently I lay there waiting for him to answer but afraid to hear it.

"No. But I came close once."

I swallow, wondering if he's going to continue and tell me what happened. He doesn't. He turns off the light and pulls me in even tighter to his warm body.

"This right here, watching you climb in bed with me and holding you will always be the best part of my day," Cain mumbles sleepily.

"Mine too," I say, before falling asleep snuggled against the man I will always love but the man whose life is about to toss me right back into hell.

****

I moan from the warmth of sunlight against my face, wondering how long I've been asleep. Yawning, I stretch and open both of my eyes to look for Cain. I'm in bed alone.

Swinging my legs around, I climb out of bed, the soreness between my legs evidence of a night of rough sex with the first step I take.

Padding in my bare feet to the bathroom, I nearly scream when I see myself in the mirror. My hair is a tangled up mess, snarly and matted to my head. Everything can wait, Cain included. I turn on the shower, pull his t-shirt over my head, and walk in.

The hot spray drenches my hair. Grabbing the only bottle of shampoo, I quickly wash and rinse, cursing along the way when I can't find conditioner. I soap my body, rinse off, and reach for a clean towel on the shelf. When I'm dry, I throw the shirt back on and make my way through this monstrosity of a house in search of Cain, in utter need of coffee.

I come to a halt when I hear raised voices from the kitchen. One I know is Manny, the other Cain, and the third I don't recognize at all.

"You need to tell her the truth man. If she finds out..." Manny says.

"Shut the hell up, fucker. I'll tell her. Jesus, don't you think she's got enough to deal with right now? Shit, Manny. You know better than anyone how much she means to me. My first priority right now is keeping her safe. And you need to find that rotten snitch," Cain says to the unknown man.

"I've told you all along who I think it is, but you've ignored me. Maybe now that your wife is here, you'll pull those blinders off of your dick and believe me," Unknown man retorts.

Do I stand here and take my chances of getting caught? I'm desperate to know who he is talking about. My back is up against the wall. I slither down the hallway a little closer only to hear Manny's voice get louder like he's right on the other side.

"Good morning!" I say chirpily, as if I didn't just hear a conversation I had no business hearing.

"Morning, babe."

I steal a smug glance at Manny as I pass him by on my way to Cain where he is leaned up against the counter in dark jeans, again with the dark t-shirt and his vest. Arms crossed and hair freshly washed, he smells edible when I reach up on my tiptoes and kiss him on his cheek.

"Jesus Christ!" Manny and unknown man both shout at the same time.

I whip around, plastering my back against Cain's front.

"What?" I screech, my eyes scanning the floor for a mouse or something.

"Dress your fucking woman, you asshole!" Manny hollers, while unknown man can't seem to take his eyes off my ass, even though it's plastered up against Cain.

"Oh, my God!"

"It sure as shit isn't, 'Oh, my God,' sweetheart. It's more like, 'Oh, my fucking God, that chick has one hell of a nice ass,'" Unknown man says.

Cain draws me in tight. His hands spanning my waist territorially.

"Beamer, enough you pervert. Calla, go," he orders, squeezing me a bit before pushing me away.

"May I have some coffee first?"

"Fuck, no. And don't come back out until I say."

Oh, I am pissed now. Is this how he thinks he is going to talk to me around everyone? Is this how all these rat bastards talk to their wives and girlfriends? Oh, no. Not me. I storm back to the bedroom like a scolded child and plop my ass on the bed. He has five minutes or I'm walking out there with absolutely nothing on and he can shove his bossy male stick up his ass.

Five minutes turns into ten. It's eight o clock and I'm beyond mad.

Raised voices are heard once again when I creep into the kitchen. All three of them stop talking and look at me like I'm intruding. And I am. I don't care. None of them have moved from their spots.

"I thought I told you-"

"Stop," I say, holding my hand up.

"Let me tell you a little something about me, which Manny should know, being that he has followed me around for a few years. You do NOT mess with me and my coffee!" I yell. "I've lived off of that stuff for six years. It's the only thing that I crave, the only thing I need, and you'd better give me a damn cup right the fuck now!"

"Damn, woman. You really are a feisty one," Unknown man says.

"And you are?"

I turn and face him, knowing full well what his name is. It cracks me up all these nicknames everyone has for each other. Makes me curious to know what they call Cain. I stick my hand out for him to shake.

"Bronzer," he replies politely, taking my hand into his big one.

"Ah. Nice to meet you. Priscilla is your wife, right?"

He grins at the mention of her name.

"Yeah, she claims me," he chuckles.

"Great. Is she here by chance? Because you see, my husband here said she would go shopping for me today, and well," I look down at the t-shirt that has now fallen off my shoulders, baring a lot of skin. "I kind of need some clothes."

"Calla?" Cain growls my name.

"Yes, dear?" I respond without looking at him, tossing a wink at Bronzer.

"Here."

A cup of black coffee appears in front of me. The rich aroma sets my nose twitching.

"Thank you," I say pleasantly.

Manny chuckles. Cain swears and I feel everyone's eyes on my backside when I leave the room to try and find some paper and pencil to spend a hell of a lot of my darling hubby's money.

"Have you ever been spanked?"

I cock my head and glare at Cain, who is standing on the threshold of the bedroom. I'm sitting cross-legged on the bed finishing up with my list. I glance at it one more time before I answer him to make sure I have all my sizes down. There's a big star next to the lingerie shop in Birmingham Hills that I know carries my favorite bras. I stick the pen behind my ear out of habit.

"Are you cross examining me?"

"Cut the smart ass lawyer bullshit. I thought I made myself clear when I told you to respect me in front of others. It's a shame Bronzer is one of the cool guys and doesn't treat his wife like shit, because I want nothing better than to turn you over my knee and crack that ass."

I grind my teeth and shake my head at this fool.

"Look, respect goes both ways. I apologize. Give me a break, would you? I mean, how was I supposed to know you would be having some man meeting in the middle of your kitchen early in the morning?"

"You didn't, and that's on me, but you prancing around with nothing covering your ass in front of my buddies really pisses me off."

His muscles are tense as I stand and approach him.

"Whatever." I wave him off.

"Goddamnit. I don't care if it's the pope who's in this house. I do not want anyone else seeing what's mine."

Now it's my turn to shout. I'm livid as hell.

"Don't you dare raise your voice at me! I didn't do a damn thing wrong. It's you. All of it is you! The way I see it, this t-shirt covers more of my body than the clothes some of those women had on last night at that party. And I am not yours. I can show my ass to whomever I want."

"Fuck. You are so stubborn. Those women's asses weren't hanging out. I'm having Priscilla buy a gunny sack, granny panties, and a damn muzzle for your mouth."

I roll my eyes.

"Yeah, good luck with that one, buddy. You'd be better off spanking me."

"Oh, you're going to get spanked, all right."

"Ha! We'll see about that," I sneer.

"We sure the hell will!"

Ugh. This man infuriates the living shit out of me. I don't know whether to love him or hate him. Bitch slap him or kiss him. I'm not done with him yet, though. I want him to admit he's jealous. It may be childish of me to pull it out of him, but I don't care. I just want to hear him say it. I'll prod on with my so-called interrogation and then when I'm done, I'll be dropping a bomb right on top of his head. He'd better be ready for a big explosion if he lies to me.

"So which one is it? Are you mad because I went back out there and asked for some coffee, or are you really mad because they saw my ass?"

His gaze stays glued to my mouth until I climb off of the bed and stand directly in front of him.

"I'm not mad, baby. I just don't want anyone else to see what's rightfully mine. Whether you believe me or not, you are mine. There is nothing in this world that will ever change that."

Cain reaches for my face, his fingers gliding down my cheek. His eyes become soft.

"You have a slight bruise right here from last night."

I know he's talking about my run in with Emerald. I noticed it this morning, too, when I looked in the mirror. I lean into his touch.

"It doesn't hurt."

"I'm glad. So are we good?"

"We will be if you get me another cup of coffee."

"That I can do."

His fingers slide to my throat, down my shoulder and arm until he reaches my hand, and clasps it with his. Even though he didn't tell me directly he's jealous, it's written all over his beautiful face, dark with scruff. I hate to put a spoke in his wheel, but it has to be done.

"By the way, here's my list for Priscilla." I hand it to him with a flourish. "I'm a woman who has expensive taste. I hope you don't mind. If you don't want to spend the money, I'm sure Manny can go back to my apartment to get some of my stuff, you know," I add, suddenly feeling guilty.

"He can't. I would bet anything Kryder knows you're here. I'm not taking any chances where you're concerned at all. And as far as the money goes, what I have is yours. It makes me feel good to be able to spend it on you."

"You know," I say, twining my fingers around his neck. "You're not as hard ass as you think you are."

"That's where you're wrong, pretty lady. I am as hard and as badass as I think I am. Now is there anything else?" he smirks.

His amusement amuses me. The minute my words come out of my mouth it will be gone.

"Tell me what the three of you were talking about when I walked in kitchen. What are you hiding from me, Cain?"

Chapter Eleven

Cain

"What are you talking about?"

Her face falls. Along with mine.

"I overheard you three in there talking before I came in. Please don't lie. If it's something I need to know, or something I can help with, then tell me. Don't leave me in the dark anymore."

She looks hurt. Lost. Uncomfortable, even.

"Please, Cain. Let me help."

I loosen her arms from around my neck and she retreats to the bed. She deserves to know everything. For the first time since the day she left, I feel the pain again. If I tell her, will she hate me? Of course she will. She's on the good side of the law, while her husband breaks it every time his feet hit the damn ground.

"I'll tell you the truth, but I need you to promise me you will keep an open mind."

She looks down to the floor then back up at me again.

"Now you're scaring me. You're in some kind of trouble, aren't you?" she whispers.

Someone has sucky ass timing. My phone rings and I pull it out of my vest pocket. Seeing that it's Priscilla, I answer.

"Yeah. I got it. I'll be right out."

Disconnecting, I shove my phone back in my vest, my eyes never leaving hers.

"Priscilla's outside. Let me give this to her and I'll be right back."

I don't stick around in the room after that. I need a moment to myself, to decide if I tell her everything or just enough to hope like hell it pacifies her enough so I can get on with my day.

By the time I'm finished giving the list and a wad full of cash to Priscilla, my mind is made up. I need for her to trust me and know I'm serious about the two of us. She's going to flip her shit when she finds out just how deep I am into being a first class law breaking criminal.

"Let's go in the other room and talk. And here, put these on. You're distracting the hell out of me knowing you have nothing on underneath my t-shirt."

The air is crackling with a thick cable of tension. I hand her a pair of my shorts. She doesn't even look at me when she takes them out of my hand. My gut twists in a damn knot so tight, I'm afraid it will never come undone, like a shoelace you can't seem to undo no matter what, so you cut it. That's how I feel right now. Like I'm about to cut my own damn heart out.

I stand there and watch her slide my way-too-big-for-her shorts up her long legs, catching a glimpse of her bare pussy when she pulls them up and ties the string.

"I promise I'll keep an open mind. I'll do anything to help you."

Her words startle me. I nod in her direction when she sits on the couch and I head for the chair. I'm in desperate need of a drink. I couldn't care less what time of the day it is.

"Do you want that cup of coffee?" I ask.

"No. I want you to quit stalling and tell me."

She looks like she could claw my eyes out. An intimidator. A fucking lawyer. Before I even begin, I know deep in my gut my wife is the one person who just might be able to help me.

"I'm a gun thief, Calla. I steal them and turn around and sell them."

I watch as shock takes over her body. All the color drains from her face. Her mouth goes slack. She gulps loudly.

"Why? How?"

"Why? I'm damned good at it. The best. And it makes me a shit-ton of fucking money. And the how? I've got my ways. Ones I'm willing to share with you if you'll become my lawyer."

She looks away from me for a moment, shaking her head sadly.

"How could your life have come to this?"

Disappointment in me is etched across her gorgeous features. I'm sure it matches my own. Every day when I look in the mirror I'm reminded of the failure I've become. The woman sitting across from me is the one person I've failed the most. I'm not who she thought I was. Or who I wanted to be. I'm a money hungry, blood thirsty criminal. I'm not about to ask her to forgive me. It may not be what I wanted to do growing up, but I enjoy what I do. I shrug internally.

I contemplate my response. I haven't had to answer to anyone in a long ass time. Calla's not just anyone; she's my life. If there is a way out of this without anyone getting hurt, or worse, killed, I will do it. For her.

"I'm my father's son," I simply say.

"Yes, you are. That doesn't mean you had to follow in his footsteps and be like him. What happened to being on the good side of life? God, Cain. Do you sell guns to kids? I mean, who do you sell them to?"

I laugh, even though none of this is funny. She sounds like a lawyer and I'm on trial already. She wants to know it all? I'll give it to her.

"No, I don't sell them to kids. What happens after I sell them isn't my concern, though. I sell them domestically to a few large buyers in New York. I do not sell them out of the country to drug cartels or gangs."

"How do you get them?"

This is the part that is going to rip her heart out. I look her straight in the eyes when I tell her.

"I steal them."

I watch her shoulders sag. She leans back on the couch, her head goes to the ceiling where she stares at a particular spot for the longest time.

"You get rid of the serial numbers."

"Yes."

"Then you sell them so they can't be traced."

"Again, yes."

"What else have you lied to me about?"

"Nothing," I lie.

Actually, this is only a half lie. I haven't technically lied to her about who my partner is yet. I just haven't said.

"Do all these people really have jobs, or are they all in on this, too?"

"Everyone has a real job, including me. Manny, Beamer, and I work together. No one else knows we front this bar to cover our tracks."

I shrug as if it's no big deal when really, it is.

"And this is where your snitch comes in? Someone here found out, or they're an undercover cop, or they're out for revenge. Am I right?"

"You're very inquisitive, baby. I like it. I'm getting hard sitting over here, admiring how you're questioning me like I've been arrested and now being interrogated by a sexy-as-hell lawyer."

She looks over to me, a deep frown line creasing her forehead.

"None of this is funny. It's both illegal and immoral. You could spend the rest of your life in prison or wind up dead."

"It's not funny at all. It's not who I wanted to be, but it is who I am," I say with an edge.

"Who do you sell them to, Cain?"

She's demanding now, her tone heavy and completely in control. Me, not so much at the moment. The answer I'm about to give her is going to scare the hell out of her.

"Salvatore Diamond."

She jumps off of the couch, her eyes becoming wide.

"Jesus, Cain. Are you serious? How in the hell did you get mixed up with the fucking mob?"

I sit there, watching her pace back and forth across the carpet. Her hands run through her hair out of frustration.

"I don't know if I want any part of this. Do you know what this means, for God's sake? It means you will never get out of stealing and dealing guns. You can't just get out of the mafia. Everyone in the world knows that. If you want out, the only way those people let you out is by killing you and burying your body somewhere where no one will ever find you. And you say you love me? You've kept me safe from a drug dealer? Well, who the hell has been keeping you safe? Who has your back?" she snarls.

I take a deep breath and steeple my hands under my chin, resting my elbows firmly on my knees.

"Your dad keeps me safe, Calla."

I half expected her to go on a rampage, but she does the complete opposite. She stays calm, acting like I haven't just tossed her into a tornado.

"I knew there was more to the reason why my parents were so adamant about keeping us apart, but never in my wildest of dreams would I have ever imagined this. You have a lot more explaining to do. And I demand to see my parents. You!"

She stalks over to me and leans down right into my face. Not so calm anymore. She's become the eye of the twirling tornado and fuck me, she's destined for destruction.

"You said you weren't lying to me about anything else!"

"I haven't." She's so close to my face. Her face bright red from anger.

"No? Are you sure? Because I have a very good memory, and I recall you telling me just yesterday that I couldn't call my parents because the less they knew, the safer they would be. Get them here now, goddamnit. I want, no, I deserve to know everything. My God. The mob! This is insane! We're better off just putting one of those guns you steal to our own heads and blowing our brains out. Those people don't mess around."

"Calla. Enough."

Our attention swings to the door. Neither one of us heard it open.

"Well, speak of the devil. Hello, mom and dad. Or would you prefer I call you Bonnie and Clyde?"

"Sit your ass down, and watch your mouth."

John Greer stalks into the room. The fucker is big. I'm talking huge. He towers over his daughter. The two of them stare each other down. Her stubbornness matches his.

"I'm a little old for you to be telling me what to do. Considering the lion's den you all have thrown me into, I think you should sit down. Or better yet, start fucking talking."

Her mouth. Christ almighty. If we were by ourselves right now and she kept on running her mouth like she is now, I'd love nothing more than to... Yeah. Fuck, I'm not going there. I palm my hands down my face, then toss a glance at Manny, our eyes saying the exact same thing. This is about to get real ugly.

Chapter Twelve

Calla

I feel like an energy field. My emotions have all of a sudden risen past their capacity; even though they've been pushed to the max, someone is still feeding me just to see how far I will expand.

"Last time I checked, I was the parent in our relationship. So if I say sit down, then sit the hell down. And if I say shut your mouth, then I mean shut your mouth," Big bad John says.

I'm not afraid of my dad, especially when his soft eyes give him away. He's towering over my tall frame trying to intimidate me. I want to laugh, no, spit in his face. My entire life has been nothing but a lie. I move to the couch and sit. Not because he told me to, but because I deserve to know what the hell is going on.

"You look like hell," my deceitful mother says.

Her long, dark hair is pulled into a pony tail. Her loving eyes that look so much like mine send me an apologetic look. She's in on this, too. Everyone is. Along with Manny, who's standing off in the corner by the door.

"Yeah, well, what do you expect?" I ask through clenched teeth. "I came here for a divorce, not expecting to be carried away by a lying, cheating, and now criminal husband."

I peer around my mother, who is now standing in front of me with eyes shooting bullets at my husband. I wonder if he steals those, too. I could use about four of them right now to shoot every one of these deceitful, mafia-loving people. Okay, not really. I could never shoot my parents.

"How long?" I demand.

It's a simple question, really. One I deserve to know the answer to. I seem to be the only one left in the dark here by the way everyone is looking back and forth at each other as if they're deciding which one of them should fill me in.

My parents sit down next to me. A fond memory flashes through my mind from when I was five years old. The three of us were sitting on the couch exactly like this while they told me our family dog was struck by a car and died. I cried like a baby, kicking and screaming for Hopper to come back. My dad held me for the longest time, stroking my hair and reassuring me that all dogs go to heaven and Hopper would be waiting there for me someday. I feel just like that little girl again. Except I'm not, I'm an adult. One who has been lied to about everything.

It's my mom who speaks first. Her hand comes to rest on my knee.

"I've been connected to the Diamond family my entire life," she begins, giving me a little squeeze. "My name was Cecily Abagail Diamond. Salvatore is my older brother."

I stand and move over to the wall, pressing my back up against it and glaring at everyone in this room. I stop when I land on my mother.

"In other words, you're a mafia princess," I say with malice.

"I used to be. That is, until I met your father and fell in love."

Her smile speaks the truth. Even though my parents would fight and argue when I was growing up, the love they had for each other was very evident, even as a young girl, I knew how much they loved each other.

"I don't understand, then. Enlighten me here, Mom, or what about you, Dad? How do you fit into all of this?"

I hold my breath and wait for him to speak. The tension in the room coils around me.

"Calla, baby. I really think you need to sit down," Cain declares.

"I don't want to sit down. What I do want is the truth from all of you."

I feel cheated, sad, and humiliated. This is a lot of information to incorporate. I'm so angry right now. With Cain I had so many questions; with my parents, I feel like they have hidden too much from me since the day I was born. My brain at this minute doesn't even know how to function. My dad gets up and puts his arm around me, tugging me into his chest.

"Honey, you're shivering."

"Please don't touch me," I whisper.

I duck out from under his arm and step away. Suddenly, the tension leaves him as if he's come to some sort of decision. I watch it roll right off of his chest. His eyes turn glassy. My knees start to buckle. I stand firm, though. I'm not weak. I'm frightened and scared for my life; for my family's lives.

"I'm a hitman," he says emotionlessly, as if he hasn't just crumbled my entire world. I've worshipped this man my entire life, and now he sits before me telling me he's a murderer.

"Y…you kill people? Oh, my God! What's wrong with you people? Don't any of you care about how badly corrupted this world is? And dead center lies my family. The untouchable Diamond family," I say bitterly.

"You've stolen loved ones away from others, Dad. Is this why you pushed me so hard to become a lawyer? Because if you ever got caught one day you would hope like hell that your daughter would defend you? Come on. Tell me. Why?

How can you sleep at night? Breathe the same air as the very families of the wives, husbands, or even children whose loved ones you've killed?"

"It's not like that, Calla."

My father looks genuinely hurt. He should be.

"Then tell me how it is. Because like I told Cain, I'm on the good side of the law. The right side of the tracks. I can't just stick out an olive branch to all of you. My entire life has been a lie. You've left me hanging all by myself on that small branch and today is the day it finally snaps and the ground I thought was underneath isn't ground at all. It's a cliff. And I keep falling, smacking my head into every hard rock along the way to the bottom."

"Jesus. Fuck. Help me out here, Cecily?"

"No, Dad. This is between me and you. Father and daughter. I'm sure she has her own poison she needs to shove down my throat. I want to know how my own father could take someone else's life?"

"I have no choice. I was born into this lifestyle just like your mom, just like Cain, and just like Manny over there. We don't have choices like you do. You wouldn't be here today if I had told them no."

"You're still not making sense to me. Were you threatened? Spit it out. The truth, all of it."

I'm trying so hard to wrap my head around this. There's no way I can. My body is looped so tensely right now.

"Our families go back a long way. My father was a trained assassin. He had me shooting targets from a mile away by the time I was ten years old. I'm not going to stand here and tell you what I do is right. What I will say is I sleep at night because I know you're safe. Your mother and I kept this from you to protect you from this type of life. That's why all those years ago when you first brought up Cain's name I prohibited you from seeing him. I didn't want my daughter anywhere near this kind of life. I never wanted it to touch you at all."

I look at him suspiciously.

"So the feud between you and Cain's dad was a lie, too?"

"That part is the truth. I hated that prick. He wanted your mother and let everyone know it. If it wasn't for the fact that he was good at getting us the type of guns we needed, I would have killed him before someone else had the chance to. And then he hooked up with Cain's mother and his obsession with Cecily stopped. Cain was born only a few months before you, and when two innocent little babies came into this world. I buried my hate for him. I don't kill people just because I want to. I kill them because they're scum. You don't get a second chance when you fuck over Salvatore."

I tilt my head and fix my eyes on Cain. He knows. He knows everything. And Manny, how does he fit into all of this? Is he a child of the mob as well? Four pairs of eyes are all looking at me. All of them gauging my reaction. Cain looks defeated. Manny looks like he feels sorry for me. My mother looks frightened, as if she might lose the one thing in her life she could never live without. And my dad, he's standing there watching me intently, wondering if his little girl will ever be able to forgive him.

Suddenly the room starts to spin and the walls begin to cave in. My legs give out and my body crumples to the floor. I can't breathe. My sweet, caring father is a cold-blooded murderer. My husband steals and sells guns. My mother is the sister to one of the world's most notorious criminals.

And me? Who am I? The wife and daughter of people I once trusted. A fake, just like them. They all play a role in this. And whether any of them believe it or not, they have left me with no choice. Either I accept the lifestyle they lead, or I find my way out of here. Disappear, and never have contact with them again.

For the first time, I am ashamed to admit I can't live without any of them. My parents' blood pumps this non-existent life I was destined to live through my veins. That's what makes my heart turn cold. And for that, I truly am my father's daughter.

"Calla!"

They all shout my name at once. Cain is kneeling at my side, lifting me up as if I weigh nothing at all and cradling me in his arms.

"Come on, sweetie. Look at me."

I do. I look up at him, and his face is so full of love and concern. I should hate him. Hate them all for the lives they lead; for the life I'm being forced to enter.

All of a sudden, I'm crushed by the dire need to be in Cain's arms. I'm right where I want to be. Right where I'm meant to be. Burying my face into his chest, I let loose and cry while he holds me tightly. I feel so lost. So sad. I don't even know my family. The two people in this world who I never expected would hurt me have completely wrecked me.

No one says a word as I let loose, soaking Cain's shirt. I need to pull myself together. There is so much more to be said here, so much more I don't know, and I'm afraid of just what that might be.

I peel my face away from Cain's chest. He cups my jaw tenderly, his thumb brushing away the wetness from my face.

"I... I'm sorry," I say breathlessly. "I'm fine."

I'm truly not fine, and they all know it. I've been kicked in the chest.

"No, you're not," says my mother, echoing my thoughts.

"I am," I insist. "Don't you see? I'm the daughter of a mafia princess. The niece of the biggest mobster in the state of New York and the daughter of a killer. How could I not be fine?"

Cain bends and kisses each corner of my mouth.

"You've been lied to and deceived by us all, but we'll get through this together. I promise."

"Sweetheart?" my dad calls to me. I'm not ready to look at him yet.

"Yeah?" I croak pathetically.

"I never wanted you to find out. The last thing I ever wanted to do was to hurt my baby girl. You've always been my world. You always will be, no matter what you think of me. I'll give you the time you need to process all of this. Cain knows everything. I'll be here when you're ready to talk."

Dad's voice is strained. I still can't look at him. I focus solely on Cain's face. His square jaw. Bright blue eyes. The way he looks down at me with worry etched all over his face.

"I love you," my mother's voice serenely whispers in my ear as I hear her kneel down on the floor with us. She puts her hand on my back. I don't want to look at her right now, either.

"I know, Mom."

"For the record, I'm sorry too, Calla," Manny says.

I don't move a muscle until I hear the door close behind them all. It's after I know they are all gone that I break down once more in my husband's arms.

The two of us stay in this position until my tears have all dried up. I have so many questions left to ask him. I need to pull my thoughts together.

Cain's phone vibrates in his pocket. I unlock my grip from his shirt and go to stand, but he holds me in place with one hand while digging into his pocket with the other.

"Stay," he simply states.

I do. If I could stay cocooned in his arms forever, right here on the floor, I would. I feel safe, untouched by the evil world outside of this house. The moment I walk out of these doors I will become someone I'm not. Someone I will hate.

"Just leave them on the porch," I hear him say before turning to me.

"That was Priscilla. She has all your stuff."

His voice is low, unsure, even, when he speaks next.

"Do you want to talk about it?"

I give a slight shake of my head.

"Not right now."

My eyes are still closed. I know they're swollen from all the crying I've done. My breathing is delicate and light. My ears keep hearing over and over again the things my loved ones said. There's an unpleasant taste in my mouth. All of my senses are screaming at me.

"All right then. Will you at least look at me?"

Rough fingertips start to stroke my cheek. A flash runs through my mind of him using these hands that feel so good across my skin to steal, hand over guns to people who use them to kill. I shiver.

"Calla. Look at me."

It's more of a demand than a statement. He thinks I'm fragile. In a way I am, but not in the way he thinks, though. My heart has been stomped on and bled dry. But here's the thing; it's what terrifies me the most. I am a lot more like my father than any of us can begin to comprehend.

When I do look at Cain, it's as if these past six years never existed and we were never apart. But we were. How can you feel a pull so strongly towards someone when in reality you never knew them at all? How can you love someone so much after being separated for as long as we have, and at the same time want to gouge their eyes out? It's a riddle I will never be able to solve. A puzzle that will always be missing the last piece no matter how hard I try to find it.

"We have a lot more things to talk about, you and I. You tell me when. If it's too much for you to handle and you don't want to know any more, then we can leave it at that until I find Kryder. The one thing I do want to tell you is, I fucking love you so much it hurts. I've hurt every day since you walked out of my life. It's killing me that you found any of this out and that it's been shoved in your face all at once. You seem so fragile and yet so strong at the same time. Your dad speaks the truth, you know?"

"I know."

Cain pushes the hair away from my face. The way he looks at me as if trying to define whether I'm real or not sends an indescribable tingle to the one place that shouldn't be tingling at all. The place that is still sore from our reconnection. I keep telling myself over and over that I don't know him anymore, but does it really matter if I do or not? Not to me, it doesn't. I've never been one to give a damn what other people think of me. I'm sure a lot of people around here think I'm crazier than a lady with a hundred cats. I don't care.

"It's just a shock, a blow right to the center of my gut knowing he kills people," I say, picking up our conversation again.

"He loves you, Calla. So does your mom. They never wanted you to know. At least, not this way."

"Well, I know now, don't I? What I don't know is how this Kryder guy fits into all of this. Or Manny. Dad said he didn't have a choice, either."

Cain lets a whoosh out of his lungs.

"You sure you want to know?" he asks, speaking as if what he has to say could break me more than what I've already heard.

"If it's the last of the big, gut-punching hits, then yes."

"Like I told you, Kryder deals drugs. I don't do drugs. I despise them. The asshole wouldn't listen, so he's gone. We kicked him out."

"And he knows about the weapons and the mob?"

His sexy lips curve up in a smile.

"He does now. He didn't before."

"What do you mean?"

"Sweetheart. What I mean is, he put a hit out on my wife. The niece of Salvatore Diamond. The daughter of a man who can silence you without the person sleeping next to you realizing he's there."

My spine goes ramrod straight.

"Holy shit. So my dad put a hit on him? That's why he's in hiding. He's scared. He knows he screwed up."

"Now she's getting the picture!" he says, lifting his face to the ceiling for a moment. "That's why we have Manny on you. To keep you safe. We've been trying to find him before he finds you."

"This is like a nightmare. Worse, even. This is a war," I whisper.

He begins to caress my cheek once again. The effects of his hand stroking my face is relaxing. I could easily fall asleep like this. I just want to slip into my own world and process all that has happened today.

"And Manny?" I ask.

He hesitates for a moment too long.

"Shit."

The way he said the word shit sends a nauseous sensation to my stomach, without me even knowing why, I can already feel this is going to be another blow to my heart. Another chunk of my chest cut open. I come to my senses and jerk away from him, standing up.

He's looking at me with pity. I hate pity. It's the worst emotion ever. Pity is for the weak, and considering everything I have found out and overcome in the past day and a half, the last damn thing I want is pity.

"Don't look at me like that," I grit out. "I'm not a charity case. I fell apart once and I refuse to do it again, so tell me, what does Manny have to do with this?"

"Calla... Manny's your cousin. He's Salvatore's son."

Chapter Thirteen

Cain

I've studied her face for the past two hours. Watched it go from happy to sad, to pain and betrayal. There are no words, nothing to try and describe the look on her face right now. I couldn't muster up a word to save my ass right now. I do the only thing I know. I go to her. Fold her into my arms. Soothing her, my hands smoothing down her messy hair.

"I'm not sure what to do or say here," I murmur, speaking into her hair.

"I don't know what to say, either. For my entire life, my parents always put me first. I know they love me, and that they want me safe and happy, but this... this doesn't make me happy. Nor does it make me feel safe. It makes me feel furious and hateful. It's like the two people who helped mold me into who I am are not the people I thought they were. They're strangers, not my parents. And my dad... I just don't understand how he could do what he does. I don't know what any of you expect of me now."

The sound of her voice is flat and dull, and her body quivers in my arms. She needs time. How much time, is up to her. Until then, I will give her the space she needs and try to come up with a plan to get us both away from here to a place where she can relax. Ease her mind. Fuck, I don't know what the hell to do.

She's my top priority. Once I know she can handle the things she's learned, then time will only tell if she's willing to lead this kind of life, the life on the other side of the tracks she was just referring to. She's the one who has to step over into unknown territory and give up her dream of being on the right side of the law.

Calla has to choose. Her family or her freedom. Those are her only two options. If she decides she can't live her life knowing the things we do and learn to accept them, then I have to let her go. I'm going right in this fork in the road. She could go left, and I would never stop loving her, always being there in the background making sure she's safe. My love for her is unconditional. It will exist forever. The thought of her marrying someone else, building a life with someone else, is unfathomable to me. I'd rather die than lose her.

I lightly brush my lips across her forehead and down her flushed face to the sensitive corners of her eyes. The bridge of her nose. I do all this while holding her delicate face in the palm of my hands. Reaching her lips, I make sure the pressure I apply on them is not demanding, but friendly and understanding. She sighs and kisses me back tenderly.

"Let me go get all your stuff from the porch."

"No, not right now. I want to stay like this for a bit longer."

"Sounds good to me," I say softly, drumming my fingers down to the hem of my t-shirt. "I hated this shirt up until now. Now it's my favorite."

She hums into my chest in agreement.

"It is ugly, isn't it?"

"It was. Now, it's not only my new favorite, it's also one I'm very jealous of."

I stop talking and splay my hand wide across her smooth stomach. I can feel her flesh break out into tiny goose bumps. She sucks in a breath.

"The truth is, if I could be anything right now, baby, I would be this shirt."

I tilt her head back so we make eye contact.

"You're crazy," she smiles weakly.

"Been called worse."

My eyes never leave hers. She is looking at me right now as if I'm her world. As if I could make all of this disappear. If only I truly could.

When I look down her body, her nipples start to poke out. I know full well I could take advantage and have her beneath me in a matter of minutes, but I won't. When I have her again, it won't be just carnal fucking. We can fuck anytime we want. I both need and want to make love to my wife.

"So tell me, why would you be this shirt?" she asks playfully. Her sense of humor is one thing I definitely missed about her.

"It's resting up against your heart. A heart I hope belongs to me. Or at least, will again."

A smile slants the corner of her sinfully delicious mouth.

"I told you. You aren't as much of a badass as you think you are."

"I'm well known as a hard ass and a bastard to all of those people out there. I may have pushed you a little too hard when you first got here. Said shit to you I didn't mean. But I can't be that with you," I say solemnly. "Just don't tell any of them, or you'll really get that spanking I warned you about. Now, I think you need some time to yourself."

She doesn't protest when she gets up on her feet and I follow.

"Go take a shower. I'll bring you your girly stuff and leave the rest on the bed, okay?"

I slide my hand down to hers, the one where her wedding ring should be. It's bare. It shouldn't be. My rings should be there. It pains me knowing I never got the chance to properly put any on her finger.

We married so hastily, so damn tired of everyone trying to keep us apart, especially our fathers.

But what she doesn't know is that John knew about us the entire time. It would kill her even more if she knew he was the one that told my dad to do whatever the hell he needed to in order to get her away from here.

I hook my fingers through hers and bring them up to my lips, casually kissing each knuckle, lingering a little longer on her ring finger. If she notices, she doesn't say anything.

I let her go and watch her retreat down the hall.

I'm a fucking sinner. An advocate to organized crime. Even so, each and every one of us would give our lives before we let anything happen to her. When she comes to terms with the situation, she will realize her identity hasn't changed. She's still their daughter. My wife. And the cold, hard fact of the matter is, there isn't a damn thing she can do about it.

* * * * * * * * * * * *

Both Manny and Bronzer are here while Calla cleans up. As soon as she left the room, I called Priscilla and asked her to bring me up a bottle of Johnny. I needed it after what went down today. Hell, I need about five more bottles of the shit.

"Fuck, man. I don't even know what the hell I'm supposed to say to her when I see her now," says Manny, looking distraught.

"Tell her the truth like the rest of us did, fucker. It's your turn to take her wrath. She's been through the meat grinder today. You grew up knowing who your family was; she grew up thinking her dad worked for a fucking bank. That every time he would leave for a few days, he was off doing business, when what he was really doing was blowing someone's brains out. She'll be glad to have someone to talk to about this. You know her better than most; she's going to trust you and the things you tell her more than she will trust anyone else."

He looks like a scared puppy who just got taken away from his mother. Bronzer pats him on the back and slides the bottle over to him.

"Damn, dude. She's a chick, and on top of that, your cousin. Chill the hell out, you fucking pussy."

I throw back my last shot and glare at Manny.

"Did you call your father yet?"

"Yup."

He slams his shot glass on the table.

"And what the hell did he say?"

"He knew already. Cecily called him the minute they left here. He wants to meet her. Said to find a way to get her to New York, and get her there today. You know how he is. When he says do something, you do it. It doesn't matter if you're family or not."

"Do you two realize how fucked up this is? We've got some crazy fucking sick bastard out there threatening to kill her. Even one of the world's best assassins can't find this sicko. Call him and tell him no. She's not leaving here until we find Kryder. If he wants to see her, he'll have to come here himself. Now that we're back together-"

"Who says we're back together?"

All three of our heads jolt in surprise when Calla gracefully strolls into the kitchen. She stops dead in her tracks when she sees Manny leaning against the counter.

She's wearing a plain black tank top that stretches across her breasts, white shorts, and a pair of black flip-flops. Her hair is pulled back in a tight ponytail. Her makeup is flawless. I can smell her natural scent from where I'm standing and my testosterone level rises. All I want to do is kick these two out of here so I can cover her entire body with mine.

She smiles at Manny but doesn't even look my way. If I didn't know the two of them were cousins, I would beat his damn ass for her having eyes for only him right now. He stands tall, although he's not the one to move first; she is. She greets him enthusiastically.

"Hey!"

"Hey..." Manny replies cautiously.

"You look great, Calla," Bronzer acknowledges before turning to me. "I'm out."

I push myself off of the counter.

"Hold up, man. I'll walk out with you. I've got some shit to do up in the office. Give you two some time to talk, yeah?" I throw a meaningful look at Manny. "Bring her up to me when you're done."

"You got it."

Calla never says a word. She nods her head, never taking her eyes off of the man she's considered her friend since he first moved here at the age of sixteen; not by choice, that's for damn sure. His parents wanted him to get an education. Manny, on the other hand, wanted to dig into the family business, feeling he was old enough to start blowing people's fucking brains out.

But that's his story to tell her if he wants to, not mine. I've got other things to tend to, like trying to find out who my mole is and getting Calla and I out of here safely.

"You look beautiful," I whisper in her ear as I pass her by.

I grab my bottle and Bronzer and I casually walk outside. I look down for a moment to grab my phone out of my pocket and run smack dab into none other than Salvatore Diamond himself.

"Hello, Cain," Salvatore greets me smugly in that way only he can.

I love this man, yet his presence here today is going to drive Calla nuts.

He gives me his usual 'long-time-no-see' hug, a medium squeeze with a pat on the back. I return the gesture along with a handshake to Beamer, who stands tall with one hell of a strange smile on his face.

"You know I mean no disrespect, but what the hell are you doing here? You're going to tip her right over the damn edge, and you know it."

He looks pleased with my sincerity concerning Calla's well-being. He knows me, knows better than most people how much I love her and that I won't ever back down when it comes to her.

"Cain, your protectiveness of my niece gives me great pleasure, but I'm a little disappointed in you not telling me she was here. I had to hear it from Cecily, who you didn't call, either," he says reproachfully.

"I had no idea she was coming. The last damn thing on my mind was calling you when I first saw her. Besides, she's safe here and you know it."

"I have not seen my niece since she was two years old. You know as well as I do that pictures are not the same as the real thing. Her being here is not the kind of shit you keep from family. She needs no protection from us."

He waves his hand dismissively, and if I didn't respect his ass, I would pull the 'I beg to differ' card on him like

Calla did me. They would never hurt her, but this lifestyle sure as hell could.

Salvatore has seen me at my lowest, and was one of the few who helped me see light in all this darkness I've been living in since she's been gone. He's the only man who told me that distance wouldn't matter if we truly loved each other. Our minds try and overrule our hearts, but love can triumph over any obstacle, any distance, and any person who tries to take it away.

No one would help me find her six years ago. Not my father, not her parents. Everywhere I looked, there were reminders of her. I gave up. I stole a shit ton of money from my father, found Salvatore's address, and forced a meeting with him. I will never forget what he has done for me. He gave me the strength and the wisdom to fight for what's mine. And here I stand, challenging him in that fight. He notices the tension in my stance and raises an eyebrow.

"Don't get all pissy with me, boy. I care about her just as much as you do. Now where's my other son?"

The boss opens his expensive jacket, shrugs it off, and tosses it on the porch like it's nothing. I bet that material cost near five thousand dollars. He wears Armani exclusively. He rolls up his sleeves.

"Well, where is he? I've got business to tend to."

I back up to grab the jacket and place it on the post leading up the stairs.

"Business? Here? You hate this city."

"Damn right, I do. It's dirty. Full of drugs. Rats. Sewers. It smells."

"And New York doesn't?" I laugh.

"Anyway, smart mouth, Detroit has just become my new favorite city."

I shoot both of them a narrow look.

"All right, you fuckers. Tell me, what the hell is going on?"

Before they can answer, I hear the sound of a car driving slowly up my path. We all turn to look.

"Jesus Christ, now what?" I exclaim.

I look from Beamer to Salvatore. Their faces stare blankly at John and Cecily, who are now getting out of the car. The three of us stand there and watch them approach. John's fists are clenched at his sides, and Cecily looks like she's ready to kill someone herself.

"You!" she shouts, aiming her finger at Salvatore. "You had the nerve to call me and tell me that shit on the phone."

"Get your finger out of my face and give me a hug. Be thankful I called you at all."

The two of them embrace, kissing each other on the cheek. My head goes back and forth between all four of them. This is some screwed up shit right here.

"What the hell is going on?" I ask loudly. "You people trying to kill her, or what? You've told her enough today, John. And you didn't speak enough, Cecily. So what brings you back to my house?"

All four of them snap their heads in my direction.

"John?" Cecily indicates for her husband to speak.

"Cain. Beamer here found Kryder this morning."

My blood starts churning. My hands clench so tightly into fists that I swear to Christ we all hear my knuckles crack.

"Where?"

"He's been right under our noses this whole damn time man. Fucking Brightmoor."

I shake my head.

"Come again? Brightmoor? As in where Emerald grew up? As in where her parents still live? Dad's old VP Monty? No motherfucking way."

This can't be. He's been right here the whole damn time.

No one says a word. All you hear is the whistle of the breeze and the shuffling of trees until John walks back to the car, the crunching of stone heard with each thunderous step. He opens the back door, reaches inside, and drags out Monty. His mouth is taped shut and his hands are cuffed. He looks as scared as a cat standing on hot bricks.

I freeze. My throat constricts, the blood that was boiling through my veins moments ago turning deathly cold. That prick. After everything my father did for him. I may be going straight to hell, but this piece of shit is about to beat me there.

"You fucking bastard! How long, you fucking grunt ass motherfucker?"

I charge at him. He falls to his knees when my fist connects with his jaw.

"I've only got one thing to say to you, you coward."

I rip the tape off his mouth and he yelps. Pussy.

With my hand fisted tightly in his hair, I jerk back his head. His eyes search me out.

"I didn't know he was the one that p...put the hit out on Calla," he snivels. "I swear to God, Cain! I was helping out Emerald. She asked me if he could live in the basement, that he needed a place to hide out from the cops."

"Emerald?" I ask incredulously.

I thrust his head back and run my hands through my hair. I cannot believe this shit!

"I'm telling you Cain. We didn't know. She's just as innocent as I am. We've all been played here."

"Aw, come on, Monty. You expect us to believe you didn't have a fucking clue? You knew he killed my father. And you fucking know why? It's because I threw his ass out of here. I don't do drugs and you know it. You, on the other hand, do. You smoke that weed like fucking crazy. It's fried your goddamned brain cells. And as for your daughter? Well, I guess she fucked up too, didn't she?"

"No. Oh, God, no, you guys. That's my little girl. She's all I have left of my wife. She's innocent, I know she is. She would never do anything to hurt you, Cain. You know this. She's been in love with you for years. Come on, man. Not her."

I look at him in disgust.

"As much as I would love to kill the both of you myself, my father-in-law is so much better at it. You see, he doesn't blink. Doesn't talk. He's going to inflict so much pain on you, you will be begging him to end your lives. But he won't. And do you know why, you stupid fuck? You've been harboring a man who has a hit out on his daughter. You are so fucked, man. I could almost piss my pants for you. After every goddamned thing my father ever did for you, you've been protecting him. He killed my father, you fucking dickhead. MY FATHER! The man who trusted you! Jesus Christ, you make me sick."

Right then, the crack of the door slamming shut cuts through the sound of Monty's whimpering. Six sets of eyes simultaneously set their sights on my wife standing on the porch with the same look in her eyes as her father. The intent to kill.

She looks down on Monty with contempt.

"My dad isn't going to do anything to Emerald. But I sure as hell will."

Chapter Fourteen

Calla

"I'm glad we talked. I can't say I understand why everyone does the things that they do. The hardest part is coming to terms with what my dad does. It's so hard to explain the feelings I have inside of me right now. I mean, how do you handle it?"

My voice nearly breaks sitting here talking to Manny about being a child born into the mafia. His mom wasn't born into it. She was his dad's high school sweetheart just like Cain and I, only they weren't forced apart by those who should love you, like we were.

I'm not a damn idiot. I know my parents, or at least my father, had something to do with Cain and I splitting up. A fresh onslaught of tears wells up inside of me knowing he had a hand in my destruction. He stood by and watched me fall apart. I'm not sure if I can forgive either him or my mother for that.

"I've grown up with this lifestyle," Manny continues. "I'm used to it. It's all I know. Everyone in the family is expected to have a certain role, whether it be to kill those who wrong the family, or become a lawyer on my father's team. Me, I had the desire to kill. I remember one time going out hunting with my dad and a couple of his buddies when I was ten years old. My first hunt and my first kill. I was so fucking happy, I couldn't stop talking about it for days, like how good it felt, and asking when we could do it again. It worried the hell out of my mother so much so that every time dad and I would go out hunting, she would nearly have a nervous breakdown. That's why she sent me here to live closer to you all."

"Really? You came here by yourself?"

Manny shrugs.

"I lived by myself during the week. And every weekend my mom or my dad, or sometimes both, would come."

"My God, you were only sixteen years old! How did they get away with letting you live by yourself?"

He gives me this, 'Seriously? We can do anything we want' look.

"And, I wasn't alone," he adds. "I knew who you were, and I knew about Cain, too. That's why I made it a point to be friends with you right away. Plus, I had Aunt Cecily checking in on me every day, not to mention your dad. Jesus, that's one scary man."

I scoff at his remark about my dad. He's never been a scary man to me. Not until earlier today, anyway.

"What did he do, beat your ass when you stepped out of line? Catch you in bed with all those sluts you used to bag in school?"

We both laugh. Manny was the new guy in school. Tall, dark, and mysteriously handsome, he climbed his way into just about every girl's pants in the entire school.

"Nah. He didn't give a shit about that kind of stuff. He just said he'd take me to the spot where he burns and then dumps the remains of his victims if I ever knocked any of them up. He was serious, too. I think that was his way of telling me it takes a special type of person to be able to take someone else's life. You know what I mean? Here's the thing, though. That's not what my parents wanted me to do. They didn't want me to be a hit man for the family; they wanted me to be a protector, one that kept an eye out for you and kept you safe. We have lots of enemies. People who want to take us out and destroy us. People who know what your father does. All families protect the ones they love the most. So I trained. I trained to be a killer. Not an assassin like your dad. Instead, someone who's not afraid to kill someone if they attempt to hurt someone we love. My first assignment after your dad trained me was you."

I do know what he means. I don't think I could ever kill anyone, but I don't have a problem with beating the shit out of someone if they deserve it, just like I did with that damn whore Emerald last night. But to actually take someone's life? I don't think I could do it.

Something Manny just said doesn't add up, though. I look at him questioningly.

"Wait. You said you didn't start looking out for me until a couple of years ago."

"That's true. I didn't."

"Well then, who did? There's no way in hell I was left out in the open on my own if this family has enemies."

"Your mom did."

"My mom?" I laugh. "She wouldn't hurt a damn fly."

"Oh, Calla. There is still so much for your pretty little head to learn. Your mom was an assassin, too."

I choke on the last piece of toast I just stuffed in my mouth, dumbfounded.

"What?" I shriek.

"I'm not even touching that subject. You talk to your parents about that."

"Jesus God almighty. I don't know any of you at all, do I?"

"Yes, you do. You know the real us. The ones that love you."

I look away, trying in vain to digest this latest piece of information. After my shower, I stared at my reflection in the mirror and searched deep into my soul. I'm a lot stronger than I thought I was, and a lot more like the rest of this family, if I can handle the things I have learned today.

I notice something furtive about the way Manny's eyes skate over mine. He's hiding something. Something big. Something he thinks I should know about. He's envisioning my reaction to whatever he has going on inside of his head. I decide to him tell me when he is ready.

There is one more question I want to ask. He remarked earlier that everyone is expected to do something for the family. Have my parents deceived me? Do they want me to be a mob lawyer? Was that my intended destiny all along?

I don't have the chance to ask; we both hear yelling coming from outside. Manny quickly draws a gun from behind his back and peeks out the front window.

"What in the shit? My dad's here, and so are your parents. Shh."

He places his finger over his mouth to tell me to be quiet when he gently opens the door. We make our way onto the porch without anyone noticing us. Manny tucks his gun into the back of his pants. We stand there listening to them talk about Kryder and whether or not he has been found.

Manny and I exchange a knowing glance. This is the best news we've heard all day. That is, until I hear Cain start to yell when my dad drags a man out of the back of the car. A man Cain punches and manhandles. A man now on the ground begging for his life.

And then I hear a name. Every time I hear that name, think about that name, I see red- the bright color of blood. Heated waves of violence take over my body.

Emerald.

I move, my flip-flops slapping against the gravel roughly. I move until I'm standing next to Cain. Everyone's eyes are on me. Watching, waiting to see what I will do.

I bend down to eye level with this scum of a man.

"You know what? I don't think you'll be around to see what I'm going to do to your daughter," I hiss. "I do believe my father has plans for you."

"Fuck you, you little bitch. None of this would even be happening if it wasn't for you. You all have to find her first, and my little girl has been fucking all of you over left and right for years. Right under your noses. And all the while fucking your man," he sneers at me.

"Watch it, fuckwad. That's my daughter you're talking to. I'd hate to blow your brains out right here."

"That's okay, Dad. I can handle it. You see, I get why you're trying to save your daughter's life. I really do. You love her, just like any parent should love their child. Just like my dad loves me."

I lift my gaze from this piece of shit and give my dad a loving look. His eyes turn soft and he nods in understanding. Yet I see a warning look in there, too. One that's telling me to say what I have to say and be done with it.

"But the thing is... and I would listen very closely if I were you... my father's love outweighs the love you must have for your daughter. My father will always protect me, just like you're trying to do for your daughter now. But the difference between you and my dad is, he never loses. Your daughter, on the other hand, lied, deceived, and obviously helped a man who wanted me dead. That doesn't sit well with me and my family. So while my dad is doing his thing to you, I want you to be thinking about the fact that I'll be doing the exact same thing to your daughter. Your daughter who was fucking my man, along with many others, I'm sure."

Then I stand. I've wasted enough words on this man.

"You'll rot in hell, bitch!"

"Probably. But just like my husband said... you and your daughter will beat me there first."

****

"Please tell me you didn't grow a pair of balls. I love your pussy way too much, baby," Cain rasps in my ear.

"Very funny," I retort.

We all stood there watching as my dad bore his fist into Monty's face, finally shutting him up, before shoving him into his car and taking off with another man in the passenger seat to places I don't even want to think about.

"I don't know what came over me. I'm shaking so bad. I would never kill her, you all know that, right?"

I tear myself free from Cain and hurl myself into my mom's arms.

"Oh, God. What have I done? Dad is going to kill them all."

"Shh. You have done nothing, honey. They did. You only stood up for yourself and for this family." Her arms feel so comforting around me. It doesn't matter how old you are, to be encircled in your mother's arms is one of the best feelings in the world.

"You can't and won't blame yourself. That is a sign of weakness, and this family is not weak," opines a deep, heavy voice behind me.

The authority and power of his speech has me whipping around to see a man who looks familiar. This is my mom's brother? Manny's dad? If I didn't know better, I would think he and Manny were brothers, now that the two of them stand side by side.

Manny is the spitting image of Salvatore, whose large frame towers over my mother and me. His eyes and facial structure are the same as the man standing next to him. It's crazy how two people can look so much alike.

"Hello, Calla. I'm your Uncle Salvatore," he says, opening his arms wide for me to step into them.

I search out Cain, who is standing behind them. He gives me a gentle nod. I'm still shaking when he embraces me, placing his hands on my face and staring deep into my eyes.

"You are simply stunning. A sight for this old man's eyes. You remind me so much of your mother. Wouldn't you agree, Cecily?"

"Yes, she does," she says, stepping between us. "My looks and her father's character make a lethal combination. And I don't mean that in a bad way, Calla. I mean it in that you're a lot stronger than you think. You're the best thing that has ever happened to your father and me."

"Your eyes tell me everything you can't say, Mom. I know you used to be a killer. You wanted to go with Dad, didn't you?"

"Used to be, Calla. Those are the three words you need to hold onto right now. I'm right where I want to be. Do I want to rip Monty, his daughter, and Kryder's hearts out? No, I don't. But before I found out I was pregnant with you, I would have shoved your father aside and killed them all without even blinking. But you, my precious one... feeling you move inside of me, knowing I helped create you... I never doubted my choice in giving that up, not once. Not for you. But as for your dad, well... it's in his blood."

I shake my head. I don't understand.

"If you can, then why can't he?" I whisper so softly, I can barely hear myself.

"It doesn't work like that for him, honey. If he could give it up for you, he would. Your uncle came here for two reasons. One, to take care of the scum who dared to try and hurt us, and two, he wants to discuss things with you. I'm putting a halt to that talk for a few weeks."

She faces my uncle head on, her back to me now.

"She needs time with her husband, Salvatore. They both deserve it. You can discuss things with her later. I don't ask for much, but this time I'm not asking, I'm telling. Give them this."

"Cecily, I'm not here to pressure her. She can have all the time in the world. In fact, I demand it." He glances at Cain. "Take her to my suite in the center for a few days. The view is impeccable."

If I didn't feel like a ping pong ball before, I sure as hell do now. So there's to be no more talk of the future, at least for now? That baffles me with the way this family acts. I so want to run to that bottle of alcohol of Cain's lying on the ground and down the whole damn thing.

"Time with Cain would be great, but really, I would love to just stay here for now," I state, holding my head high with a confidence I'm not so sure I actually have right now. I'm pretending when deep down inside I'm fucking scared out of my goddamned mind.

"Very well. Stay here and enjoy yourselves. I will be in touch. Right now I'm taking my son with me. We have some things to discuss ourselves." He kisses both my cheeks delicately and shakes Cain's hand. "Cecily, you need a lift?"

She nods, indicating that she'll be along in a minute. Salvatore places his hand on the back of Manny's neck and the two of them begin to talk as they stride to his car.

"You call me later, sweetheart," Mom demands.

"Of course," I say with a heavy sigh. All I want to do is eat, climb into bed, take a long nap, and pretend this isn't my life. That none of this is actually happening.

"Talk soon, Cain." Mom leans up and grazes his cheek.

I nearly soar out of my skin when someone's phone rings. Salvatore reaches into the pocket of the jacket he retrieved off the porch then holds the phone up to his ear, leaning up against his car.

"John."

We all listen intently at the sound of my dad's name.

"What the hell does this mean?" he growls into the phone.

Something's not right. Is my dad hurt? What's happening? The thought of him being hurt has my heart racing. I grip my mother's arm for support. Everything was under control when he left.

"Fucking find her. God damn it. She's a stupid bitch. Where the hell could she have gone?"

"Oh, no," my mom whispers.

"Motherfucker!" Cain roars.

Salvatore hangs his head and shoves his phone back into his pocket. When he lifts his head back up, his ice-filled eyes scare me.

"They can't find Emerald. The whore never showed up for work. You all know what this means?"

Everyone acknowledges him but me. I have no damn clue what this means.

"It means we have another goddamned snitch. Cain, it's up to you to find out who the fuck it is and bring that motherfucker to me."

"Don't worry. They'll find her," Mom says to me comfortingly.

Knowing now everything is all right with my dad, I'm not worried at all. In fact, I'm the opposite. For the first time in my life, I see blood. Blood dripping from that bitch's mouth as I pummel her to death.

"Salvatore," I call out.

"Yes?"

"When they find Emerald, have them bring her to me."

At that statement, he studies me closely. Then, without saying a word, my uncle, the leader of this family, the man I had no clue existed until a few hours ago, folds his tall frame into the passenger's side of the car, which pulls off with my cousin at the wheel and my mother in the back. Fifteen minutes ago no one would have been able to convince me to kill anyone. Now I've come to one conclusion. I truly am my parents' daughter.

****

"You're staying, then?"

I feel him behind me. So close, his breath caresses the back of my neck.

"Do I have a choice?"

His lips graze the hollow of my nape.

"Yes. You always have a choice."

"Then I choose to stay. Under one condition," I rasp, angling my neck the way he likes it.

"Anything."

"We're reconnecting, Cain. For now, there will be no touching and no sex. Absolutely nothing."

He spins me around in his arms, his handsome face dropping.

"Nothing?"

"Well, you can kiss me. Hold me. Talk to me. I want to know everything about what it is you do. If I'm staying here, it's time I learn exactly what my husband does."

"I'll do whatever you want me to do, as long as you're by my side. And as long as I keep hearing you say, 'my husband.'"

Chapter Fifteen

Cain

I'd be a bigger asshole than I already am if I didn't say the past five days have been miraculous with all the bonding Calla and I have done.

We've laughed, talked until both of our jaws hurt. She hasn't left my side once. Things around here have been relatively quiet since the news of the disloyalty of both Emerald and Monty spread like a wildfire.

Everyone is looking for her. Everyone. Yet we are all stumped as to her whereabouts. She has no connections, nothing. I've wracked my brain to the point of exhaustion trying to figure out who in the hell would help her. Everyone around here hates her, except for Coon Dog. Fuck, my knuckles are still raw from beating his ass trying to see if he's the one. He stood there and took it.

Dumb ass. I know it's not him. Of course, I never expected that Emerald had it in her to turn on me, either, even though I treated her worse than the slut she is.

People do some crazy ass shit. I knew Emerald was obsessed with me, but for her to go to the extreme of helping that dickless prick Kryder by keeping him in her house this whole time, and worse, involving her father, still surprises me.

Even so, she's the one to blame for her own father's death. I can only imagine the kind of suffering John inflicted on him before he finally put him out of his misery.

This family is all about protecting the ones they love. Friendship means nothing to Salvatore and John. Cecily, either. Their blood does. Especially a young, innocent daughter or niece. Principles run high. Honor, solidarity, and then vengeance. Very few people get a second chance, and Emerald has fucked up in a way she will never be able to fix.

She may not have had a clue that she was disloyal to the wrong people, but she sure as hell will find out once she's located. Makes me sick to even think I kept her around for years. I feel like it's all my damn fault. I should have listened to Beamer. All this time, he kept saying he suspected something was off with her, and I didn't listen.

'Nah, man. She's too hung up on me to do anything as stupid as helping Kryder.'

Those were my words, over and over. Fuck. Is she right under our noses like Kryder was? Is her accomplice one of the old club members from when my dad first started up? Someone who hated the fact that I took over when he died? One of the bitches around here I screwed?

"Who the hell is it?" I holler, swiping everything off of my desk. All of it lands on the floor with a loud crash.

Calla strolls in, taking in the destruction. I love it when she walks into my office. I love hearing her voice every day. She's proved me wrong in every aspect. She's perfect. She listens. She doesn't smart off. Well, not in public, anyway.

Not that she's met too many people. This damn place is quieter than a library, guarded tighter than Guantanamo Bay thanks to my father-in-law, who refuses to let anyone but Priscilla, Bronzer, and Beamer in.

"Who's what?" she now asks. "Jesus, Cain. What's gotten into you?"

"Whoever's helping Emerald, that's who! I've got work to do. I need to get the hell out of here and get it done, but I'm not leaving here until I know who the hell it is. This has gone on long enough. My life with you has been taken away. I can't even take my wife out to dinner or take her for a long ride on the back of my bike. Shit, I'd even enjoy taking you shopping all day just to be able to get the hell out of here. I want you to be able to go to Canada and get your stuff. Redecorate the house. All I want to do is start my life with you, the life that was stolen from us years ago. If they don't find that stupid bitch and whoever the hell is dumb enough to help her, I'm going to lose my shit!"

God, why did I quit smoking again? A smoke sure would hit the spot right about now. The bar phone has been ringing nonstop with members wanting to know why they're not allowed in. I finally had Priscilla set the answering machine to pick up after one ring. They can leave a message. I'm not dealing with them right now. Salvatore's people from New York are crawling all over the place; it's like a damn war zone out there. He wasn't on edge like this when Calla was in Canada, but now that she's here, he trusts no one. And Manny? He's off doing my job. Now I feel like Calla did when she first arrived here and I told her she wasn't going to leave. Except I'm trapped in my own damn territory.

"Whoa there, mister. Who crawled up your ass this morning?"

And there's her smart little mouth. The one she's been hiding for the past several days. The one that would look good wrapped around my dick.

"Nothing's crawled up my ass. You can come over here and crawl on my lap if you want," I challenge slyly.

Calla strides farther into the room.

"I've told you to go. Go do your work. I can go stay with my parents. I know you're going crazy being locked up here. So am I."

Her hair is down today, hanging halfway down her back in loose waves. Big and messy. How I would love to grab a handful of it while I'm buried so far inside of her that all she can think about is begging me to give it to her harder. Or to feel it whipping around me as we take a ride to wherever we want to on my bike, this time not having to hide from anyone or only going so far because she has to get home. I want the whole damn world to know she's mine. I've waited years.

These past few days not being able to touch her have been torture. I get where she's coming from. The night she first came here, we fucked like wild animals. Our desperation for each other was so intense, it was bound to happen.

I've had enough waiting, though. I want her, and I know she wants me. Every part of her body tells me she does, from the way she watches me get dressed in the morning as her eyes roam over my body, to the way she kisses me, pushing her body up against mine. I feel her heat. Her body trembles whenever I kiss that spot on her neck.

And then there's her legs. Her legs are longer than Eight Mile Road. Is there a fork somewhere down Eight Mile Road? If there is, I'm not going left or right. I'm plowing the motherfucker right in the middle. At least, that's where I'm looking to plow right now.

My dick gets hard from just the thought of her, but when I touch her, he turns into a beast. A mad, angry fucker. Whenever we've gone too far, she pulls back mere seconds after she realizes what she's doing.

I'm a mess. Pushing my chair back a few inches I thump my head down on my desk.

"Seriously?" she asks.

Her toes move into my line of sight. They're painted a bright pink. Yesterday her mom finally came over with a doctor. They won't give her any form of birth control until they're sure she isn't pregnant. So now if we do have sex in the next few weeks, I have to use a condom.

After the doctor left, they spent most of the day tucked inside our house, painting each other's nails, talking, and drinking wine. I'm glad she has that close relationship with her parents. The other day I asked Calla if she had grown a pair of balls, but I should probably check myself to see if I've grown a pussy, with all this whining I'm doing inside my own head.

"I know what you need. Sit up, babe," she commands firmly.

"I am sitting up. Take a look," I taunt, looking down at my dick. It's hard. He's just as horny as I am and he's fucking killing me.

"I can see he's standing at attention. If he wants some attention, then please sit back."

He most definitely wants attention. I end my inner wrath. She's once again boosted my thoughts. If she's going to do what I hope she is, I'm all for it.

My fingers reach up and slide down her cheek as my gaze takes her in hungrily. The hunger for me in her eyes stares right back, so full of love, patience, and forgiveness.

"You deserve the fucking world, baby. I want to give it to you. I'm an ass."

Her tongue darts out and licks the entire outer edge of her lips. My fingers leave her jaw, tracing around the same spot she just licked. She is so beautiful. I don't deserve her.

"You can be. But I know what your problem is. I have the same exact one. You know what I mean?"

Her hand glides down my chest, stopping at the waist of my jeans. She flicks the top button open.

When she ducks her head, her teeth grab my zipper and tug it down. Christ almighty, I knew she was a naughty girl. Fucking hell.

She nips the tip of my cock with her teeth, jerking me off of the chair.

"Fuck me," I moan.

"I'm about to, with my mouth," she says seductively, all the while tugging my jeans off of me.

I lift my ass to help her. When my jeans are down around my ankles, Calla leans in again, her dark hair flowing everywhere. I grab it and tug it hard while she continues tormenting me. I could lose my load right now and her mouth hasn't even touched me.

"I'm loving seeing you on your knees, although it should be me on my knees begging you to love me forever, telling you my heart is finally healing. Good Lord, you have no idea how hard you make me. How badly I crave you deep within my bones."

"I feel the same way. All these years, I never wanted to acknowledge to myself that I have always felt you here," she admits, placing her hand over her heart. "But right now, I need to feel you here."

She squeezes my dick. I grit my teeth.

Her small, delicate fingers pull my briefs down and my cock springs free. Her eyes go wide as she does a double take, looking up at me then back at my dick. Son of a bitch. I've been so enthralled in what she is doing to me that I completely forgot about my tattoo. She gasps loudly, her hands flying up to her mouth.

"Oh, my God. You crazy man!"

All kinds of questions flicker through her eyes. Some I'm willing to answer, and some I'm not.

She hesitantly reaches out and runs her index finger down the stem of the white lily.

"Did it hurt?"

"It hurt. Not as much as losing you did," I tell her, speaking the God's honest truth.

Her eyes turn sad.

"When did you do it?" she whispers, her smooth finger continuing to glide up and down my dick.

I've waited six years to show her this. Tell her why I marked myself. And now I can't seem to get the words to escape past my throat.

"Cain. It's the most beautiful thing I've ever seen."

Her head bows, her hair once again falling all around her. I can't see her face, but I can feel, though. And when her tongue takes a swipe across the tip of my dick, all I can do is to lay my head back and relish in the fact that she is here. It's her. Her mouth making love to my cock. Her long, dark hair spread across my stomach, draping down my legs.

I'm finally believing I have my life back.

Chapter Sixteen

Calla

I'm astonished, nearly rendered speechless when I get a good look at Cain's glorious cock. I've never seen anything like that tattoo in my life. A single, perfectly drawn out white Calla lily runs up the front of it. I want to explore it. Lick it. Suck it. Hell, devour it.

I'm no slut; I have had only two lovers since our breakup, but I haven't given a blow job since the last time I gave one to Cain. What inexperienced teenagers we were. I was so surprised when he told me one night while we lay in the dark on the bed that he has never let anyone else give him a blow job, kissed another woman, or even gone down on one. I told him not to say shit to try and make me feel better; I didn't expect him to keep his dick in check while we were apart. He said he always knew we would get back together, or at least, he was bound to try.

So now I sit here on my knees in front of the man who I love with everything I have. I start at the tip, placing small kisses around his opening, swirling my tongue up and down the front and licking the now enlarged head. My hair veils my view of his face, so I can't see if he's enjoying what I'm doing. He sighs, his thigh relaxing under my touch. His hands firmly set into my hair, giving me the confidence to carry out this sexual act. God, I'm confident in almost everything I do, but right now I am fucking nervous.

Please, babe, love this. Let this be the best damn blow job of your life.

I'm on an exploration of this beautiful dick. Good God, it's like one of those hot, sunny days where you want your

Popsicle to last forever. I've never wanted to please him more than I do now. I don't care how wet I am, or how much I want to feel him inside of me; this is all about him. His pleasure. His relief. Him. Just him.

I barely take in the tip. I could never take him in all the way before; there's no way I can now. He's so much bigger. So thick and so hard. I wrap my hand around the base and inhale his scent. Relaxing the muscles in my jaw, I work my way down, taking in more and more, my movements syncing with the up and down gliding of my hand. My tongue swirls around, tasting his erotic flavor.

"Fuck, baby. So damn good. I want to see you," he grits out, grabbing two handfuls of my hair.

He's panting; his eyes are so dark, the darkest I have ever seen them, but there's a spark beneath those hooded lids. I squeeze his balls with my other hand. Rolling them, gently caressing.

"I... Hell!" Cain yells out, his head flopping back against his chair.

I know he's close just by the way he's twitching in my mouth. His moans become mine. My desire to taste him takes over. Small whimpers of craving escape from my throat. I suck harder, lick more. His balls tighten in my hand.

And then I taste him. His come. His sexiness. It tastes like him. I swallow it all, licking my way up to the tip and dipping my tongue into the small hole. My hand releases his balls while the other stays firm around the base of his shaft. His eyes open, gazing down into mine. A smug smile tugs on his lips.

"Fucking hell. Am I in heaven? I must be. That mouth of yours is heaven. I'm so ready to go again."

My brows shoot up.

"Really?"

Cain releases his grip on my hair, smoothing it out, then he stands up and tugs his briefs and jeans on leaving them hanging open. Before I know what's happening, he lifts me up under my arms and throws me over his shoulder. I squeal, this time happy to have a prime view of his tight, sexy ass. I know now I can grab it and squeeze it. Do any damn thing I want to do to it. It's mine!

He's on a mission. In four long strides, we are at the end of the bar and I'm flipped over onto my back with my legs dangling over the edge and my hands pinned over the top of my head. The most excruciating agony develops between my legs. I could scream.

"Spread those legs, baby," his throaty voice growls.

I don't even think about it. I scoot my body up, the cool, glossy surface of the bar grazing my overheated skin. I spread for him, planting my feet onto the wooden surface. He takes a few moments to enjoy the view, running his hands up my legs until he hits my thighs. He presses them gently to open me wider.

"What are you doing?" I ask when he goes around the bar.

He reaches underneath, then lifts up a bottle of tequila along with two shot glasses.

"Grabbing this, and these."

"Tequila?"

"They say it makes your clothes come off."

I scoff.

"You don't need that to make my clothes come off."

"Oh, but I do," he insists, twisting off the cap and filling the two glasses. "You see, my love, we're about to have our own little party. Take your top off, but leave that lacy red bra on."

He lifts one of the glasses to his mouth and drains it, his eyes never leaving my face as I sit up and pull my top over my head, tossing it behind me.

"Shit. You have the nicest tits. They're beckoning me to lick them."

He guides me back by placing his hand on the back of my head until I'm laying down again. My chest heaves, the ache between my legs growing more intense by the second.

"Do you like tequila?" he asks, raising the second shot glass. I watch him, mesmerized, as he places the shot glass right above the swell of my breasts.

"I love tequila," I say breathlessly.

"Me too. Now don't move. No matter what I do, stay still. Understand?"

I nod my head and watch him intensely when he dips down, opens his mouth, and takes a nipple into his mouth through my bra. I gasp when he bites down on it. The shot glass wobbles slightly.

"Don't spill it," he warns, unclasping the front of my bra with his long fingers. Pulling the cups to the side, he exposes my breasts. He stares in awe, licking his lips, then cupping one of them in his hand, palming it and rolling his finger across my peaked flesh.

"You're killing me here, Cain."

"No. You're killing me. You have no idea how badly I want you. How much I love you and want to worship every part of this body."

My chest rises and falls. The glass tips to the side. He swoops down, licking right between my breasts until he reaches the shot glass, then opens his mouth and tips the contents back. He goes and pours two more shots while I lay here in a trance, my insides shaking.

"Here."

I sit up, expecting him to hand it to me. He doesn't. He grabs a handful of my hair, tilts my head back, and devours my mouth with his. The bitter taste of tequila has never tasted so good when he strokes his tongue against mine. It seems like eternity before either one of us comes up for air. My hands roam underneath his t-shirt. God, he's so hard. If I didn't love every part of his body, I swear, I would find some super glue and leave my hands right here. Pure male muscle, all man and all mine to do whatever I want with.

"Keep your mouth open," he commands, breaking away from our kiss.

He brings the shot glass to my lips; I watch his every move as he pours the clear liquid down my throat. I swallow, my nose scrunching up from the burn as it flows down my throat.

He guides me back down, then moves to the end of the bar to unbutton my shorts. I lift up while he yanks them down along with my panties, exposing me bare.

His hands scrub down his face before he looks back at my bare pussy.

"I've never seen anything so flawless in my life."

His words hit me straight in the heart, in ways I have dreamed about for years.

"Now here's the real test, babe. I'm going to eat this pussy like it's breakfast. And you are going to stay perfectly still. Got me?"

Oh, I got you all right, you pussy tease.

I'm engaging in this game he's playing, enjoying myself very much. But goddang, I want him naked.

"I'll stay still and play along... if you take your clothes off first."

He lifts a finger and wags it.

"Patience."

"I don't have patience. I'm a law student. A sex deprived law student who wants her husband. Now, my clothes are off. I'm naked and spread out on top of this bar."

I spread my legs farther in illustration, reaching down and pulling the lips of my pussy apart. He looks down and then back up at me, a smart ass grin on his face. Inside I'm laughing my ass off. Our lives are beginning to form into what I know will be a challenging yet fulfilling life. Both of us are control freaks, but it makes it all the more interesting. And it sure as hell is making me want him all the more.

I dip a finger and inch or so inside of me. He growls. Pulls his vest off. Yanks his t-shirt over his head. Jeans and briefs fall on the floor and then there he stands, all six foot plus of my man with a dick as hard as this wood I'm lying on. I have a perfect view of the lily stretched wide across the top.

My man thinks fast. He grasps firmly onto both of my wrists and climbs on top of me, bringing my arms up and over my head again.

"My courtroom. My rules. Keep those hands above your head, your legs spread wide, and hold still."

I moan in frustration when he presses his cock into my center. He removes his hands from mine, picks up the shot glass, and slides his body off of mine. He delicately places the glass on my stomach, which is now moving up and down, twitching and clenching just as badly as the apex between my thighs.

"You smell down there like you want something. Like you need something."

He strokes his dick in his hand. I lift my head and watch him, trying desperately to endure this anguish building inside of me.

"I want you," I say carefully.

"Oh, you're going to get me, all right. But only if you hold still and don't spill that tequila."

Then his head is gone. It's in my pussy. One swipe, two. I'm not going to last long at all. I'm too goddamned turned on. Then he stops and licks around my outer edges. He tenderly rains kisses with his wet tongue down one leg and back up the other then gives me another swipe between my legs, followed by a nip of my clit.

My stomach and chest are clenching forcefully, but now I really don't give a shit if the tequila spills or not. I want him.

He does this move one more time. I lift my head and see him bend down and retrieve a condom from the pocket of his jeans. He tears it open with determination and rolls it on, fire shooting from his eyes into mine.

I'm starting to shake. The bastard has a smug look on his face. He knows he's getting to me.

"I swear to God, if you don't take that shot glass off of me now, you're going to sit right there and watch me finger fuck myself!" I screech.

"Don't tempt me. I would enjoy it."

Before he can reach the glass, I snatch it up my own damn self and drain it.

"It seems there needs to be some order in this courtroom," he says huskily. "Someone doesn't want to listen to the judge."

"Yeah, well I'm the lawyer who's fucking the judge!"

He raises an eyebrow.

"Not yet, you're not."

"Cocky bastard."

He shifts his body slightly, fiddling with something under the bar. All of a sudden the room explodes as the sound of an electric guitar comes out of the speakers directly above us. The deep voice of the lead singer of Foghat fills the room as he sings the opening lines to 'I Just Wanna Make Love to You.'

The song is instantly recognizable to my ears.

I'm thrown back to years ago when we would listen to music like this, ear buds in our ears as we rode down the highway on the back of his bike. Cain used to sing this song to me, along with so many others.

He pulls my body towards him, his dick perfectly lined up with my entrance.

"The judge calls a recess while he sees the lead defense attorney in his chambers."

Then he drives his dick straight in, slamming it up against my walls. My ass comes off of the bar as I revel in the wonderfully full sensation.

"You feel so good," he murmurs, stroking slowly.

I can hear my pulse strumming in my ears along with the erotic music as I watch him watching himself move inside of me. He continues to slide in and out at his slow pace, taking me higher and higher until I feel my back arching with my impending orgasm.

"Oh!"

I gasp when he suddenly slams in hard, stretching me even farther.

"You look like a dark haired goddess on top of this bar. I love seeing your body flushed, the scent of your pussy and the sweat between your breasts mixing with the oxygen filling my lungs. Hearing you groan and pant as my dick makes you come. I love you so damn much, Calla. Now hang on, because I need to pound this pussy. I want to own it. Consume it. Drive you crazy until you come for me one more time."

That speech may have just stopped me from breathing for a bit, but oh my hell, he feels so good. One hand grips tight onto the edge of the bar while the other hand moves over one of my breasts, rubbing hard and fast across my nipple.

"So beautiful," he moans. "Get there, sweetheart."

His pounding is persistent, moving as fast as the hard strokes of the guitar blaring in our ears. I can't help myself. I bow up, digging into the wood of the bar with my nails, I'm holding on so tightly. Cain shifts back and stills. His dick twitches and I feel the warmth of his release penetrate through the thin layer of the condom. We come together, just the way it should be.

He jumps down and pulls off the condom, looking up at me with a gleam in his eye.

"This trial has been reconvened until tomorrow morning because the judge will be in his chambers all day!"

Chapter Seventeen

Cain

I'm sitting on my deck grilling chicken for dinner and sipping on a beer while I listen in envy as Manny tells me about the M-24 sniper weapons he lifted- from a fucking pawn shop, of all places.

"Shit. You better not get your ass caught. You driving them to New York?" I ask, flipping the chicken.

I stick my phone between my chin and shoulder to free my hands and listen as Manny scoffs at the thought that he would ever be that stupid. I close the grill and take a long pull of my beer, catching sight of Calla in the kitchen doing her thing. I watch her thoughtfully for a moment.

"You know, Calla told me earlier her dad would help get us out of here. We should come with."

The more I think about what she said today, the more I want to get the hell out of here. We'd be safer at Salvatore's house than anywhere else.

"Tomorrow it is, then. I'll call John. You know his ass will want to come. Cecily, too. All right, buddy. Watch your back. Later."

I hang up and call John. We talk for a few minutes about tomorrow. My instincts were right. He wants to come with, which is fine by me. I'm sure Calla will love having time with both of her parents, as well as getting to know Salvatore better. He can talk to her while she's there.

You wouldn't think we would need protection from someone as dumb as Emerald, but the truth is, she isn't dumb at all. She's played me for a damn fool. I don't trust her or whoever it is she is working with not to somehow follow us.

I toss my phone onto the small table by the door and walk into the house, stopping dead in my tracks when I see Calla standing at the stove naked, stirring whatever she's making with one hand while texting someone with the other from the phone I returned to her the other day. I have the notion to both slap her ass and claim it at the same time.

"Are you my dessert?"

She jumps, the wooden spoon and phone falling from her hands onto the floor.

"God, you ass! You scared me!" she shrieks, placing her hand over her heart.

"Sorry, not sorry, babe."

She bends down, her plump ass going up in the air, right along with my rigid cock.

There's my dinner right there. No way am I eating this chicken, not when I have the damn gourmet special staring me in the face.

Slipping back through the slider, I cut off the grill. Let it burn; I don't care. That ass is mine!

"Stop!" she laughs when my arms come around her and my hands palm her naked breasts.

"Put the spoon down."

"No, I'm starving. And I'm talking to Mrs. Henry. She has all my things packed up. Dad's going to get them tonight."

"Give me the spoon. And say thank you to Mrs. Henry."

Fuck. I'm so damn turned on I don't even recognize my own voice. I've never had the desire to fuck someone's ass before. Hell, I've never had the desire to screw anyone but her, ever. The other women were completely erased from my mind the minute I laid eyes on her again.

I press my dick into her backside and she gasps.

"Oh!"

"'Oh' is right. Why are you naked?"

She places the phone and the spoon down on the counter, then reaches for the knob on the stove and turns it off. I squeeze her breasts one more time and swipe my hand up her neck, pushing her hair off to the side to kiss her sweet spot.

"I'm hot," she says finally.

"I agree," I say mischievously, making her gasp again when I pinch her nipple. "So tell me the real reason why you're standing in the kitchen naked?"

"I want you."

Thank Christ the window in the kitchen is high enough that no one can see her. She's just as sinful as I am. This playfulness is the way it should be, doing whatever we want to each other whenever we want. I lightly bite into her neck.

"I want your ass. Do you trust me?"

"I do. I mean, I trust you, but I guess I've never thought about doing that before."

She starts to rub her ass up against my dick.

"I've never done it before, either. But fuck, I want to with you. We don't have to; I can just make love to you. But you're naked and standing in our kitchen. You knew exactly what I would do when I saw you, so I know you want it just as bad as I do. You just tell me how."

My fingers begin to roam all over her silky flesh, around the curve of her ass to the front of her pussy. It's hot and wet. I can feel the heat radiating from it before my hands even cup over her mound.

"My ass," she exhales.

I swallow back my nervousness. Hell yeah, I'm scared. This is new territory for me, too, but it's one I'm eagerly anticipating will bring us both to one hell of a damn climax.

"You sure?" I swallow hard.

"Very sure."

Grabbing both of her ass cheeks in my hand, I roughly squeeze them.

"I'm going to fuck it hard, Calla. There's no way in hell once I get my dick in that tiny little hole in this voluptuous ass of yours that I'm going to be able to hold back."

"Do it. Fuck me until I scream your name. Fuck me until I can't walk tomorrow."

My eyes close, inhaling her. God, she's intoxicating. And she's mine.

"Come on, babe. This can all wait."

I follow her down the hall to our room, watching her ass sway back and forth. She holds her head high. That's my wife walking down the hall in front of me. My self-assured woman. A naughty one. A man's dream wife. My jeans are off the minute we hit the room. She places herself in the middle of the bed, smiling brightly when she sees me stroking my dick, stalking her way.

"My hand would feel so much better, don't you think?" she asks.

She doesn't sound scared at all. She shifts until she's centered in the bed, spreading her legs wide. I can see from here her pussy is already wet. My dick is screaming, pussy or ass. Either one is fine by me, just as long as it's hers.

"It definitely would. Touch yourself. Feel how wet you are and spread it around your tight little hole for me."

She does. Her hand glides down her body and separates her folds. She starts rubbing her clit in quick circles. Jesus Christ.

"Stop!" I yell out.

She doesn't listen; she just keeps pleasing herself. Her pants are getting louder and I'm going to come just watching her get herself off. My dick sits in my hand, long forgotten.

I climb on the bed and grasp her hand. She looks up at me in annoyance.

"Turn over. I think my hand would feel much better, don't you?" I ask gruffly.

When she flips herself over and her ass is hiked up in the air, I slap it hard, causing her to look over her shoulder in surprise. I bend down and kiss the spot I just slapped.

"That's for walking around the house naked."

"I'll walk around naked more often, then, if I'm going to get spanked every time I do it."

I roll my eyes at her smile.

"You're beautiful," I tell her, changing the subject.

Even though I'm about to take her ass, I want her to know I think she's the most amazing, talented woman I have ever met.

"I love you," she declares.

The most beautiful words ever. I don't care if anyone calls me a pussy for thinking so. When you hear them come out of the mouth of the woman you love with everything you have, those words would be any man's favorite.

This act is so intense and delicate that I would never dream of doing this with anyone else. Gazing down at her ass, I think back to many dreams I have about her over the years, making love to her in every way possible and then flipping her over and fucking her so hard that neither of us can move.

I was put on this earth to please her, take care of her in any way I can. This may have originally been my idea, but seeing her juices practically dripping out of her weeping pussy I know it's something she wants, too.

Not wanting to delay the pleasure, I slowly run my finger up her slick center, my dick dying to slip inside of her with no condom. Just a few more days, I tell myself. My hand goes to her hip, holding her in place the moment I touch her puckered hole. She moans loudly and deeply as I begin to coat her with her wetness, loosening her up. She's so soaked.

Back and forth I go between her ass and her pussy, hungry to be inside of her in this way and watch her fall apart. My fingers are so wet now that I easily slide in the tip of one. She's so tight.

I bend down and kiss her between her shoulder blades.

"You all right?"

"More than all right. I'm dying here. I want you in me."

The vibrations of my silent laughter rumble deep in my chest. Never would I have thought my sweet Calla would turn into a woman of such power and confidence. When it came to sex back then, she was never the aggressor. Once we got into it, she would ride my dick like it was her last day on earth, but she never spoke her mind. Not that I cared. I've always loved her for who she is. This new wild side of her I fucking crave.

My eyes are so heavily lidded that I can hardly see straight. I want in there. I want to hear her scream.

I remove my finger. I have no idea if she's lubricated enough, so I reach over and grab a condom from the nightstand. Her head lays flat on the pillow. One glimpse of the gleam in her eyes and the smirk on her face is all I need. I rip the packet open and smooth the latex over my cock. I take a deep breath, aligning it with that beautiful little hole.

She winces when the tip pushes in slightly. I hold back just a little until I feel her body relax.

"Let me know if it's too much, baby. We can stop at any time. I'm more than happy to slip inside your tight pussy. The choice is yours."

Her ass squirms and my dick gets harder.

"Take me, Cain. I'm not scared at all. I want this with you. I want everything with you."

I inhale deeply again, only this time it's not for fear of hurting her; it's those words. Fuck, those words mean as much to me as when I hear her say 'I love you.'

I drive myself in inch by inch. Once I'm fully sheathed, she nearly shoots off the bed. I've never felt anything so tight on my dick in my life. I could come right now.

"You all right?" I tenderly ask.

"Yes, but if you don't move that big dick of yours, I'm going to spank your ass," she grumbles.

And there she is. My hardcore control freak. The woman who has changed in so many ways. I have no damn clue how I can even move in and out of her when she's this tight, gripping me like a pair of damn pliers. I'm not going to last more than two minutes.

"You're so tight, babe. Play with yourself. You feel so good I'm not going to last long at all."

Her hand glides down. Her breathing matches my own; hard, heavy, and loud. My movements start to pick up.

"Cain!" she cries out.

Her hands move fervently on her pussy. I hear how wet she is. How close she is. A few more pumps and she screams my name as she comes.

The way she yells out my name is so outrageously engaging to my soul that I come hard. Gripping her hips, I still myself. I never want to come down from this high. Never want to leave this bed. And I never want to go another day without her.

****

We ended up having to eat BLTs instead of the dried up, burnt chicken we neglected. We laughed hard when we looked at it after I brought it into the house.

"You're walking funny," I observe, an hour after we've gotten cleaned up.

I'm serious. She is. I know she's sore but too stubborn to admit it.

She also has another one of my shirts on. We're in our room packing so we can leave early in the morning. I want us to be in New York by nightfall.

I swat her ass.

"Go run a bath and soak for a while. You don't need all this stuff. Your dad has all your clothes. Go."

"Join me," she coaxes.

"I need to make one quick phone call and then I will," I promise, tossing the last bit of stuff into my bag.

I watch her retreat into the bathroom and wait to hear the water start. I snatch up my phone and walk down the hallway completely out of her earshot.

"Cain. Is everything all right?" asks Cecily, sounding out of breath on the other end.

"Everything's great. I need a favor."

I hear the smile in her voice.

"Of course."

"Well..." I scratch the back of my neck. "I never bought Calla a wedding ring. I have no clue what the hell to do. I thought maybe you might be able to help me, maybe get someone to come to Salvatore's house so we could look at some."

I hesitate, her silence making me nervous.

"Hello. You still there?"

She clears her throat before speaking.

"Well, I would love to help, but I'd like to show you something first, if you don't mind."

"Sure," I say, more out of confusion than anything else.

She must catch it in my tone. She knocks me back when she speaks again.

"I have my mother's wedding rings. They're stunning. I think Calla would love them."

I'm in shock. Family means everything to all of us. She would love to have those rings. Hell, I would love to put them on her finger.

"That's perfect. Those would mean the world to her."

"I think so, too," she agrees. "I'll get them out of the safe. We can get them sized and cleaned up."

A deep hole has just been filled in my heart. There are a few more demons I've been holding back from her, ones that are intimate, and that up until now, I have kept to myself. It's time to finally let go of my past. But first, I have to go make sure my girl is okay.

"I can't believe how fast this fills up," Calla says when I help her into the tub and sink down behind her. My lips go straight to her neck, my arms circling her waist.

"Nothing but the best for you."

I nuzzle into her neck. She has her hair piled on top of her head, her neck exposed. I love that spot on her neck just as much as she does.

She slumps down further into the water. My lips leave her neck, giving me the perfect opportunity to answer the question about my tattoo I've been avoiding.

"The other day you asked me about my tattoo. Do you remember?"

"Yes, and you evaded it very smoothly," she remarks.

I hold back my laugh. I should have known she wasn't fooled.

"You may think I'm crazy for getting it, but my reasons are my own. You and I have been with others..."

I hate the fact we both have. There isn't a damn thing I can do about it, so I continue on.

"...but no one has ever seen that tattoo but the person who put it on me, myself, and now you."

She goes to speak, but I press down on her stomach and she halts.

"Listen. Not only has my heart belonged to you since the first day I saw you, my entire being has, including my dick. What you and I had back then meant more to me than anything. I never had any type of real, honest love until I met you. I grew up with a father who I know loved me in his own way, but who lied and deceived me my entire life. I know my mom loved me before she died, but I was so young, I barely remember her. We were young. We fell in love. That love never once died for me. The whole time you were gone was spent cleaning up the mess my father made of this place. I turned it into something I wanted. Something as honest as possible, given that everything I did behind the scenes was illegal as hell.

But you... I needed to have a part of you with me. And well, that's where I decided to put it. It was either there or over my heart. It felt too sacred for me to put it over my heart. I put it the one place I always wanted you to be. And I don't mean that in a dirty way. It's just that, every time we made love back then, it meant the world to me."

I wait while she absorbs what I just told her, wondering if she thinks I'm fucking crazy. Finally she sits up, straddling my lap. Tears stream silently down her face, a look of love and admiration in her eyes. I let out the breath I was holding. Her tiny hands cradle my face.

"That's the most beautiful thing I have ever heard," she whispers.

"You think so, huh?"

"I know so," she affirms, leaning down to brush her lips over mine.

I kiss her longingly.

"One more thing and then I'm done. No more secrets."

"These lips have never touched another woman's. Only yours."

Her shocked expression leaves me tense.

"You mean to tell me you've never kissed anyone? How? I mean-"

I place a finger over her mouth.

"No one. I can't take back the things I've done. Everything I did, I did to protect you. Kissing is an intimate act, and those other women meant nothing to me. I meant nothing to them. But you? I would do anything for you. There isn't another person on this earth who I want to kiss, or let my lips touch theirs, or let my tongue touch any part of their body. No one."

"Oh, God, baby. I... I don't know what to say."

Tears keep rolling down her face. I hate making her cry.

"Don't say anything. Except promise me you will never leave me again. No matter what happens. No matter how tough it gets, or what life throws at us. Just don't fucking leave me, all right?"

"Never. I get it now. All of it. I'm coming to terms with it all. I've accepted it all. My family. You. Everything!"

She grins, then smiles. It spreads wide across her face.

"Now kiss me. It seems those lips have been deprived for way too long."

I have no problem with that at all.

Chapter Eighteen

Calla

"Really, Dad? A toy hauler?"

I laugh at my dad when he, my mom, and Manny climb out of his truck.

"These fuckwads want to bring their bikes. And between you and your mother and all of your clothes, you would think we were moving there, for Christ's sake," he grumbles jokingly as he climbs up the steps and swoops me up into his arms.

"You look so happy. I do believe we have our baby girl back, Cecily. Who would have thought that this dickhead over here was the one who would bring my girl happiness?"

"Fuck you too, old man," Cain retorts from behind us.

"You're not my type, asshole."

Dad sets me down, lifts one of the suitcases, and retreats to the back of the hauler.

"This is going to be a long ride. Good thing I brought my computer with all those Nicholas Sparks movies we love to watch," Mom says, winking at me. We are both suckers for those movies.

The drive seems to take forever, but when I see the New York City skyline all lit up the closer we get, I exclaim in excitement.

"Holy shit!"

Dad catches my attention in the rearview mirror.

"It's something else, isn't it?"

"It's remarkable. I've never seen anything like it."

Salvatore lives on Long Island, right on the water. I crane my neck when we cross over the bridge only to head east away from the city.

I haven't been deprived by any means; my parents and I traveled everywhere when I was growing up. Now that I know what my dad truly does, I almost bust out laughing, remembering all those times we went to Disney World.

He never once complained about having to go on any of those rides with me. Always my protector. Always holding my hand, showing me his love until I grew into a teenager. Even then he would always kiss me goodnight whenever he was home, or if I was already in bed before he got home, he always looked in on me.

Now as I watch him steer us through the traffic with ease, I can honestly say that I love my dad even more. Not at all because of the things he does, but simply because he's my father, the man who is still protecting me to this day.

His phone rings. He's short with whoever is on the other line. I'm assuming it's a job by the way his eyes flicker back and forth between the road and me, where I sit between Cain and Manny, who are both busy on their computers.

Everyone has a job to do in this family at the moment but me. Do I feel left out? No, not at all. I want to finish school and make a life with Cain. Build on it, and eventually have a family. My gut feeling tells me I will finish school. However, I'm more than curious what Salvatore wants to talk to me about.

Both Cain and I think he wants me on his team of legal defense. One of his consigliere, as they call them. A confidant, advisor. It baffles my mind. I've researched the mafia online until I was about ready to throw my computer across the room. I know I'm family, but everywhere I've looked, they typically don't have outsiders as one of the closet people to the leader. I mean, hell... they're pretty much the only ones who can argue with the boss and get away with it. So why me? Being family is one thing; being a minnow in a shark infested ocean full of lawyers is another. And if that's not what he wants, then what the hell could it be?

"Lost in thought, cuz?"

Manny snaps his laptop shut and sits it on the floor in front of him, shifting my way.

"Just wondering what your dad wants to talk to me about," I say, hoping he might know.

"You'll find out soon enough."

I nudge him in the side with my elbow. I'm more than ready to get out of this damn truck, anyway. I want a shower, some decent food, and a bed. That's a simple enough request, if you ask me. And let's not forget my clothes and shoes. God, I cannot wait to slip into some heels.

"I know you know what your dad wants with me, Manny. I'm a lot smarter than you may think," I whisper in his ear.

"I know you know, smart ass, but it's not my place to tell you. It's his. My father is one of the most laid-back men in this business. But he expects loyalty, honesty, and most of all, respect. I love my father, and no matter how much you sit there with your little lip sticking out like you're eight years old, I'm not telling you."

He gets another nudge, this one harder.

"Goddamn, that hurt."

"What hurt?" Mom, Dad, and Cain all ask at the same time.

"He deserved it."

"Like hell I did!" He points into the darkness. "You see that ocean over there?"

I look at him like he's nuts. It's so dark outside, I can't see a thing.

"Yeah, didn't think so. That ocean is scary as hell at night, and if you don't keep your scrawny ass elbows out of my ribs, I'm going to toss you in it."

Mom and Dad start laughing, and then Cain and Manny join in.

We are all still cracking up when we stop at a street light. Then everything happens so fast. Bright lights shine into the truck. Dad draws his gun and screams for everyone to get down, but we are hit by a massive semi before anyone can move.

I hear my mother screaming for my dad as Cain grips me tightly. The semi isn't stopping; we're bring pushed. I can feel the truck being lifted off of it axles.

My dad is yanking on the door handle, trying to get it open.

"Motherfuck! Fuck! Fuck! Get me out of here, goddamn it."

I'm panicking. We all are. I'm in the middle with no seat belt on. It's my own damn fault. I didn't put it on after gawking out of every window in awe of the city lights. I'm being pulled, tugged, and yanked in every direction.

"I don't have any goddamn fucking control of this thing!" my dad screams.

I see the gun come up and he shoots a hole in the window then beats it with his fist until it gives.

"Oh, my God, he's shooting. He's hanging out of the car. Dad, noooooo!" I scream, reaching for him, only to be jerked back by Cain.

After that precise moment, my mind is a fog. It feels like someone hit the slow motion button on a horror flick, only this isn't a movie. This is really happening. One moment Manny and I are teasing each other like family members would, and the next we are getting hit by a truck. The thundering noise echoes throughout the darkness, the grating sound of metal against metal, twisting steel, and screeching tires.

The lights from the dashboard illuminate the horrific scene as my mom's head jerks forward, the seatbelt digging into her flesh as the truck begins to flip. I scream in terror as I watch my dad being ejected from the vehicle. Suddenly we come to a stop. Cain and Manny try to get out of their seatbelts as Cain hangs onto to me for dear life. It's chaos. There's no other way to describe it.

There are no noises now. No yelling, no screaming. Everything has gone from the lightest shades of gray to the darkest black. I don't know if I'm dead or alive. If I feel numbness or pain. If I'm moving my hands and feet or not. Nothing. If I'm alive, then why can't I hear my family? Where are they? Am I alone? Thrown from the truck like my dad?

Is this the fear one gets right before death? You try to inhale a breath, not even knowing if you truly are. I feel detached from my body. If this is it, then take me. Take me so I don't have to think about my family. Take me so I can breathe. Just take me!

"She's coming around."

My muscles constrict. My heart starts pounding. All of my limbs are weak and tingling. Yet, that voice, it doesn't sound like the sweet voice of an angel. It's rough, deep, and more like the voice of the devil. I'm going to hell. That's where I am, just like Monty said. The voice is gone now. I'm floating. Floating through nothing but blackness.

"Wake her up," a brooding voice says close to my ear.

"I've tried. Her eyelids flutter every now and then, but then the bitch is right back out again. She's been banged up bad. Bruises and cuts everywhere. You really should let me see if she has any internal damage."

Is he a doctor? Please let him be talking about me. I'm not dying. Not being sent to hell.

"She gets nothing. If you don't get her to come to within the hour, it's your ass right along with hers, Doc."

I feel an arm on both of my shoulders shaking me adamantly.

"Listen, girl. You need to wake up. At least for a few minutes."

"Pl…please. My family."

My eyes flutter open, trying to adjust them to the bright light. I can vaguely see an older, gray-haired man leaning over me. He's too close. His eyes show years of wisdom mixed with something else. Compassion? I just don't know. The devil as we know him is the king of tricksters. But something tells me this isn't the devil and I'm not dying.

At least not yet, anyway, I think to myself, remembering the other person's threat.

"It's about damned time you came around. That will be all for now, Doc. Thanks."

The voice I heard earlier is coming from my left. I turn my neck towards it.

"It's you and me now, Princess."

I'm unable to open my eyes all the way, but I am able to get a glimpse. If I were able to gasp or cry out, I would.

He is the scariest man I have ever seen. He's not much older than I am. His head is shaved bald and he wears a black patch over one eye. A thick scar, old and healed, runs from the center of his forehead all the way down his cheek. It's ugly and twisted, as if someone had sliced him with a jagged knife.

The scruff on his face matches his voice. Coarse, rebellious, and dirty. But in spite of the scar and patch, this man is downright sexy. This is a smoothly polished professional who I have no doubt is a trained killer.

His eyes tell a story. A long, fucking scary ass story. I've been trained how to read people, and my observation tells me he's seen and done some horrific things in his life. What I want to know is, what does he want with me?

I shake my head trying not to think about what he is going to do. He presses my shoulders down with so much force I can feel my bones start to rattle.

"Get off me!" I scream to the best of my ability through my scratchy and sore throat.

He withdraws his hands.

"You have it in you, I see. Good to know."

I'm seething. My body is bruised from head to toe. I remember the accident. The way I was tossed and flipped around in the truck. Everything. Now that I know I'm not dead, I want my husband and my family.

He took me from them. But how? How did he get away with me without anyone coming to save me? There is no way my dad, Cain, or Manny would just let someone take me. My mother, either. They would all fight. Unless... Oh, God. No!

"Where's my family?" I demand.

He doesn't answer me. He swings his head slowly to the right, his demeanor becoming uncompromising.

It takes every bit of energy I have to lift my head, using my elbows to hold me up. I cry out as pain shoots down my neck and arms. In the corner of the room is a man who has his back to me. He's leaning over a man whose head is slumped down, resting on his chest. Those clothes he has on. I recognize them.

A bloodcurdling scream escapes me when I see the man pick up a long, shiny knife and bring it up to the light. He examines it closely, twirling it around in his fingers. My cries and pleas are ignored as my abductor laughs.

"You sons of bitches! Let us go! Do you have any idea who he is?"

I'm hauled up by the hair and dragged off of the table. My body crashes to the floor. I'm too weak to try and fight. Too bruised, too battered, too shocked.

"Let her take a look at him. Let her see what's about to happen if she doesn't help me get everything I want," he says, looking down at me. His eyes bore into mine.

"This is the kind of torture you father inflicts on people when they won't give up the information he wants. Only I'm not your father. I won't end his life, not until I've drained every ounce of blood out of him. Not until I get what is rightfully mine. I want you to watch, and if you disappoint me and look away, I'll instruct Raymond here to do the exact same thing to you, except he likes to play with women before he tortures them."

No words come out of my throat, as it is choked with my sobs. Tears drip steadily down my cheeks, landing beside me on the cold, tile floor.

Raymond doesn't say a word. He licks the tip of the knife. His eyes are crazed, darting back and forth over his target, who slowly lifts his head. Oh, God. Please don't look at me. I don't think I can bear to see him. When his almost unrecognizable face comes into view, I scream.

"Manny!"

No! What have they done to him?

Chapter Nineteen

Cain

I stare out the window, studying the view of the Long Island Sound from Salvatore's house. It's been two days since Calla and Manny were taken from the accident and not a word of their whereabouts.

By the time the paramedics got to the scene, they were gone. Both of them. There were no witnesses to the accident to give anyone a description of who took them. Yet Salvatore knows. He knows there would be only one person who would do something like this. One person who was biding his time and waiting to strike. He has my wife. He has my best friend. And he's a cold-blooded killer. A hitman seeking revenge against his family, who shunned him for his actions and betrayal.

I've been left in the dark while Salvatore works with his men to try and find them. No one has heard from him in years, so why now? Why all of a sudden would he come back and take two innocent people? Why wouldn't he take John or Cecily? It doesn't add up. I know there has got to be more.

Guilt surges through my veins. I'm the only one who came out of this nightmare unscathed, except for the knot on the side of my head where I must have gotten on impact when the truck flipped and crashed into a building. Cecily has a broken arm, bruises on her face, and burns across her neck and shoulder from the seatbelt. John is banged up all to hell. He's got stitches in his forehead and some broken ribs. It's a damn miracle any of us are even alive.

Cecily is going crazy, crying constantly over not knowing where her daughter and her nephew are. John has been bandaged and is gone, looking for a man who is known to do worse things to his victims than even himself. I need to be out there helping instead of here with my hopeless thoughts. I just got her back. I need her. We need them both. Just like me

"Fuck!"

I can't stay here anymore. They're out there somewhere, I know they are.

"Cain."

I turn around to the sound of Salvatore's voice. He strides in with the same clothes on from yesterday, looking like shit. There isn't any other way to describe it. He hasn't slept from his worry, just like the rest of us. His wife, Lola, is going out of her mind. She's normally so calm and collected just like Cecily, and now she's just a shell of a woman. She is guilt-stricken, blaming herself for all of this.

"Any news?" I ask Salvatore, veering away from the window.

"Not a damn thing," he sighs in frustration.

"They're out there, I know they are. I can feel it in here." I pound my fist against my chest.

"We'll find them. Look," he says. "I know you feel helpless here, but if I let you go out there to help with the search and something happens to you, I will never forgive myself. I need you here. I need you to take care of Lola and Cecily while I'm gone."

His sudden change of course has me puzzled.

"I thought you said you were staying here in case he calls?"

"I can't stay here anymore. It's me he really wants. It's me who he thinks destroyed him and kicked him out of this family. I need to make myself visible. He wants me and he knows he can't get to me here. I'm going to make it easy on him."

"He'll kill you," I caution him.

"He won't kill anybody until he gets what he wants."

"Salvatore, you need to tell me everything. You need to tell me why in the hell your oldest son would turn on his family."

"I'll tell you why."

Lola stands in the doorway. Her once strikingly beautiful dark hair is unkempt and there are dark rings around her eyes. Her mouth set in a tight line. For a fifty-one year old lady she's always looked so much younger than her years, but today she looks well past her age. This has got to be hard on her, knowing that one of her children has taken the other and is doing God knows what to him.

"Lola," Salvatore warns.

"Don't 'Lola' me. Damnit, Sal. Cain has a right to know. That's his wife out there somewhere with Royal, and he deserves to know why. So either you tell him, or I will. You have no other choice."

The two of them study each other powerfully. For the first time since I've known Salvatore, I see fear mixed with pain in his expression. The way he looks at Lola, telling her with his stare how sorry he is, makes me wonder even more what the hell is happening around here and how it affects Calla.

"Very well. Shower, Cain. Meet me downstairs in the kitchen in half an hour. We will tell you everything."

With that he puts his arm around Lola, pulls her in tight to him with a kiss on the top of her head, and leaves me standing here with envy. He's able to hold his wife, while mine is out there somewhere with a man who must have done something beyond my wildest imagination for

Salvatore to cast him out of the family. To make Royal want to take his brother and cause him harm, his own flesh and blood. I can only hope that Calla is as strong as we all believe her to be.

I jog quickly down the stairs, through the foyer, and down the long hallway to the back of the house to the kitchen after showering and changing into a pair of jeans, a black Sinners t-shirt, and my boots. Several people I do not recognize at all are standing or sitting in the kitchen, all of them with guns in holsters dangling at their waist or hints of the outline of a gun tucked in the back of their pants. A map is spread out on the table.

"Any luck?"

Several of them turn towards me, either shaking their heads 'no' or giving me a slight chin lift. Salvatore excuses himself from the table and makes his way toward me. With a squeeze on the back of my neck, he leads me out of the kitchen, down the hall, and into his office where he shuts the door behind him.

"Take a seat," he tells me, indicating the chair directly across from his desk.

I sit. He shifts around the desk, sitting in his own chair.

"I'm going to get right to it. No bullshit. No lies. Although I will tell you this; what I'm about to tell you is not an easy thing to hear, nor is it easy to tell. I love both of my sons. But Royal, he's not right. That boy has some demons inside of him."

He pauses, looking out the window for a moment, his eyes glazing over. Finally, he speaks in a low, trembling voice.

"My oldest son is a killer. And I don't mean a killer like John. I mean, he gets a thrill out of killing people. He gets off on it."

"Jesus Christ! You mean to tell me he kills people for the hell of it?"

An unsettling numbness wells up inside of me. Panic instantly hits. Salvatore's not telling me everything. He places his elbows on the desk, steepling his fingers and resting them on his chin.

"We haven't heard from him in ten years, not since the day we kicked him out and told him he was no longer a part of this family."

He closes his eyes. I can tell this is so hard for him to say. To discuss this with me.

"Royal works for Ivan Solokov. My son is now known by the name of... Scarface."

I stand up abruptly, leaning forward.

"You have got to be fucking kidding me? Jesus Christ! He's known to cut people up into tiny pieces with knives. He leaves them unrecognizable, and he has my wife!"

"Listen here, goddamnit. I feel your pain. I feel it here, in the pit of my soul. That man is not my son. He may have my blood running through his veins, but he is not my child. He's the prodigy of the devil himself. And he has my son, too. He's seeking revenge on Lola and me. The only way he can hurt me is to take away Manny. To leave us with nothing. He knows how strongly I feel about family. That may sound like a contradiction, but that monster... Fuck, he turned on this family, all for greed. All for power. He knew when the time came, I would turn the reins of the family over to Manny and not him. As far as Calla, I don't know what he wants with her."

I begin pacing the room, his words crippling me.

"Do you think he will kill them?"

I stop at the window, my hands shoved deep into my pockets. My mind is wandering all over the place. I should be out there looking for them, not stuck in here. I'm no use here. Not to them. The walls in this huge house are suffocating me.

"Do you want the truth?"

Salvatore is behind me now, his hand on my shoulder.

"I already know the answer. You don't have to say a thing."

"Ivan's big into drugs. He always has been."

Goddamnit, this is going to be worse than I've imagined.

"The first time Lola and I suspected he was on drugs, let's just say that shit didn't go over very well. He was only fifteen years old. I forced that boy to do a drug test and sure as shit, traces of heroin were found."

All of a sudden I feel sick. No wonder Manny jumped on board when I wanted that shit away from the club.

"He was regularly in and out of rehab up until he turned eighteen. We did everything we could to try and help him. Lola was a mess. And Manny, he always used to look up to Royal, until one night he came home so high, he beat the shit out of Manny. Broke him arm, busted up his jaw. A few days before that I had told him I'd had enough. If he wasn't going to straighten himself out and prove to this family and to himself that he was man enough to beat his addiction, then we were done. He would not lead this family, Manny would. That night was the last night I ever saw my son."

I face him now. His pain pours out of him. To lose a child to drugs and to know the kind of person they have turned into has got to destroy a man.

"Don't pity me, Cain. I can see it in your eyes. I love Royal; he's my son. But I will never condone the things he does. I'm no better than he is in certain ways. I'm not a law abiding citizen. Fuck, I've killed, too. But one thing I will never do is turn against my blood." His eyes turn icy and resolute. "We will find them. That I can promise you."

Standing before me is a man who has more power than anyone I know, but if I had to guess by the look on Salvatore's face, he's trying to convince himself more than he's trying to convince me.

"Come sit. There's a few more things I want to go over with you, which I think will convince you I believe what I'm saying."

Jesus, it's like he just read my mind. We each take our seats once more. Salvatore turns on his computer. As we wait for it to boot up, he proceeds to tell me something I should have known the minute he mentioned the word drugs.

"You don't have another narc in your club. It's always been Emerald."

"How can that be?" I question.

"Every bit of information she found out, she told that dirt bag Kryder, who then went back and told Royal."

"What the fuck? How do we know this to be true? I mean, how the hell did you find all this out?"

"I have my ways. It may take time, time we don't have right now."

I walk around to the other side of his desk and I stare him down.

"Don't hide shit from me, Salvatore. You're like a father to me. How did you find out?"

"I've been on the phone with many people, asking if anyone has spotted Royal. He's been hanging out the past few nights at The Rose Garden. It's a nightclub in Times Square. I have video surveillance from the club."

He leans forward in his chair and opens some files on his laptop, then turns it around and slides it over to me.

There they are, cozying up to each other at the bar. Another shot shows them kissing. Her back is to me in this one. It's her though, I know it's her. I continue to click. There are several shots of them on the dance floor, then back at the bar. The video comes to an end as they exit.

"Where is she now?"

I'm going to burn her alive. Listen to her scream.

"I'm going to assume she's with him."

My heart stops beating. Whatever type of revenge Royal wants on his family, she knows absolutely nothing about anything. They'll kill her. I can't even think straight. My wife is a strong woman. But to withstand being drugged, or even worse, beaten and tortured? She won't be able to handle it.

"John's due back anytime," continues Salvatore. "I have resources everywhere, including quite a few cops who tend to turn their cheeks the other way when it comes to my business affairs. He's here in New York, I know he is. He won't do anything quietly; he wants my attention. He wants me to feel fear. He had my fear the moment I found out he took those two. We just need to find them before he sends me his message."

"What message might that be?"

I swallow down the answer I already know in the back of my throat.

"He'll torture one of them while the other one watches. He'll video the whole thing. I know how his sick mind works."

Chapter Twenty

Calla

"You monster!" I scream.

"Who are you?"

His ferocious, intimidating laugh would normally scare me. I see Manny looking at me through one eye. The other is badly bruised and swollen shut. He's been brutalized. Blood is everywhere. How he can even be alive at this point is beyond me, but that one eye, the one that is barely open, is pleading with me to keep my mouth shut. There is no way in hell am I going to lay here and watch him be tortured. Or worse, killed. My head starts spinning, my stomach rolling from the sight in front of me.

I'm thrown back down by this animal. I kick and scream at him to let me go with all of my might, hurting myself even more as I struggle to get free.

"Come over here and help me tie her down!" her roars.

"Fuck you, you bastard!"

Somehow I'm able to get one arm free. I bring it up and claw at his face with my nails. Blood instantly pours out, dripping everywhere.

"Leave her alone, Royal. Or would you prefer me to call you Scarface.

It's Manny, his voice small and barely recognizable.

"Fuck off, little brother."

My eyes go wide. I stop trying to get away. All I can hear is 'little brother.' I look closely at the beast towering over me. The resemblance is there; that single eye is identical to Manny's. I'm going to be sick. These two are brothers. I don't understand.

"So, now you know who I am," he sneers, glancing down at me.

I recognize it in his tone, too. They sound so much alike. I'm in such a daze that I don't even see or hear the other man come around to the opposite side of the bed until I feel a prick in my arm.

"No, Royal! Fuck you! It's me you want, not her. Fucking leave her alone, God damn you!"

"Manny."

Is that me talking? Whatever it is they just shot me up with has my head foggy. A euphoric feeling travels through my veins. My skin is burning up, itching everywhere, but I can't scratch it. I can't move. At least my body doesn't hurt anymore. Are they tying my hands down? My legs? I can still hear someone thrashing about, screaming and hollering. I don't know how long this lasts. Maybe seconds, minutes, hours? I'm alert. At least I think I am.

"Wake up, princess."

A series of sharp slaps is delivered to my face. I become more aware of the stinging the more I come back to consciousness.

"You had quite a little nap. Now, up you go."

I start to gag the minute he lifts me up.

"She's gonna lose it! Toss me that bucket," he says.

I start to heave. Some of it lands on the floor before the bucket is shoved under my face. I throw up until there is nothing left, and then I dry heave until I feel rawness in my throat. I swipe my mouth with the back of my hand. The acidy bitterness I taste makes me want to puke again. He shoves a glass of what looks like water in my face.

"Drink."

My throat burns. It hurts worse than anything.

"I don't want it."

"It's water. Believe me, I know you want it. Your throat is so tight, you can hardly breathe. So unless you want more of what Raymond gave you, you will drink this."

I take a small sip and he forcefully pulls it away. It does nothing to help the burning sensation in my throat.

"Better?" asks the man I know as Scarface.

No, I'm not better, but I'm not about to tell him I want more water. Fuck him.

Then it all comes back. I heard someone say 'brother.' I can't remember who, but I know someone did.

"Manny is your brother?" I ask.

My throat is so dry, it hurts to even talk. His intense orbs glare into mine.

"By blood, yes."

"I don't understand. If he's your brother, then why are you doing this? Why hurt him?"

He chuckles that evil laugh again, his eyes turning cold as ice.

"I'm an outcast to them. The evil one. The fuck up. And he's about to get what is rightfully mine. I can't let that happen. He will die first, princess."

Why he's calling me princess has me perplexed. My mom is a princess, not me. I know very little about this life; only what I've been told. And no one has told me about him. I can see why. He's an enemy who has obviously been waiting to strike.

"You look a little mixed up there, Calla."

The sudden use of my given name shocks me; however, I will not show my fear. I'm the daughter of John Greer. No way will I let my fear be known to this man. I trust my family. Whatever reasons they had for banishing him from the family, I stand by them.

"You're sick! That's your brother! He's my family. You won't get away with this. Whatever vendetta you have, you may as well give it up now. My dad will find you, you son of a bitch, and when he does, you're going to wish he hadn't."

"You mentioned family. I'm your blood, princess. You know, it really is too bad you and I are on opposite sides. A beautiful woman with a sharp mind can be very dangerous. I could see myself actually liking you."

"Screw you. You're not my family. If you mean nothing to them, then you mean even less to me."

Malice is what I feel for this man, although he's not really a man at all. I'm now within an inch of his face. His undamaged eye scans me meticulously, observing my strength. All of it comes from being the daughter of John and Priscilla Greer. I may not have known the true lives they have lead, but one thing they taught me was to never show your fear.

"You're a snake. A cowardly one, at that. I promise you cousin, you're going to die from your own venom."

"Snakes strike when you least expect, Calla. I want you gone just as much as I want my brother gone. And as far as John goes, I want him to come. It's just too bad that by the time he does find us, my dear little brother will be dead and so will you. I have plans for you. You'll be gone before they get here and if we're not, I'll take care of him. It's about time he retires, anyway."

"Fuck off. He'll destroy you," I spit at him.

"I'm going to let that slide, just this once. John's good. Very good. But don't think for one second that I'm not better. Now, you have a show to watch. Unless you want me to shoot you up with more of this?"

He pulls a syringe out of his back pocket.

"I'm not watching shit. And you can take that and shove it straight up your ass."

He quirks his brows and shoves the syringe into his pocket again.

"Is my heroin not good enough for you? Do you want something better? Cocaine, perhaps? Crack? You name it, I've got it."

I'm momentarily shocked speechless.

"No cocaine, either? That's too bad. Did you know cocaine can heighten your sexual arousal? It delays your orgasm but it increases your sex drive. Raymond over there would like nothing more than to show you just how much it improves his sexual performance. Would you like me to let him show you?"

He grips my chin and jerks my head towards this man named Raymond.

"Go to hell, both of you!"

"You know, I've had it with your mouth. Raymond, bring me some tape and put that chair over there right next to my brother. She's going to watch."

I struggle against him when he lifts me up and carries me over to the chair. Manny's head is now slumped down, the blood on his face now dried up. I squeeze my eyes shut as tightly as I can. I fight to get away. My hands are pulled severely behind my back. This time, I feel my shoulder pop. Pain shoots down my arm and I cry out. Neither of these unhinged men pay any attention as they tie my hands behind my back and tape my mouth shut.

"Secure her good, Raymond," Royal firmly commands.

The minute he leaves the room, Raymond takes advantage of my situation.

"Very pretty," he chuckles, running his dirty hands up my leg. Once he has his nasty hands on the inside of my thighs, he pushes them open. Tears form in the back of my eyes. My voice is muffled, incoherent behind the tape. He continues his exploration, sliding his hands up my sides, brushing the underside of my breasts. He stills, leaving one hand around my neck, the other one reaching for the tape on the floor. I continue to watch him, horror stricken, as he tapes my body to the chair.

Do not show fear!

He drops the tape back on the floor and spreads my legs again. That's when I notice this dumb fuck hasn't taped my legs. I could easily kick him with the heel of my shoe. I've never loved my six-inch Louboutins more than I do right now. These things are weapons, and somehow I'm going to use them. How they've managed to stay on through everything, I will never know. One thing I do know is, if I ever have a son, his name will be Christian.

Raymond slides his body backward a few inches. Lifting my leg, I kick him square in his balls, digging the point of my shoe in as far as I can until he crumples to the floor screaming.

"I will get my chance to fuck you, bitch!" Raymond screeches with hunger raging out of him.

I lose it, and aim my foot straight for this bastard's dick again when the door opens. I'll be damned. My eyes go wide as saucers as I see Royal's arm is draped around Emerald, of all people. This slut really gets around.

"Raymond, what the fuck are you doing, man? Get your ass up."

"This cunt kicked me in the balls before I had a chance to tie her feet!" he complains, stumbling when he tries to stand. He leans forward, still cupping his balls.

Anger is such a cruel bitch. She arises inside of me even more at the sight of that fucked up bitch stalking her way towards me.

"Remember what I said, baby. Do not touch her. You say what you have to say and then leave and wait for me."

Royal's eyes are glazed over with fury and something else. Oh, God. They're both high. I can see it all over her face when she stands directly in front of me. One would think a professional killer would want to be lucid enough to complete his job. No wonder this family is so dead set against drugs. He's a user.

"Come on, Royal. You know I want to slice this bitch's throat."

"She's hurting enough as it is. Get over it. Say what you need to say. When the time comes to kill her, I told you. She's all yours."

Holy shit. These people are fucking crazy!

"Did you hear him, you fucking bitch? I'm going to have so much fun with you. And here's the kicker; your husband is going to watch. He is going to watch me rip every piece of hair out of your head. He's going to watch me do so many things to you. I'm going to end you. You have no idea how much I wish I could do it right now. That I could pick up Raymond's knife over there and slice you open from here to here," she signals from my chin to my crotch.

I do my best to hide my fear from her, too. I'm not giving up on the fact that my dad is out there. They will stop at nothing to find Manny and me.

"Enough! Come here!" Royal commands, and she goes to him. He puts his hands all over her. On her ass. In her hair. I'm gagging behind this tape, sickened by the sight in front of me. This woman has no limits. She's a traitor and a whore. For the first time in my life I want to kill someone, and my target is standing less than a few feet away from me. I'm going to beg my dad to let me be the one to pull the fucking trigger to place this bitch right next to her father in hell.

Finally they pull away from each other and he watches her walk away. Once the door is shut, he turns his disgusting gaze back to me. Sick asshole. I know he reads my expression. He smirks and paces lethally towards Manny. My heart plummets.

"Make sure she watches," he orders, pointing at me.

Raymond comes up behind me, forcefully gripping the sides of my head and jerking it to the disturbing picture in front of me. He compels my eyes to stay open.

"Wake up, little brother. It's time to party."

He slaps Manny on the face several times. Manny mumbles something I can't understand, his head wobbling from side to side. I watch in grief stricken horror when he grabs Manny's hair and yanks it back.

"We have unfinished business. I need you awake. Come on, brother."

Manny says nothing. His eyes are almost dead. I fear for his life now, this man who is my husband's best friend. My cousin. He has kept me safe for years and now I have no way of helping him.

I don't know where Manny gets the strength, but all of a sudden he rears his head forward even with the tight grip on his hair and slams his forehead into Royal's nose. Blood pours out and Royal stumbles back, stunned.

"Fuck you, Royal. You can do whatever the hell you want to me, but you will never control Dad's empire. You will die right along with me."

Royal straightens up, wiping the blood from his nose.

"So, you're not such a little pussy after all. Let's see how much you got left in you after I do this?"

He punches Manny swiftly in the gut, causing him to jerk forward as if he is trying to catch his breath. I scream behind the tape as Royal picks up that long knife, studying it for a bit. He looks his brother dead in the eye.

"I think I need to send a message to Mom and Dad, don't you?"

Oh, no. Please, no. I can't bear to watch this. Manny's hands are tied to the arms of the chair. With one swift and heavy swing of the knife, Royal chops one of Manny's fingers off.

A chilling cry echoes through the room. I'm nearly suffocating from my tears. Manny is rocking the chair back and forth violently as he tries to get a grip on the pain. I swear, I can feel it. I observe the blood trickling onto the floor, trying to count every drop. There's just way too many. It won't stop bleeding.

"Bandage him up. Leave her there and then come outside."

Royal is holding his brother's severed finger in his hand. He's abhorrent, immoral. How could he do such a thing to his own brother? I scrutinize the knife when he drops it on the floor. How I wish I could pick it up and carve his darkened heart out of his chest.

"Do not touch her. You hear me?"

I almost wish Raymond would get close enough to touch me. I would do my damnedest to kill him, and then go after Royal and Emerald.

I will not show my fear.
I will not show my fear.
I will not show my fear.

Stone-cold eyes give me one last 'I told you so' look.

"You should have stayed in Canada, princess."

I watch him with baited breath, struggling to hold back my tears. All I can see in my mind is Cain's handsome face. The way he holds me and touches me. He and my parents have tried to protect me from this for all these years. This is exactly what they had been afraid of. The despicable, unhuman people in this world. People who have no conscience and no morals. People who turn on their family. I will never give up on them.

Royal grabs a laptop and slams the lid closed, then strides out and slams the door behind himself, leaving me alone with Raymond and a crying, screaming Manny.

"I bet you're one hell of a fuck. I'm itching to touch you, but instead, I will give you more of this."

A syringe appears in my vision. I shake my head back and forth. Then I feel it. The slow, burning feeling in my veins. Like a warm hug from a loved one. The tape is ripped off of my face. My eyelids become heavy.

"Don't sleep too long, princess."

I don't know how or when I fall asleep after that, but I do. It's a restless sleep filled with nightmares of the torture I've witnessed. All I do know for sure is that Manny and I are alone now. It's dark in this cold, dreary room. I think Manny is calling my name. Or is it another dream?

"Calla." I hear it again. "Son of a bitch. Calla!"

I know I'm making sounds. I can hear them. They may be muffled, and more like grunts, but I'm trying. My head is heavy. My body feels warm and tingly, like an ocean wave is flowing over my skin. It leaves and comes right back again. I shouldn't feel this good. Am I high? No, I can't be.

I'm right here, Manny. Over here, I keep saying.

Why can't he hear me? Where is he and why does he sound so strange? He sounds like he's hurting. He's in pain.

"Calla."

I jolt up. I'm shivering with cold. My stomach rolls once again and all I can do is dry heave, gagging and coughing until I feel like I'm crushing my ribs.

"Manny."

"Oh, thank Christ. You're alive."

The agony in his voice mixed with the pain in my shoulder has me bawling. I cannot control it anymore.

"Shh. Calla, listen to me. Please stop crying. I need... I need you to be strong. You have to listen to me."

"I'm so sorry," I sniffle.

"Calla. You cannot show weakness. You have to be strong if you want to get out of here alive." His tone has now turned to misery. "No matter what they say or what they do to you. You do not say a thing. Do you hear me?"

"Yes. Are you okay?" I manage to get out.

"I'll be fine. It's you I'm worried about."

"I'm fine. They keep drugging me with heroin, though. I hate it."

"That's his drug of choice, always has been, even when we were younger. I'm surprised he hasn't overdosed on that shit yet."

I hear him let out a heavy sigh. Oh, how I wish I could see him and make sure he really is all right.

"Listen, they'll be back here soon. I know they will. He knows Dad won't give up until he finds him. Royal has crossed the line this time. He's broken a contract."

All of a sudden Manny stops talking. All I can hear are his sharp, shallow breaths. I'm worried for him. The excruciating pain he must be in triples the pain I am beginning to feel now that the heroin is wearing off.

"Manny, talk to me. I... I'm so sorry. I can't do anything to help."

I wait for what feels like an eternity for him to answer, and when he does, his voice is strained. He's fighting to try and get out every word he can.

"Royal works for the Russians," he winces. My heart is breaking for him. "My dad and the Russians have an agreement. You stay out of my way and I stay out of yours. The Russians deal with drugs, prostitution. You name it and they do it."

Another deep breath escapes him.

"I'm going to tell you the truth. All of it. Unless they find us, he'll be back to kill me, Calla. You need to prepare yourself. Fuck!" he screams.

"How do you know that?"

"Because this is one of my dad's warehouses. He wants us to be found. He's fucking nuts. Just stay calm and keep your mouth shut. I don't think he wants you dead. He's going to use you for leverage or some sort of negotiation. No matter what happens to me, you have to promise me you will not fight him."

"I don't know if I can promise you that."

Manny doesn't say anything after that as once again, bright lights shine down on us.

"You're both awake. This is great. Now it's Manny's turn to watch. You wanted her baby, come and get her. Just remember she cannot die. I need her alive."

I turn my head just in time to be punched in the face by none other than Emerald herself.

Chapter Twenty-One

Cain

I've never known true fear until today. Salvatore's words gobble up my every thought, working my imagination overtime. I've heard of Royal's work. He's messy. He never cleans up. How he has gotten away with this for as many years as he has is beyond me. Ivan obviously has cops in his pocket just like this family does.

But this is a completely different story. He has my wife and my best friend. I need to get the fuck out of here. Lola is a mess, Cecily is a mess, and John was due back here hours ago and no one has heard a damn thing from him.

The front door flies open. A disheveled looking John walks in holding a box, violently kicking the door shut behind him.

"Jesus, man. Are you all right?"

He's white. His hair is a mess. I know he's in pain. He refused any pain medication from the doctor. Told everyone his mind needs to be clear.

"Where's Salvatore?" he says sharply as he walks past me towards Salvatore's office. "And Cecily and Lola?"

"I'm not sure where they are. In their rooms, maybe? I've been in the family room going out of my mind."

"Let's just hope they stay where they are. They don't need to see or hear this."

His voice sounds rougher than normal. Something is wrong, I can feel it. Whatever happened is troubling him in a bad way. A way that he wants to keep from the ladies. I don't like this feeling at all.

Breaking his fast paced stride, he crouches down, placing the box on the floor and his hands on his knees. I'm by his side in an instant.

"John. What the fuck is wrong?"

A dark shadow crosses over his face.

"Fuck me!" he roars, crumpling to the floor.

Salvatore pushes through his office door.

"What the hell?"

"Hell if I know. He came barreling in here with that in his hand. Asked about Lola and Cecily and then collapsed on the floor."

Salvatore reaches for the box.

"Don't open that!"

John gets off of the floor, his entire body shaking, and snatches it up. He's got to be in pain, not only from the accident, but for Calla and Manny. I've never in all my years of knowing him seen him so agitated.

"In your office," John demands.

The three of us walk in. Salvatore shuts the door and locks it.

"I need a drink."

John moves to the cabinet, grabs a bottle of Johnny, twists the cap off, and guzzles it like water. Without putting the cap back on, he sets it back on the top of the cabinet, turning to the both of us and exhaling loudly.

"Goddamn it! You better tell me what the hell is going on and now!" Salvatore shouts.

"Shit. This was delivered at the gate about five minutes before I got here. I told them I would bring it up. It's... fuck!"

He runs a hand through his already messed up hair.

"It's what?" Salvatore moves to him, takes the box out of his hands, and lifts the lid.

"Jesus Christ!"

"What is it?"

I move to the two of them. My stomach rolls when I see the bloodied finger laying in the box alongside of a flash drive. Salvatore stands there, unable to move. The finger has got to be Manny's. Good God, he was right. They are torturing him.

"How? How could my own son do this? How could I have failed as a father?"

Once again I'm helpless as I watch a man who is like a father to me beat himself down with despair, mourning the loss of one son while grieving for the other. When his hands start to shake, I take the box from him, my stomach churning.

Closing the lid on the box, I quietly back up to leave the room. John has his hand on Salvatore's shoulder, his eyes on me nodding towards the door for me to go. I make my way up the stairs and down the hall to my empty room; the room I was going to share with my wife. The room where I was going to give her the ring that is now sitting on top of the white dresser. Cecily cleaned it up and gave it to me this afternoon. She went on and on about how stunning it was going to look on her daughter's finger, and how it was going to mean so much to Calla to have it. And now I can hardly bear to even look at it.

Moving across the room to the closet, I open the door and place the box with Manny's finger on top, covering it with the extra blanket on the top shelf. I don't even bother shutting the door. I have to see what's on this flash drive. I have to see her. I have to see him.

I turn on my computer, tapping the drive on my leg waiting for it to boot up. Once it does, I plug the stick into the USB port and wait.

The sight before me has me standing up, gripping the sides of the desk hard. My teeth clench together. There she is, taped to a chair while a man holds her head in place. I'm going to kill him for touching her. Slice his goddamned throat and watch him bleed out.

Calla's eyes are wide with fear. She's busted up. Her eyes are swollen. Her face and arms have bruises and gashes running up and down them. But she's alive. If it weren't for the irony of the situation, I might laugh right now. After everything she has been through, she still has on those sexy as all hell spike-heeled shoes she demanded John get for her before we left.

I don't take my eyes off of her until I hear a scream I will never forget in my life coming from just a few feet away from her. I stare at the back of a man's head while he's crouched down on the floor. I know this is Royal. He stands up, giving me my first view of Manny.

"Aw, fuck!"

He's screaming, rocking the chair. And then I notice it. There in the corner. Crates. Large crates. I know this place. I know exactly where it is. It's a storage unit for the guns Manny and I steal. I've been to this place more times than I can count.

With shaky fingers I stop the video. I pull the flash drive out, shoving it into my back pocket before opening the dresser drawer and pulling out my Glock and clips. I shove the gun into the back of my jeans, racing down the hallway and down the stairs. My boots thump loudly as I go. I swing the office door wide open, not even bothering to knock.

"I know where they are," I say breathlessly.

Four pairs of eyes are centered directly on me.

"Shit."

Lola and Cecily both stand. I can only look at my mother in law. I cannot bear to look at Lola. She has to know what's about to happen. Either one or both of her sons will be dead by the end of the night. I can't even begin to imagine the pain and heartache she must be feeling right now. The same as Salvatore. He knows better than anyone how things like this go down. He is the first to speak.

"Where are they, son?"

"He has them at the warehouse in Queens."

"Are you sure?" This comes from John.

"Yes, I'm sure, for Christ's sake! Let's roll."

I don't give them time to follow me. I'm down the hall and out the door as fast as my legs will go. I try to block out the women's screams, yelling to all of us to please be careful and bring their babies home. I shake my foggy head, clear my thoughts, and focus on what lies ahead.

By the time Salvatore and John get to the car, I have it raring and ready to go. John hops in the front and Salvatore in the back. Tires squeal as I race out of the drive.

"Open the gate," I hear Salvatore say heatedly. Then he's on his phone, every word clipped to whomever he is talking to. I pay no attention.

"My God, boy, are you trying to get us killed?"

John's hands are gripping the dash. I'm weaving in and out of traffic, speeding like a bitch and running every red light, driving heedlessly.

"He's right, Cain. You can't cause an accident; it will delay us getting there. Besides, I already have guys surrounding the place."

I'm so in the zone. So ready to see, touch, and hold Calla. The only thing on my mind is getting to her.

I slow down and don't say a word, my eyes trained on the road ahead. The closer we get, the thirstier I get for blood.

"Pull in here," Salvatore commands.

We're about a quarter of a mile from the warehouse. I swing the car into a vacant lot.

John points to the side of the building where a narrow paved path leads to the back of the building.

"Around back."

My fist grip the steering wheel tight. I'm ready.

"What is this place?"

"One of my buildings. It's empty. I have several men meeting us here."

I'm stunned. John must see it in my expression when we come to a stop alongside several other cars. At least a half dozen men are standing around with rifles on their backs, cigarettes hanging out of their mouths. I put the car in park, cutting the engine. I grab the keys and go to open the door.

"Cain."

John grabs my arm.

"You need to get your head on straight right the fuck now."

We have a stare down. I know he's right. I've never done anything like this before. I take a few calm breaths before speaking.

"Tell me what you want me to do. Just don't tell me I have to wait out here. I need to see her just as badly as you do."

"Fuck! You listen to me. I want Royal. Calla may be your wife, but she's my little girl. And no matter how much blood has been lost between Salvatore and his son, he won't kill him. But I will. I go in alone."

I slump against the headrest. My heart explodes in my chest, bouncing around like a fucking ball.

"I know you want to see her. Hell, I know better than anyone the means you've gone to, to protect her. But Cain, this is not a job for you. I'm not saying you can't pull the trigger in that sweet ass Glock of yours," he adds wryly.

I chuckle. The motherfucker doesn't miss a damn thing.

"What I'm saying is, I'm trained for this. I already have so much blood on my hands. I won't allow you or Calla to have to live with the shit that runs through my head every day. I love the both of you too much. I have no clue where my daughter's head will be at when I get her out of there. She's going to need you to be strong for her. Be that man."

Shit, he's scaring the hell out of me. I know he means well, but fuck me if he's not in a roundabout kind of way telling me he's not sure if he will come out alive.

"What I need you to do is tell me exactly where in that warehouse they are."

The faint smell of cigarette smoke fills my nostrils. John is the one man who I know will get her out alive, even if it costs him his own life. I recite two times exactly what I saw on that flash drive. His demeanor shifts from burning rage to the coldest of ice.

"I hope Salvatore and Lola will be able to forgive me for this. I'm not letting Royal off easily, not by a long shot. I'm going to make that piece of shit suffer. By the time I'm done with him, he'll regret the day he caused this war against his father. No one touches my daughter."

With that, John is gone. I sit in the car, my face looking up into the dark, clouded sky. I don't know if John was trying to convince me or himself that he would come out of there alive. It's the first time John has left me with any kind of doubt. Shit is about to be real, and son of a bitch if I'm not worried.

Salvatore turns from his position outside of the car, his eyes filled with regret and sadness. He knows what's about

to happen. How could he not? John works for him. He's also
very aware of the type of cold, hard killer his son is.

I run my hands through my hair. I need something,
anything, to help me keep my mind from its negative
thoughts. A cigarette. Smoke inhaling through my nose. Into
my lungs. That's what I need.

Exiting the car, I bum a few from one of the guys, then
sit back in the car and fire it up. I suck in the deep aroma,
letting it fill my lungs before I exhale. It does nothing. I put
it out just as quickly as I lit the damn thing and lean my head
back. I watch two ambulances pull in. The EMTs get out and
shake hands with Salvatore. I watch him work his magic
with all the men around him.

I don't envy him at this precise moment. He's a good
man, a decent man. One who doesn't deserve to be fighting
the unknown of what's happening inside his warehouse. He
didn't even see what was in that video, and yet, I know he
knows. He's aware of everything. Controls everything. I stay
focused on him. He may be acting in control right now, his
words rough and his smile tight. But he's not. His shoulders
are slouched. He keeps checking his phone and his watch.
The building up the road.

I survey him until I feel like I have him all figured out.
Until I see him look once more toward the building. The
building that holds my heart.

"I want to ask you something, Calla."

I remember that moment so well in my mind. The way
her eyes got huge. The strange look she gave me.

"What? That you want to marry me?" she'd teased, her
head lying in my lap. We were at the park that day. Moms
were pushing their children on the swings. We were
surrounded by laughter, though somehow it seemed it was
only the two of us.

"How the hell did you know I was going to ask you?"

I puffed out my chest like the badass teenager I thought I was. She pushed herself up off of my lap and started jumping up and down, screaming.

"Yes! A thousand times, yes!"

We talked it all out. Planned it all out. Thought we would have the world at our feet and that no one would be able to keep us apart again. Little did we know the very same day she became my wife, she would be ripped away from me by the one person I trusted. And now when I finally have her back, have a chance to prove to her that I love her so damn much I ache, I can't do anything but sit in this car and stare at that front door. Willing it to open.

Chapter Twenty-Two

Calla

My head is thrown back by her punch, though it barely scrapes the surface of the pain my body is in. She hovers above me, her tiny frame seeming so much smaller than I remember. Drugs will do that to you. Make you lose your appetite. The only craving you have is the desire for your next hit, your next score, or whatever the hell you call it. She's a fucking druggie.

I tilt my head to the side, doing my best to try and muffle the sounds of my cries from the sudden jolt to my shoulder. The numbness from holding it still for so long causing a surge of the worst pain I have ever had to progress its way down my arm.

"You're not so tough now, are you? Cain's not here to protect you this time."

She puts her face up close to mine.

"Do you know how long I have waited for today? A long time. I've loved Cain ever since I can remember, and then, Boom! Out of nowhere comes you. You stole him from me, and now you're going to pay."

The bitch lunges at me, clamping a vice-like grip onto my shoulder, her fingers pressing deeply into my wounded flesh.

"Aaggh!" I scream out in agony. "Fuck you!"

I spit in her face.

"You weak cunt. That's the best you got? You're fucking pathetic," I hiss.

"Calla. Shut the hell up."

Manny speaks with a thick tongue, his words scarcely intelligible.

Royal steps in front of his brother, backhanding him across the face.

"You shut the hell up, brother. This isn't your call. Emerald, hurry the hell up. You have five minutes to play. And guess what, sweetheart? I've all of a sudden changed my mind."

Changed his mind about what? He glances down at his watch, lightly tapping his fingers on the face.

"Since the two of you are clearly testing my patience, I've decided to kill you both. Do what you want with her, she's no use to me. He can watch this time," he says, flicking his hand.

I watch in horror as he walks over to Manny whose eyes are pleading with mine to hold on for as long as I can.

"Then I'm going to fuck her up good," says Emerald with ill-suppressed glee.

She grabs a handful of my hair. I can do nothing but cry out. The view of the room changes as I land with a loud thud on the floor. Emerald yanks and tugs, walking backwards, pulling me by my hair. My neck and shoulders scrape across the coarse cement. I squeeze the backs of my legs up against the chair as they smack up and down.

Manny is screaming for Emerald to let me go. The farther away I get from him, the more panic arises. I feel the blood drain from my face. My mind tells me this is the end. You're about to die.

She lets go of my hair. My neck muscles volley to stay upright. I'm left there for a few seconds, barely able to catch my breath.

"Let's see how you like this? Three, two, one, go!" her voice squeals.

My body goes stiff as a board. I've lost all motor skills, though I'm entirely cognizant of my surroundings. I've never been electrocuted but that's what it feels like. My entire body starts to convulse. My side is on fire from whatever she is pressing into my skin. She's tormenting me in raw, horrendous fashion. All I want to do is die. I grind down hard on my teeth, afraid I will swallow my tongue. And then it's over. The convulsions stop, but the burning in my side is still there. I breathe in and out as best as I can. I hear a loud clunk next to my ear and I slant my head to the side to see what it is. She used a Taser gun on me.

One of her feet steps on my head, then both of her feet come together, squeezing so much pressure on my skull that I feel it down to my toes. I begin to choke. I feel vessels popping in my brain. All the while she laughs. She knows she has me. I'm restrained. Even if someone took the tape off of me now, I'm too weak to fight.

"Royal told me how much you love this. I love it, too. Did you know too much of it can kill you? Cause you to have a heart attack?"

I try to talk, but nothing comes out but a gurgle. The needle in her hand gets closer and closer to my neck. I feel her weight when she sits on my chest. I feel the sting of the needle, not in my neck, but in my arm. Once again, I feel the burning sensation rushing through my veins. The feeling I have... it's worse this time. I can't explain. I have only a second before she is up and off of me. My eyes roll into the back of my head.

My vision is blurry. I watch her stand up, her small frame towering over me now. Seconds tick by. Her foot, decorated in a pair of boots, appears over the top of my face. A cruel smirk crosses her face. I close my eyes, bracing for the impact of her slamming that boot into my face.

My lungs burn with each small breath I try to take. This is it. I'm going to die. My entire life flashes before my eyes. All those happy memories of my childhood. My parents' excitement when I would open my favorite present on Christmas morning. Curling up on my dad's lap for him to read me a story. Making cookies with my mom. The look on Cain's face when he first told me he loved me. The moment he kissed me after we got married. The happiest memories of my life. I wait.

Nothing happens. Opening my eyes, I peer up at her, my mind clouded. Her doll-like features are frozen in shock, her eyes vacant and cloudy as she slumps down onto her knees. Blood and matter drip down onto my chest from the gunshot wound right between her eyes.

Emerald slumps forward, her dead body lying halfway across mine. I know I'm screaming, unable to move with her body pinning me down. I hear feet shuffling.

"Greer! You cock sucker!"

The hoarseness in Royal's voice is strained. He's been shot.

"Dad?" I barely manage to squeak out, beginning to gurgle. The potent taste of blood sits in my mouth.

"Manny? Dad?"

Silence. A strange sensation floats through me. All I see is white, the colors slowly shifting darker until all I see is black.

****

I wake up suddenly in unknown surroundings, blinking profusely to adjust to the bright lights shining above me. I try to talk. I try to move. I can't do either. My memory is so confused, I begin to panic.

"Calla."

The sweet sound of my mother's voice hugs me. I can feel her hand on top of mine.

"Sweetheart. Don't try and move."

Unable to move my head, my eyes search out her voice. Tears flow down her face. Her appearance is unlike her. She's pale, and there's a silent void in her eyes.

I need to know what happened. Where am I? Where's Dad? Manny? Cain?

"Water," I manage to croak out.

She brings a Styrofoam cup with a straw to my lips. I take a small sip. The coolness of the water does very little for my parched mouth.

"I know you have a lot of questions. However, I have been instructed by the doctor to keep you calm if you were to wake up before he gets back."

Calm? Why? What happened? What is she not telling me? My lids become increasingly heavy again. I try to fight falling out of consciousness. It's no use, my body is too weak. I drift back into the unknown where everything once again is the awful color of black.

"Mom?" I jolt awake this time. The room is dark.

"Calla, baby." I hear him. Cain. He sounds so tired.

"Jesus, baby. You're awake."

"My shoulder," I say.

"It's fine. You're going to be fine." He bends and kisses me on my cheek.

"Manny?"

"He's fine, too. Both of you have been through hell and survived."

"My dad?" I can't see him. It's too dark.

"Cain?" I begin to panic.

"I'm right here, my girl."

I lift my hand, trying to find anything for it to come in contact with for support. I feel the warmth of someone's hand. My dad's hand. I squeeze it. My body begins to tremble. I attempt to stifle my sobs at first, to show my strength. It's no use. The salty tears fall down my face to my quivering lips.

"Hey, no crying. I'm here. You're safe."

A warm hand presses against my back. I would know that hand anywhere. Every time it touches me, I feel myself come to life. My adrenaline soars and my heart rate picks up, all from the simple touch of his hand. He moves it in slow, comforting circles, a small token to try and help me drown out my sorrows and misery.

"I don't want to go back to sleep. I want to know what happened. I need to see Manny. Please," I croak.

"I'm right here."

Manny's voice has me more alert than before. I'm happy to hear them all. Irritated doesn't begin to scratch the surface that I cannot see them.

"I need to see you," I say.

I'm welcomed with silence once again.

"Seriously?" I question, my irritation turning to anger. "I'm not a child. I want to see him."

The click of a light switch comes from the corner of the room. A soft yellow glow cascades from the lamp. My dad is the first person I see, just like so many mornings when he would get me out of bed and help get me ready for school.

"Where's mom?"

He has a slightly impressed grin on his face.

"She's upstairs taking a shower."

"Upstairs? Where am I?"

"We're at Salvatore's."

I go to speak but my dad silences me with his finger.

"An ambulance brought both you and Manny here. No hospital, sweetheart. Too many questions would have been asked if you were taken there. You've been treated with the best doctors around, Calla. We have round the clock nursing staff here. Do you understand what I'm trying to tell you?"

The hospital part catches me somewhat off guard. I contemplate what he said for a moment, although I understand more than any of them think I do. My dad, or someone, cleaned up after it all. Knowing my father, he hasn't left my side not once. Neither has my mother. Neither has Cain.

"I understand everything, Dad. I do have to say though, you look like shit," I blurt out. He smirks.

"You think? I probably smell worse than I look. I haven't showered in four damn days."

"Four days? That's how long I've been out?"

He lifts his eyes from mine to Cain's.

"Dad?"

He exhales.

"You've been in and out for two weeks, Calla," Cain says from behind me.

My body is stiff. How I manage to flip over to face him is beyond me. This is my first glimpse of him in two weeks. He has days of scruff on his face, his eyes bloodshot from what I guess is lack of sleep.

"Two weeks?"

That's impossible. In and out without even realizing that two weeks have passed? Something is not right.

"What is it you three are hiding from me? Is something wrong?"

I may feel weak and somewhat lost, but for God's sake, if I can handle what happened to me, then I sure as hell can handle whatever they are hiding from me.

"Dad. Please?"

His eyes dart from mine to Cain's. Whatever it is, it's bad. The last time I saw this pained expression on my dad's face was the night he told me he was Salvatore's hitman. I'm starting to become agitated.

"I'm not a child. I have a right to know!" I insist.

"All right, calm down. It's not you. You're going to be fine. The doctors had to keep you in a drug-induced coma. You were so banged up. So drugged up. Hell, with the amount of heroin they injected into you in such a short period of time, we're damn lucky you're alive."

I rest my head back on my pillow, grabbing both Cain's and my father's hands. Manny stands at the end of my bed.

"I'm so sorry, baby. I had no choice but to allow them to keep you under," Cain whispers.

"It's okay. I'm just a little taken back. I knew they drugged me. I knew it was heroin, but my God, enough to truly kill me?"

I lift my head. The pain in my shoulder is merely an ache.

"And what about you, Manny? Are you really okay?"

He looks great, actually. Traces of yellowish color spread across one cheek and under one eye. Other than that, he looks like Manny.

"I'm fine. My pinky finger is gone."

He lifts up his left hand to show me his bandaged up stump.

"Oh, Manny. I'm so sorry," I say sincerely.

"Stop. There will be none of this 'I'm sorry' bullshit. We survived. Very few people do. If anyone should be sorry, it's me. I couldn't do a damn thing to save you from the shit my brother was doing to you and then that cunt. I hope she is living the true meaning of hell right now. Burning for eternity is too good for that dumb bitch."

I can't help myself. I start to laugh. I laugh so hard my stomach starts to hurt.

"So true!" I finally say. "And your brother is right there with her."

The room goes eerily quiet. I look at all three of them in confusion. Again, an unsettling feeling overwhelms me.

"Royal's not dead."

Manny stops laughing before those dreaded words come out of his mouth. I feel myself gripping their hands even tighter. Tight enough to feel a stinging sensation.

"Shit. It's my fault," says my dad. My lips begin to tremble.

"I don't understand."

"Calla. Listen to me. I shot him in the shoulder. It's the first time I have ever missed a mark. This is on me. I lost focus."

I really take in my dad's appearance. This is bothering him more than he is letting on. I'm back to the eyes. Always the eyes. He's beating himself up over this. I won't allow it.

"Dad, no," I say sternly. "You did what only my dad would do. You saved your daughter's life. There's no fault in that. You all know as well as I do I would not be here right now if it wasn't for you. Don't ever say or think anything like that again."

Dad and I have a very severe stare down. An ill feeling settles over me. There's more to this story. These three can't hide things for shit. The stiffness in my dad's posture gives that away for damn sure. I continue holding his gaze, my eyes telling him I will never blame him for this. His holds a promise. A promise that he will indeed find Royal and destroy him for what he has done.

My father is the first to look away. Me, I stand firm. I could never blame him for anything. One thing is for damn sure. After everything that has gone down, I have made up my mind that I will do whatever it is Salvatore wants me to. Family always comes first. Royal may not have loyalty to this family, but I do.

"When did you become the wise one? Huh?" asks my dad, stroking my cheek.

"The day I was born. The day I became the daughter of Johnathon Weston Greer."

Chapter Twenty-Three

Cain

Two people can be connected in such a manner that the health of one loved one can relate to the health of the other. It's a true fact.

The moment I saw Calla being carried out of the warehouse, I died right there of a broken heart. Her beautiful face was beaten beyond recognition. She was unresponsive, her limbs dangling like wet noodles. If it wasn't for the EMTs who reassured John and me repeatedly that she had a pulse I would have sworn she was dead.

That night, seeing her in the state she was in, not knowing whether her heart was going to give out on her from the amount of heroin that was pumping through her body, I knew I couldn't live without her. For six years I did everything in my power to protect her from this life, and in a matter of minutes, those years rolled into one nightmarish night after another as I sat by her side, waiting, talking to her about anything.

I'm not ashamed to cry. I'm human. I've cried a lot these past two weeks. Grieved, even. There will always be danger in the life I have chosen to lead. Calla was cast into it with her eyes closed. She now comes out with them wide open. My God, I'm so in love with her. She wakes up and one of the first things she wants to know is if everyone else involved is okay.

These past two weeks watching her go in and out of consciousness dragged on longer than the past six years did. She would wake up screaming and thrashing until the nurse would come in and give her medication to slip her back under. I never want to go through anything like this again.

This family has been through enough. Royal must pay. War has been declared now, against one man. No one has seen or heard from that son of a bitch since he somehow escaped right under our noses. John shot him, this much we all know. How he managed to slit the throats of two of Salvatore's men and get past us is still a mystery. He's now a wanted man. A man who has betrayed the honor of his blood. He will be caught. He will be tortured. And he will die.

I lay here next to my sleeping wife, holding her in my arms while she sleeps peacefully on my chest. My own body wants to give in and sleep, but my mind isn't letting me as it continues to race like a horse. I have to tell her the rest. I've tried so many times to come up with a way to tell her. To find the right words. She's been through so much. But this, this could destroy her. Every time I think about it, it breaks my damn heart.

I envision the day when the two of us can live a normal life. At least, as normal as it can be. When we can finally breathe easily. Fall asleep without worry. She doesn't know it yet, but we will be staying in New York. The club has been turned over to Beamer. With Kryder gone, the Savages are no longer a threat to them. That part of my life is over. Our new life together will begin here. I know her, she will agree. She is loyal to her family. Loyal to me.

For the past week I have sat in this room alongside Cecily and John constructing plans for our new life here. They, too, will be living here until this war with the Russians is over. Until Royal is found.

"You awake?"

Calla's sleepy voice brings me out of my thoughts. The sound alone puts a smile on my face.

"Yeah."

I pull her into me as tightly as I can without hurting her. She still has some healing to do. Her face and legs still have slight bruising. Her shoulder has pretty much healed. She has to be stiff and sore from lying in this bed for weeks, though.

"I know there is more you're not telling me. I can handle it, you know?"

She braces herself up on her elbow. The light from the bathroom casts a shadow over her gorgeous face. The nursing staff has taken good care of her, giving her sponge baths and cleaning her hair with some kind of dry shampoo shit. She still steals my breath away.

"Ugh. This fucking thing is driving me nuts," she moans.

"What thing?"

"This catheter. I want the damn thing out. It's disgusting."

I chuckle.

"It's not funny. What time is it anyway? I want out of this bed. I want a shower. I want to brush my teeth and eat some real food."

"Is that so?" I ask, laughing even more.

"Come here," I beckon, placing my hand on the back of her head, gently coaxing her back down on my chest.

"I'm not sure what time it is. I would guess somewhere around six."

Daylight is starting to peek through the slit in the curtains.

"As far as a shower and all those other demands, you have to wait for the doctor to clear you."

"Great. He better get here soon then, damn it," she sighs in frustration.

"Your mom came in after you fell asleep. She called him and he will be here at eight."

I leave her to her thoughts, waiting patiently for her to start probing me with questions. She's back to her inquisitive ways. Who's to say what she'll be like after I tell her everything? Will she want me, blame me? I have nothing to hide from her. I will tell her the truth about it all. Salvatore will fill her in on the rest.

"So," she begins. "My first question is, how is Manny, really?"

I feel a tug on my heart hearing her first question is about Manny's health.

"Honestly. He's fine. He's bound to find Royal. He's tough, just like you. Trust me. He's good."

She clutches my shirt in her hand, exhaling a breath into my chest.

"I'm glad. What his brother did to him... I can't even begin to describe what it felt like to see."

I contain my rancid thoughts, burying them in the back of my mind. She doesn't need to hear how I feel. The things I want to do to that slimy bastard.

"Do you want to talk about it?"

Right after I speak those words, she stiffens in my arms.

"Not really. Someday, maybe."

I sense her hesitation. I won't push her. She can talk about it whenever she's ready.

"And my dad? How is he?"

"Seriously, baby. He's good. Everyone's good. We've all been too busy worrying about you, making sure you were healing, to deal much with anything else. I mean, I'm sure your dad is kicking his own ass for what happened. You nailed it on the head, though, when you told him he did the right thing by taking out Emerald first. He knows that. You need to let him deal with it. Let him answer to himself. The only person who is blaming your dad is himself."

I start rubbing her back in slow, lazy circles, applying light pressure to try and relieve some of the tension I can feel coiling up. She moans when I find a small knot.

"I'm just worried, that's all."

"I know you are, and I love you even more for it. Just trust me. Trust him, okay?"

"I do," she says without any hesitancy in her voice at all.

"Any more questions?"

It's like I can feel her mind working up against my chest.

"I want to move here," she divulges. I hold back my grin.

"Really? I hadn't thought of that. I would have guessed for sure you would want to go back to Michigan or possibly Canada to finish school."

She sits straight up in bed, her eyes darting to mine in suspicion of my sarcasm. She adjusts the IV and the rubber cord to her catheter and faces me with a matter-of-fact look.

"Spill, Bexley," she commands.

Her demanding nature is damn near a turn on. If she wasn't still healing, I would turn her over my knee and spank her.

"Whatever do you mean?" I say innocently.

She tilts her head, shooting some wicked daggers at me with her eyes. The morning sun is now peeking through. Like I said, my woman is absolutely stunning, even with her hair halfway out of her ponytail and no makeup on. Life is coming back into her eyes. And here I lay hiding the one thing that will dull them.

Finish up this conversation and then tell her. Get it over with.

"I kind of took it upon myself to sort of move us here over the past week," I admit.

She surprises me by bursting into laughter. It fills the entire room, her bright orbs glistening. Fuck me if I'm not about to crush her.

She abruptly stops laughing as quickly as she started.

"There's more, isn't there?" she whispers.

I nod and take a deep breath, preparing myself to tell her.

I reach for her hand, stroking it gently. I can't look at her, not yet. The doctors said the best way to tell her was to just say it, but the words are lodged in my throat. When I finally do speak, I don't even recognize my own voice.

"You were pregnant, Calla."

"I... was?" she asks faintly.

I find the courage to look at her.

"You miscarried, babe."

"Oh, my God. They didn't manage to kill me, so instead they killed our unborn child. A baby we never even knew we were going to have."

She stares at our joined hands, placing them both across her stomach.

"I'm sorry, Cain."

"Calla, no!"

I sit all the way up, cradling her face in my hands.

"No. It's not our fault. Losing a baby is a tragedy. Neither one of us knew. We both have to grieve, both together and separately in our own ways. Never think this is your fault or mine. It's not."

It damn near kills me to see the pain in her eyes. The silently falling tears.

"I just... I guess I need time to deal with it."

"Take all the time you need. We'll get through it together, I promise," I tell her, resting my forehead against hers.

Her eyes close. The two of stay this way for several minutes, grieving for our loss. She pulls away first, a sorrowful smile on her lips.

"We're going to be fine," I whisper.

"Yeah, I know," she whispers back. "I love you, Cain. I've loved you all along. We were apart for so long, both of us changing in so many ways, yet here we are a month later grieving the loss of a child we will never meet."

Calla's eyes conquer mine once again. Hers filled with heat, mine filled with want. Hers dart to my mouth at the same time mine flit to hers. We meet in the middle, our mouths opening up to one another's.

A lot of information is pouring out of this kiss. I'm telling her that this is the beginning of our new lives together. She's telling me she trusts me in taking care of our future. Both of us letting the other know how much we have desperately missed each other. This is nothing like the raw kiss we first shared a month ago after seeing each other the first time. This kiss is telling each other that we only have one life and we want to share it. Life is too damn short to not share it with the one you love.

I hold her face gently in my hands as my tongue intertwines with hers. I could kiss her forever. It's short lived, though, when we are interrupted by the sound of three throats clearing. We break away, Calla's face beet red.

"Well. I was on my way in here to check on my baby girl since I haven't had the opportunity to really have a conversation with her yet, but I can see that she seems to be perfectly fine."

Calla's brows rise, her spirit lifting slightly when she sees her mom.

"You look beautiful, Mom."

Calla reaches out her arms to her mother. I get up off the bed. The two of them stay in a long embrace. Cecily inspects Calla, fussing with her pillows and introducing her to the doctor. John and I stand leaning up against the wall, arms crossed. Neither one of us can take our eyes off of the two women before us. Calla needs her mom right now, and she needs to talk to the doctor.

I push myself away from the wall, giving John a glance. He follows me out the door. I say nothing. Neither does he. All of us have known she lost our baby and have had the time to grieve. Now it's her turn.

****

"There she is!" Lola greets Calla in the kitchen.

"My God, you are the spitting image of your mother when she was your age!"

She leans in, pecking both of Calla's cheeks.

"I take that as a compliment," my wife grins. "It's a pleasure to finally meet you."

I sit back in my chair at the kitchen table, watching Cecily and Lola fuss over Calla as if she were a child. I know she's itching to get the hell out of here. The doctor told her she had to take it easy for a few more weeks, and then set up a follow up appointment to see her in a few weeks.

She looks great. Perfect. I watch her in awe as she delicately picks at her food. Small portions is what the doctor recommended. She wasn't too happy about that at all. My girl is craving a cheeseburger, of all things. Knowing her she'll get what she wants one way or another.

"Excuse us, ladies. Gentlemen, shall we talk in my office?" Salvatore suggests after he greets Calla.

He whispers something in her ear and she nods her head, glancing my way with a wink. I wink back, knowing all too well he feels it's time to address her. See where her head's at. As her husband, I wish he would give her more time. I know better than to ask, so I bow out of the kitchen like a dog with my tail between my goddamned legs. My mind reels, not only with worry for her. It's everything. I'm a thief. I haven't had my hands on a new gun in a long time. I get off on the way the smooth, cold steel feels when I glide my hands down it. Fuck me. I miss it.

"Manny. What the hell dude? When did you get here?"

We do our usual bro hugging bullshit. He follows us into the office, closing the door securely behind him.

"Just got here. Calla doing all right?"

He nods in my direction when I take a seat. He doesn't need to ask me if I told her. The true meaning behind his question is captured in his tone.

"Yeah. She is."

Manny spreads his arms wide jokingly.

"So, what's up, Dad? Why are we all here?"

"Sit your ass down, punk," Salvatore says, waving to a chair. "We're damn lucky, you all know this, right?"

"We do. Any news?" John asks.

"On the whereabouts of Royal? Nothing. He's vanished. My guess is he'll be gone for quite some time. I did have a phone conversation with Ivan this morning."

He looks at John, gauging his reaction. John's nostrils flare. His hand clenches tightly around his coffee cup.

"And?" John lifts his head, meeting Salvatore's eyes.

"He knows we have a hit out on Royal. He stands by his word. He knows nothing. He's insistent that Royal acted on his own. Our families work together on this. Am I clear?"

John goes to speak. You can see the poison running through his veins, feel his need to kill Royal himself. Salvatore silences him. When Salvatore silences you with his hand, you listen, it doesn't matter whether you're family or not.

"I believe him, John. Why would he start a war? He has no reason to. I stay out of his way and he stays out of mine. This isn't the 1920's when families fought against each other for control of empires. Sure, there are families who hate each other. Shit, I can't stand Ivan. He has no respect for anyone. I don't like the way he conducts business. I definitely don't approve of drugs or prostitution. We stand together on this. You and I together. We've talked about this. It's not easy for me, either. For years after Royal left, I listened to my Lola cry herself to sleep many nights, and there wasn't a damn thing I could do to ease her pain. I listened to her pray for his safety. For him to return home and get the help he needed. We both still mourn for the son we lost, my own goddamn flesh and blood in a living, breathing, monster of a man. But what can I do? I can do right by the people who have done right by me, or I do nothing at all. I'm doing what I have to do, not what I want to do."

Manny jumps up.

"We kill him, that's what we do! Fucking wipe them all out."

"Sit the hell down, Roan!"

Whoa. That's the first time in years I've heard Salvatore call Manny by his given name.

"No, damn it, I won't! Do any of you know what it's like to be restrained? Feel helpless as you sit back and get brutalized by your own brother? Watch a woman who you've sworn to protect be drugged, bound to a chair, and beaten? Do any of you know how that feels? Those visions rattle around in my fucked up head every day. I close my eyes and I see the hatred in Royal's face. I take a shower, I see his face. Everywhere I look, I see him. My own brother, who tried to kill me. He failed at that, yet he still managed to take something precious away from all of us. Do any of you know how much it killed me to see them torture her like that?"

Manny starts to pace the floor. His breathing is heavily labored. His hand is clasped at the back of his neck.

"Manny," Salvatore stands and walks cautiously towards his son. "I'm sorry son."

He opens his arms wide. Manny stands there for several long seconds. This is the moment we've all been waiting for, that we've all talked about. Manny has kept this all to himself. He hasn't spoken a word about it at all, up until now.

Out of the corner of my eye, I carefully regard John's reception of hearing the things that Calla was subjected to. Neither he nor Salvatore have mentioned the video since that night. The flash drive has been destroyed, stomped into pieces by the heel of my boot and scattered somewhere alongside the road. There was no need to save it, it's not like this crime will be reported to the police and Royal will be prosecuted. His punishment will be death. His body will be disposed of just like Monty's, Emerald's, and Kryder's were.

It's late in the afternoon the next day by the time we leave the house with John and Cecily and head toward the city and our new apartment. Make that two apartments. John and Cecily own one in the same building.

After Manny's breakdown, Salvatore called an end to the meeting and asked Calla if he could come to her and talk, leaving her very suspicious as to what's going on. Then he packed a bag and took off with Manny.

I'm worried about my friend. Either he's really beating himself up over this, or something else is going on. What? I'm not sure. I can't even bring my own mind to try and conjure up what these two have been through. Calla seems to be dealing with it fine. Then again, she's really only had a little over twenty-four hours to think about it. The loss of our baby. The beatings. The drugs. When I tried bringing it up last night before bed, she told me she wasn't ready to talk about it. I'm not going to push her; she'll talk when she's ready. But as a man, to have to sit there and know you can't do a fucking thing to help a person you care about, let alone a woman being abused and damn near killed, I can't even fathom the kind of shit going through my best friend's head.

That brings us to right now. We're riding in the back of a hired car to deter any suspicion from us.

"Are you nervous?" I whisper into her ear, the tall buildings of New York City coming into view.

"Anxious is more like it. I can't believe we're staying in a penthouse on Park Avenue. It's crazy."

I pull her into me, her breath blows warmly across my heated skin. The smell of her hair envelops me. My dick goes nuts, even with her mom and dad sitting in the seat opposite of us. I exhale and will the son of a bitch to keep himself in check, my brain telling him she's still hurting.

"Calla. I almost forgot. Here."

Her mom digs through her bag on the floor then slants forward, handing her a large envelope.

"What's this?"

I look up at her mother, who sits back at ease with a shit-eating grin on her face.

"Nothing major, just some papers my mom printed off for me."

I seize the envelope right out of her delicate little hands.

She laughs, not even trying to attempt to take it back.

"It's an application for the NYU School of Law. Happy now?"

I kiss the top of her head.

"Very fucking happy."

Chapter Twenty-Four

Calla

I have never seen a building so tall, the outside so modernly constructed in my life. Craning my neck towards the sky, I stare up.

"How tall is this building? And please don't tell me we're all the way at the top?"

Cain's arms snake around me from behind.

"Not all the way. About three quarters up. I'm not sure how tall it is. Enough to give us a perfect view of the city. You're going to love it."

The idea of being able to see the city excites me, although it may take some time to get used to. Heights and I don't seem to get along very well. I remember the time my parents and I were on vacation. I had been so determined I was going to go on the new roller coaster. The minute we started the slow climb up, I squeezed my dad's hand in a death grip and wouldn't let go. As we started to descend, my stomach flew into my throat. I had to hold my breath all the way down, scared out of my mind.

Dad thought it was funny. Me, not so much. Especially when the moment we jumped off, I threw up all over the place. Not a pretty sight for a thirteen year old girl to have her head shoved into a garbage can while she throws up her lunch.

I chance a glance at my dad, who retrieves the last of our bags out of the back of the car, tips the driver, and gives me a knowing look as if he is remembering the same thing as I am.

"It's nothing like that roller coaster, Calla. Now grab one of these suitcases and move your ass."

I comply without delay, grabbing the handle of the suitcase and following behind my parents inside.

"Wow."

I freeze for a moment, giving myself time to check out the lobby. It's very chic and extremely elegant. A red wall runs down one side. The other side is all windows and doors leading back outside. Black and white leather furniture is grouped into small seating areas. My heels click across the marble tiled floor, when I have to pick up the pace to catch up. The sound is delightful.

My favorite pair of Louboutins survived that horrible night I would just as soon forget. Even though at the time I would have loved nothing better than to have been able to stab both of Emerald's eyes with the heels of my shoes, now I'm thankful I didn't.

I continue on, feeling safe, shoving that night deep into the back of my mind. We stop briefly at the security desk where I'm introduced to two of the security guards. Both men are young and good-looking.

"It's a pleasure to finally meet you," they say in unison.

The bigger one of the two eyes me from head to toe. Cain growls from behind me.

"Nice to meet you, too," I say politely.

"Let us know if you ever need anything Mrs. Bexley," he says.

I return his smile.

"Thank you."

We make our way toward the elevator, leaving the two men behind. I elbow Cain.

"Jealous?"

"No. The opposite. They can look all they want. Now if they touch..." He quirks up a brow.

I roll my eyes.

The elevator dings just as we approach.

"We're on the 49th floor and you're on the 50th," Dad says as he pushes both buttons. The elevators close and we ascend rapidly. Even the elevator floor is marble. Good lord.

I'm anxious to see the inside. The view. To soak in the tub overlooking the city that Lola went on and on about. I pray my stomach will be able to take it. I'd hate to disappoint Cain.

I know he built his house back in Michigan with hopes of us living there. We haven't talked much about why he wants to live here. When we were younger, he did always talk about moving away from Detroit, with all of its drugs and violence, but there's just as much, if not more, here.

Not to mention, no one knows Royal's whereabouts. Everyone seems to think he has left the state. Salvatore is convinced he's left the country. You would think I would be frightened after everything I've been through, but I can honestly say this is the safest I have felt since I first learned about my fate, and all the things I never knew about the six years I lived on my own. Maybe it's the fact that my parents are close. Or the reality of Cain and I really trying to make our marriage work. Whatever it is, I'm ready to put the past behind me, and eager to start my new life with the only man I will ever love.

Mom hugs me before she steps off the elevator.

"Call me when you're ready to fill out the paperwork for NYU, sweetie."

"I will."

I turn to my handsome father. My protector. My lifesaver.

"Dad."

He pulls me into his arms.

"Thank you," I whisper into his ear.

He holds me tight for the longest time, then releases me, kissing my forehead and sighing heavily.

"I'm proud of you, sweetie," he winks at me as the doors of the elevator close.

"And I'm proud to be your daughter. Both of you," I say to myself.

The minute we walk into the apartment, I gasp.

"Oh my God!"

It's more like a damn mansion sitting on top of the world. Dropping my bag, I gawk, jaw slack. The foyer is slick with dark wood floors. I bypass the living room and head straight to the kitchen, which is all white except for the slate gray tiled floors. It has a large window that overlooks the entire city. The Empire State Building. The MetLife building. This view is remarkable. I can't wait until nighttime to see it all lit up.

Cain's arms encircle my waist. I lean back against his shoulders, taking it all in.

"Is this where you would stay when you came to the city?" I ask inquisitively when I enter the living room, greeted by more windows overlooking another part of the city. The walls are all white, the modern furniture a deep, rich tan.

"I stayed here a few times. Not many."

He grabs my hand and leads me into a giant office lined with shelves of books. A sleek wooden desk sits in the center.

"This is amazing."

Cain's eyes hit mine. A hint of mischievousness glimmers in his deep set eyes.

"Come here," he beckons, extending his hand out to me. He pulls me down the hall and into the biggest bedroom I have ever seen.

You could live in this room. Off to the right sit two deep gray couches underneath yet more windows. There is also a chaise lounge next to a fireplace, and another desk.

The large king size bed sits on the other side of the room, facing the windows.

Cain sweeps me up in his arms, carrying me in the direction of the bathroom.

"What are you doing?" I giggle lightly.

He sets me gently down.

"This is heaven!" I exclaim, sliding my eyes to the claw foot tub sitting by a window. There is a walk-in shower off to the left and a vanity with two sinks to the right. Gravity pulls me in the direction of the tub.

"Take a bath. Relax. I'll make us some dinner," says Cain.

I raise my hands in defeat.

"No argument from me."

I smile happily and kiss him tenderly on the lips.

"Do you need a pain pill?"

"Nope. I have everything I need right here."

He stares at me for a long moment. I can tell his mind is working, wondering if I'm telling the truth.

"I'm good. Really. Now, I'm starving."

I try and shoo him out.

"Let me see what I can find to make. Lola had her housekeeper stock us with food."

"Cheeseburger!" I holler at his retreating back.

"I knew it," he yells back.

I sigh, taking in my surroundings. I could definitely get used to this.

I lay my head back, staring out into the late afternoon/early evening skyline of New York City. My muscles tight from lack of exercise loosen up. It's my brain that won't relax, won't stop twitching. I've hidden my memories well and I will continue to do so from everyone.

It's like I'm doomed to relive the entire night from beginning to end, over and over. Drugged. Punched. Manny. Screaming. Royal's seedy, repugnant eyes. Emerald, fixated on killing me. The loss of our baby, a baby we would have loved so much. It won't leave me alone.

Will it ever go away? All I can see is the cutest little blue eyed, dark-haired little boy, wrestling around on the floor with his father, or sitting on my lap while I read him a story. I splay my hands across my belly, saying a silent prayer to give me the strength and courage to carry on.

This is the first time I've been alone to be able to cry, and mourn the loss of a baby I never even knew existed. The tears flow out freely, and I let them. When I've cried my last, I puff out a breath and submerge my body under the water, allowing pleasant memories of the last time I did this back at Cain's house take hold over the disturbing ones.

I bolt upright, thinking I might catch him again, but the doorway is vacant. Laughing inwardly, I reach for the soap when a wave of the scent of cooking burgers hits my nose, shooting straight to my stomach. I hurry up and finish bathing, and drain the tub. I moan from the soft feel of the plush bath mat between my toes.

Wrapping the oversized towel around my waist, I pad out in to the bedroom. Not having any idea where my clothes are, I open the closest dresser, squealing in delight when I see all of my bras folded neatly on the top shelf. Choosing to be bold, I reach for the red lace push up with matching panties. I pull out a few more drawers until I find my

University of Windsor t-shirt. It's old and has a hole under the arm, but it's the softest shirt I own. I love it!

With a plan in my head, the nightmares get shoved aside. I hang the towel up and stroll out of the bedroom in search of that cheeseburger.

****

"I'm exhausted, you ready for bed?" Cain asks as soon as I hang up the phone with my mom. During dinner, I devoured my cheeseburger at the kitchen table. Notice I said table. Cain wanted to sit out on the deck. I may love the view, but I'm not ready to see it from there yet. As it was, I stood frozen in the kitchen when Cain told me he was grilling outside. No damn way am I ready to go out there. Maybe never.

He leans down and lifts me up like a child, carrying me all the way to the bedroom, where he lays me down softly on the bed.

"The doctor cleared me for sex."

A grin tugs the corners of his mouth.

"Really?"

He reaches into the back pocket of his jeans, pulls out his wallet, and sets it on the nightstand. Then he unbuttons his jeans. I watch them, holding my breath when they drop to the floor. His half-hard dick permanently marked with its sign of ownership springs free.

"Yeah," I hiss, breathing out heavily. I sit up, whip my shirt over my head, and throw it down by his jeans.

"Fucking hell," he growls, staring at my boobs spilling out of my red bra.

I lay back, spreading my legs wide and walking my fingers down my stomach slowly until they edge across the waistband of my matching panties.

"You like?" I ask playfully.

"Don't," he warns, placing one knee on the bed.

He removes my hand and straddles me. He grabs my other hand and entwines them both with his.

We kiss deeply, passionately, and very slowly. My hands start to roam everywhere when he releases them finally. I've missed him.

"I want you," I say after he's been feasting on my neck for several minutes.

"I want you, too."

He reaches for his wallet, pulling out a condom. He tears it open and slides it down his cock. It's a shame to cover up. Just a few weeks until I see the doctor and it will never have to be shielded again.

My bra and panties have long been tossed somewhere. Our bodies are naked and sweaty. Cain dips his finger inside of me as he slowly kisses and licks my neck. When he hits my clit with his thumb, I begin to moan, his name falling from my lips. Teasingly he makes his way down my body with his tongue, stroking lightly down the center of my breast and circling around my belly button, stopping just shy of my aching core.

"Cain!" I cry out when his mouth hovers over my clit, his warm breath causing me to damn near come on the spot.

"I got you, baby."

He nips at my clit, fingers pumping steadily. Then he withdraws his fingers and replaces them with his tongue and mouth.

Oh, God. This man and his tongue. He runs it in slow, delicious circles up and down my entire pussy. He licks, then sucks, dipping his tongue inside repeatedly. I squirm beneath him until I come hard, screaming his name.

"I'm going to make love to my wife now. Nice and slow," he says, removing his mouth and replacing it with his dick.

He slides inside of me leisurely. I arch my back, taking him in as deep as I can. He begins to move slowly, in and out. Making love to me sweetly.

"Mrs. Bexley, I'm going to make love to you so attentively that your body will know personally that I am so much in love with you that every part of me belongs to you."

He thrusts in and eases his way back out again. His hands move to my ass, tilting me upwards to drive in deeper.

"I love how you smell and taste. I love the way you feel beneath me. On top of me. All around me. I love how naughty you can be. How sweet you can be. I honest to God love you, Calla."

"I'm so in love with you," I whimper, holding back the happy tears that want to flow freely.

He drags himself out to the tip and presses back in. My walls clench around him.

"I'm yours, Cain," I vow, clawing my nails down his back.

My release builds as we kiss tenderly, coming together. No roughness. We gratify each other completely, solidifying that we are each other's universe.

"That was..." I begin to say.

Cain beats me to it.

"Fucking hot!"

I roam my hands across his solid chest.

"Yes, it was. It was perfect."

"I have something for you," he says, reaching into the nightstand drawer and pulling out a black velvet box.

He places it on his chest, right next to my hand.

"Your mom gave this to me. She thought you might like it. It belonged to your grandmother."

He lifts the lid.

"Oh, my God! It's beautiful!" I exclaim softly.

"I don't know much about jewelry. Your mom said it's two carats."

He takes it out of the box, lifts my hand to his lips, and then slides the wedding set onto my finger.

My hand starts to shake as I hold it up to the light. The round diamond sparkles, the small diamonds all around it glistening. It's an exquisite piece.

"Thank you!" I squeal, raining kisses all across his chest. "I will never take it off."

****

"Well, good morning," I say, blinking in shock at the group standing outside my front door.

Salvatore, my parents, Manny, and Lola all step inside the apartment. I thought this meeting would be between Salvatore and myself. I presumed wrong.

My mother wastes no time at all grabbing my hand and staring down at the ring on my finger.

"It's right where it belongs," she murmurs, running her finger over the diamond and then placing her hand on my cheek.

"It's exquisite. Thank you, Mom."

"You're welcome, honey," she says, pulling me in for a tight hug.

"We hope you love your accommodations," Lola says as we all take a seat in the living room.

"Love?" I question. "I'm more than in love. Thank you for letting us stay here."

"Nonsense," she says with a flick of her hand. "I can't remember the last time I even stayed here, it's been that long. It's yours for as long as you like."

"Thank you," Cain and I say at the same time.

"Let's get down to business, shall we?" Salvatore suggests before turning to me.

"Calla, I'm delighted the two of you decided to move here. It makes what I'm about to ask you a lot easier."

"The answer is yes," I say boldly. "I would be honored to work for you. That is, if I'm accepted to NYU."

He regards me for a moment. They all do. I feel like I'm being dissected by several pairs of eyes. I sit up straight, my shoulders firmly back.

"What?" I finally as, unable to stand the silence anymore.

"You're a very bright and observant young woman," says Lola.

I glance over at her and she looks happy. Her smile is infectious. Her dark hair is pulled up on top of her head. The silver streaks splattered throughout shine from the steady streams of light coming in from all of the windows.

"Thank you," I say graciously. "However, I'm not feeling very observant at the moment. Something tells me you all know something I don't."

"Ah. That's where you're wrong, Calla," says Salvatore, eyeing me shrewdly. "You see, this observance of yours, the way you can read people... it's a gift. The moment I saw the way you handled that slimeball Monty, I knew you were the right person for this job. You're loyal and trustworthy. After the challenges of the past month, you have shown yourself to be courageous, independent, and unafraid to speak your mind. This, my dear, makes you a very powerful woman."

Now that I look at everything that has happened in the past month, he's right. I've taken my husband back after six years. Absorbed the news about my father being a cold-blooded killer and that my mother is also an ex-killer and the sister to Salvatore Diamond. Discovered that Manny, or should I call him Roan now, is my cousin.

I still cannot believe after all this time that his real name is Roan. A man who followed my every move for the past several years. Internally I laugh at that one. If I was that observant, I would have picked up on the fact I had someone following me most of the time. Either that, or he's very good. The latter sounds much better.

"By answering yes before I asked also goes to show you trust me. You trust all of us in this family to do right by you. That is why I'm here to tell you, your intuition is correct. We do want you on board with my counsel team. Although, you will not be working for me."

I open my mouth, not knowing quite what to say. The wheels turn in my head. If he doesn't want me working for him, then who?

With a nod from the head of the man in charge, Roan steps forward.

"You will be working for me."

Epilogue

Two and a Half Years Later

"Good lord. I hate this weather," I say to Stefano, one of my associates, as we take the elevator to the top floor where our offices are. 57th Street, of all places, just a stroll up the road to 5th Avenue and I'm in shoe heaven. Not today, though, in this bitter cold winter air.

I shiver in my boots, not so much from the cold, but because they are the ugliest pair of things ever to grace my feet. If I were to walk out the door of our penthouse with my heels on, Cain would have a fit. Safety first. Not that I blame him, really, with the still-unknown whereabouts of Royal. I know all too well how one can make themselves disappear, although my circumstances were a little different. I thought no one knew where I was, but they all knew all along. Especially the man I was running from.

It all worked out for the best in the long run. I just wish it wouldn't have taken six damn years away from us.

"Your dad bring you in this morning?" Stephano asks in his Italian accent.

He's quite a bit older and I've been working with him for three months now, but God, his accent gets me every time.

"Yes. You would think I was still a child. He's the worst of the bunch."

I take a sip of my coffee. Everyone here knows what happened to Manny and me. Everyone has been on high alert for over two years, waiting for Royal to strike. I'm hoping he's dead somewhere, either by my father's hand or from a drug overdose. Either way, I hope he's rotting in the farthest corner of hell alongside all the rest of them.

My dad has practically devoted the past couple of years to sticking by my side, making sure I get to school and now work safely and returning me home if Cain's not around to do so. They guard me more now than they did when I was in Canada. I feel like I'm in grade school all over again the way he fusses about me all the time. For a man who pulls a trigger for a damn living, he sure is a softy.

I pull my hat off of my head when I enter the office. The phones are buzzing. All the secretaries with their head pieces at their ears are chatting away.

"See you in a few minutes," Stefano says as he goes one way and I go the other.

"Going over the Belmont case one more time before it starts?" I question.

We've been burning the midnight oil the past several weeks over this case. It's my first big trial as an assistant defense attorney for one of Salvatore's men who is being prosecuted for computer hacking. One little slip up and he was caught, although we are searching for the proof we need to somehow prove he was set up.

An inside job that should have been an easy one for him, went sour the minute he hacked into a Mexican drug cartel's personal computer system. Brian Belmont is one of the best black hat hackers around. He should never have been caught.

To say I'm nervous would be putting it mildly. This case will take months, another reason why everyone is on high alert. The least mention of drugs sends everyone on a frenzy looking for Royal, so I understand why Brian did it. This family is leaving no stone unturned. No option untouched in their search.

Which leads me now to the two men sitting in my office when I enter. Cain approaches and takes off my jacket for me.

"Hey, babe," I greet him.

"How's my sexy wife?" he asks, kissing me briefly on the lips.

"Irritated," I grumble, sitting in my chair and pulling off my ugly boots. I toss them in the corner and slip my feet into my leopard print Valentinos. Cain slips his sexy self into a chair across from me. God, that ass of his still gets me wet.

"Work from home. I've told you this."

"Ha! I would never get any work done."

"Maybe a little."

He smiles that big smile of his. I'm going to have a wet spot in my chair before I even start my day.

"Every morning and every night," he licks his lips.

I roll my eyes.

"You two are nasty. Can you at least wait until I'm gone, for God's sake?" Roan chips in.

"I don't know, man. You have me sitting in my wife's office at eight o'clock in the morning. She's dressed in a tight skirt that shows off her ass..."

"Cain, stop it," I laugh, interrupting him.

"Can't be helped," he shrugs.

"Anyway, I thought you had an early meeting this morning."

I look between Cain and Roan. He no longer goes by Manny now that he's the underboss and second in command behind Salvatore.

"You're our meeting," Roan says.

"I'm confused."

I give my husband a snarly look, my glare asking, "Why didn't you drive me in this morning?"

"What?" he holds his hands in the air. "I had a meeting before this one."

"Sure you did."

My attention goes back to my boss.

"Please tell me you're not in any kind of trouble. You didn't knock up some chick, did you?" I tease, although it wouldn't surprise me.

He's a damn slut. I wouldn't be surprised if half the chicks he bangs don't pay him for sex. He may be my cousin, but I'm here to tell you he is hot. He's bulked up so much over the past two years, it isn't even funny. Not to say my husband hasn't done the same, because he has. These two live in the gym every chance they get.

"Hell, no. You know I wrap it before I tap it," he winks.

"Yuck," I scowl.

"Yuck is right. I hate those damn things. You need to settle your ass down and find you and your dick a nice, warm, and cozy home to live in," says Cain.

"Would you stop? That shit will never happen. Not all of us are destined to be as lucky as you and find someone as wonderful as Calla, here."

Roan flashes a shit-eating grin my way.

"Are you trying to butter me up, Roan? Because if you are, you have about, oh, two minutes to tell me what it is you need. I have a meeting I need to get to."

Just then, there is a knock at the door and I go to stand.

"Excuse me."

"I'll get it. Stay off your feet."

Cain gets up and greets Stefano.

"I'll be right there," I tell him and then glare at these two.

"Actually, he's part of the meeting."

All three of the men stand across from me on the other side of my desk.

"What's going on?"

Roan walks to my desk, placing his palms down on the edge and leaning into me.

"You've heard of Alina Solokov, right?"

"Ivan's daughter? Yes. I've met her a few times. She's extremely nice. Why do you ask?" I inquire, confused by the subject.

"Well, it seems that several years ago, she and my brother had quite an affair. When she left to go study abroad, it broke him. My resources tell me he has never gotten over her."

I peer around Cain to gauge his reaction. He just lifts a brow.

"Okay. Well, what does this have to do with me?"

"You're going to befriend her. Set her up with me."

I jump out of my chair, feeling my blood pressure rising by the second.

"I most certainly am not! That's like... oh, I don't know. Playing with fire? I cannot believe you would even ask me to get in involved with something like this. And you?" I point at Cain.

"How could you go along with something like this? Same goes for you, Stephano."

"Relax, Calla. You won't be in any type of danger. Alina doesn't even have a relationship with her father. They've been estranged since she was a child. She wants nothing to do with him. Do you honestly think I would agree to put my wife's life in danger?"

I rub my temples, staring down at my coffee cup and wishing to God I had something stronger to pour in it.

"What exactly is it you want me to do?"

"She lives with my daughter on the upper east side," Stephano chimes in. "I've invited both girls to have lunch with you and me tomorrow. It's simple, really. We're at lunch, and along comes your husband and cousin. You see, we have it all worked out."

Stefano and his damn accent. I don't like it anymore, or this idea. Not one bit.

"You said 'befriend' her. I wouldn't exactly call her my bestie after one lunch."

"You let me take care of the rest. You just be there tomorrow. Feel her out for me before we arrive," Roan says.

"Fine. Just this once. I really hope you know what you're doing."

"I know exactly what I'm doing. If my brother is still hung up on her like rumors say, then my guess is, he knows she's back in the country."

"You're putting her in danger, Roan," I whisper.

"She'll be in even more danger if my brother gets to her first!"

Acknowledgements

I'm acknowledging you, the reader. The one who continues to support, to message, and to define the very reason why I continue to write. Thank you for believing in me!

To my family and friends. My life is balanced with all of you in it.

To Skye Turner. You and I were at the right place at the right time.

To Brendan James. The story behind this cover is, in one word, EPIC.

I could carry on and thank so many people but... in Kathy style, please leave your review and get on to the next book. There are many more of them out there waiting for you!

51363498R00157

Made in the USA
Lexington, KY
21 April 2016